Sugar & Spice

Christine d'Abo

LYRICAL PRESS
Kensington Publishing Corp.
www.kensingtonbooks.com

Lyrical Press books are published by
Kensington Publishing Corp. 119 West 40th Street New York, NY 10018

All Kensington titles, imprints, and distributed lines are available at special
quantity discounts for bulk purchases for sales promotion, premiums, fundraising, and educational or institutional use.

Special book excerpts or customized printings can also be created to fit
specific needs. For details, write or phone the office of the Kensington
Special Sales Manager:
Kensington Publishing Corp.
119 West 40th Street
New York, NY 10018
Attn. Special Sales Department. Phone: 1-800-221-2647.

First Electronic Edition: February 2019
eISBN-13: 978-1-5161-0666-0
eISBN-10: 1-5161-0666-0

First Print Edition: February 2019
ISBN-13: 978-1-5161-0667-7
ISBN-10: 1-5161-0667-9

Printed in the United States of America

Praise for Christine d'Abo

30 Days
"Well-developed and engaging characters, major and minor, lead to conflicts that feel both realistic and fresh, and difficult subjects are handled with empathy and gentle humor. Romance fans will delight in this sweet and spicy expedition."—*Publishers Weekly* STARRED REVIEW

"Perfect for folks seeking a well-written, hot read with substance." *Library Journal*, STARRED REVIEW

"Christine D'Abo crafts a rare treat in *30 Days*, a book that's equal parts sexy and heartwarming, fun and deeply emotional. Bravo!"—*New York Times* bestselling author J. Kenner

30 Nights
"Dd'Abo turns up the heat and promises a fast-moving and fun story capable of making one swoon with delight and sigh with pleasure. Readers will get a kick out of Glenna and Eric's out-of-this-world chemistry, but will be even more entertained watching them try and hold back their true feelings for each other."—*RT Book Reviews*, 4 Stars

"Steamy...Delightfully stimulating and kinky...Well worth reading."— *Publishers Weekly*

Also by Christine d'Abo

Sugar Sweet
30 Days
30 Nights
Submissive Seductions

Chapter 1

"Oh my God, I just found the perfect thing for you!"

Kayla Arnold looked up from the menu she'd been vacantly staring at as her best friend Simone fell into the chair opposite her. Simone had been twenty minutes late for their weekly lunch date, which meant Simone had become fascinated by something. And given her entrance, that meant Kayla was about to be in trouble.

Closing the menu, Kayla took a steadying breath before she folded her hands, looked at her friend and smiled. "Hi."

Simone frantically arranged herself and her belongings, before she finally settled, resting her elbows on the table and her chin on her clasped hands. "Hello my wonderful friend. And you won't distract me from my good mood with that brooding look of yours."

Kayla had to fight a smile. "But brooding is my best skill."

"It's not fair to the men of the world if you steal all their good moves." Simone squirmed in her chair as she released her hands and picked up the water glass. "Aren't you going to ask me what I found?"

"I'm more than a little terrified to do that." Still, Kayla knew there was no point in delaying the inevitable any longer. "What did you find for me?"

"The very best website in the world." Simone's blond ponytail swung as she pulled out her phone and began to type. "I was conducting an interview this morning when I found out about this."

Simone's fingers flew across the keys and within a moment, she held out her phone. Kayla snorted as she took the phone and leaned back in her chair. "A sugar daddy site? Aren't I a bit rich for that?"

"Not to *be* a sugar baby, silly." Simone pushed up her glasses and grinned. "You should be a sugar mama."

Kayla stared at the screen, blinking away the first three responses that had popped into her head. Simone was her dearest friend, and one of the few who'd known her before her business Fashion Finds hit big and made Kayla a multimillionaire. She'd been with Kayla through her rise to fame, her whirlwind marriage, and subsequent divorce. She knew most, if not all, of Kayla's deep, dark secrets.

"I have no intention of being anyone's mama. Or anything else." Simone always meant well when she'd show up with one of her crazy schemes, but Kayla knew better than to give in to them. "Feel free to sign up yourself though. It might be fun picking out some young stud for you to ride."

Simone's giggle-snort blew an errant strand of hair that now flitted around her face. "I'm not rich enough to even be looking at this site. It's millionaires only. That's so not even close to my bank account."

"If you did PR for me, rather than be a journalist, you might inch a bit closer to that goal."

"Oh please. Toronto needs me. I'm an intrepid reporter, digging up dirt on…well, whatever the Toronto Record wants me to dig up."

"Wasn't your last article on the best places to get sushi?"

Simone sighed. "So much sushi. So freaking good."

"You're too much of a precious soul to exist in this world. And I'm not signing up for a site like this."

She could only imagine what would happen if someone on the board of directors found out about a stunt like that. The water cooler gossip would be impressive. "Where did you find out about this?"

Simone looked around the restaurant before she leaned in. "Do you remember a few months ago, Vince Taylor and all the noise around him and a mystery woman?"

Kayla had crossed paths with Vince over the years. Toronto might be large, but certain social circles were far smaller than most would assume. "I remember. He went online with a *mea culpa* if I remember correctly."

"What you might not know is how they met." Simone lowered her voice, her brown eyes sparkling. "Guess."

Kayla leaned a bit closer as well, enjoying the unexpected silliness of the moment. "They met on the sugar daddy site?"

"They met on the sugar daddy site!" Simone shouted, then cringed as the couple at the table beside them looked over. She waved briefly before turning back to Kayla. "And they looked so happy when I interviewed them. Marissa is so sweet—that's her name, Marissa—and smart. She's a student, and we got talking, and she told me all about it, even though Vince was giving me that brooding look. But you really do it way better than he does." She snorted again and pushed her glasses up with her finger. "You should sign up too."

"I have an idea." Kayla stood and brushed the wrinkles from her linen pants. "Why don't we plan a fun night out, just you and me."

Simone stopped moving and looked at her for a moment before the smile slipped from her face. "You're not going to do it."

"Darling, you know I'm not into relationships."

"But this isn't about that."

"What's it about then?"

Simone stilled, and the energy around her changed as she grew serious. "If you must know, I think you're lonely. And it's killing me to see you like this."

Was she?

Stuck in a rut—yes. Heartbroken—maybe at one time. But lonely?

She happened to like her life.

Kayla's day always started the same way. She'd wake up alone by four AM to get to the gym on time to meet her personal trainer for her session, where Mike pushed her as far as she'd let him, then a bit more until she could no longer think. She always had time to shower and dress impeccably before making it to the office by seven. Her day would inevitably be filled with meetings until it was finally time for her to go home. She'd end her day with a single glass of red wine and a soak in her tub.

Every day, except needing to attend the occasional birthday party, holiday event or corporate all-hands meeting. The routine had become a boon, a salve to her wounded soul after her husband had walked out on her five years ago.

Kayla needed the familiar, even craved it. She'd promised herself that she wouldn't let anything send her down the emotional rabbit hole of despair that she'd fallen into when Christoph had so politely ended their marriage and broken her heart.

Her throat tightened, forcing Kayla to swallow more than once. "I appreciate this. I know I haven't been the best friend you deserve. Not recently. But signing up for a sugar daddy site isn't the answer."

"You don't know that." Simone began to play with her napkin. "According to Marissa, and Vince too, it wasn't what either of them had expected. It worked out to be so much more."

Kayla reached across the table and squeezed Simone's hand. "Thank you."

"For what?"

"For caring so much about me."

Simone squeezed back. "Always."

When Kayla finally pulled back, she made a point of putting on her best smile. No sense in making matters any more uncomfortable. "How about this? Let's order the most expensive thing on this menu and talk about your idea. My treat. After, we can stop for pedicures at that spa you like so much. And if, after that, I'm still not convinced that this is the right idea for me, you'll promise to let it drop. Deal?"

Not that she had any intention of seeing the idea through, but it was better for both of them if she humored Simone. She knew by the time their toes dried, the idea of Kayla being a sugar mama would be off the table.

Simone cocked her head, and after a moment grinned. "Deal. I'm not worried though. I know you'll agree to do it."

"We'll see. For now, let's find our server."

"And wine. I'd love some wine." Simone looked around until she frowned at the restaurant clock. "Is eleven thirty too early for wine?"

"Never." Kayla caught her waiter's eye, which got him moving.

If she were fortunate, Simone would soon forget about this website and Kayla would be able to get back to her regular—and yeah, lonely—routine.

* * * *

Devin was ninety percent certain he was hungover. He cracked open his eyes and tried to lift his head from the couch pillow before a bolt of pain lanced through his skull.

A hundred percent certain. What the hell did I drink?

"Ray?" He barely managed to get his roommate's name out and had to swallow a few times before trying again. "Ray?"

"Hmm?"

Devin opened his eyes for real this time and saw Ray face down on the floor, the Xbox controller still in his hand. "You alive?"

"Hmm."

"Hungover?"

"Ummhmm."

"Pancakes?"

"Nah na."

"Can you form words?"

Ray lifted his head and looked around the room. "Words are hard."

"Food?"

Ray opened his mouth to say something, before rolling to his hands and knees. Devin didn't need his PhD to know what was coming next.

Thankfully, Ray made it to the bathroom this time before he got sick. "Bacon and eggs, it is."

Rolling to his feet, Devin had to give himself a moment to ensure he wouldn't be joining Ray, before carefully padding to the kitchen. He pulled out the bacon and eggs without being fully aware of what he was doing. He was trying to remember exactly what had happened last night.

They'd had an Xbox LAN party, joining up with a bunch of people from their ethics class. There had been some bragging that had needed addressing, something about who was better in Overwatch. Cassie had kicked all their asses, as was right and proper in the world.

Devin's mind tried to pull out the remaining details that had been dampened by the alcohol as he cracked six eggs into a bowl. They'd been teasing someone about being single. Cassie, maybe? And then there was something about online dating...an account?

He tossed the shells and picked up a fork as Ray came out of the bathroom. "That's better."

"You managed words." Devin beat the eggs as he turned to Ray. "Hey, did we set up a profile for Cassie on a website? Or something like that?"

Ray frowned. "Don't know. Sounds like something we'd do."

"She'll kick our asses if we did."

"I'll text her." Ray pushed papers from the counter and retrieved his phone. "She'll laugh at us for being hungover."

"I told you not to bother going shot for shot with her. East Coast girls can hold their liquor." Devin knew better than partying like this. He rarely drank to excess, but last night had been unusual.

Yesterday he'd defended his PhD. And it hadn't sucked.

Yay him!

Unfortunately, that meant he didn't know what to do with his life now. Well, not beyond drinking too much and playing Overwatch.

"Ah shit." Ray was staring down at his phone; a hand pressed to the side of his head.

"What? Is Cassie threatening to come over and kick your ass?" He looked back over at Ray when he didn't immediately respond. "What's up?"

"Well, apparently, I told Cassie she should get a sugar daddy."

Devin snorted. "So she'll be over in five minutes to kick your ass, or—"

"Naw, we're cool. She said she'd do it if one of us signed up for it first."

"None of us are gay, so that won't work."

"Apparently, there are women on the site too. Not many." Ray started scrolling through the site. "I guess I'd agreed to do it."

Devin tried to laugh, but it hurt his head too much. "That's fucking hilarious."

Ray flipped him off. "You did too, asshole."

He set the frying pan down on the stove a bit too hard, and the resulting *bang* sent a wave of pain through his head. "What do you mean I did too?"

"We both did. Cassie didn't." Ray held out his phone for Devin to see. "Millionaire chicks."

For half a minute, Devin had been freaking that he'd done something stupid. But the quick look through the site showed him he didn't have much to worry about. "It's mostly dudes on here. And I hate to tell you, we're not exactly material for rich women to be chasing after."

Ray scratched his fingers through his hair. "Speak for yourself. I'm prime meat, baby." Ray's face drained of color before he turned and bolted back to the bathroom.

Turning back to his breakfast task, Devin continued to look through the few profiles of the rich and famous on the site in between tending to the food. It was more than a little strange seeing all of the men looking for younger women to pamper. Devin couldn't imagine what those women would have to provide in return for the money, and it was probably for the best if he didn't. Faces of women, some of whom could be his classmates, smiled at him from the computer screen. Their profiles highlighted their likes, interests, and desires.

Curious, Devin moved the mouse to select the profile they'd created for him in their drunken stupor. The picture had apparently been taken with the laptop camera, its slightly fuzzy image in stark contrast to the others he'd seen. He wore a sloppy grin, one that shouted he was more than a little intoxicated.

His profile was filled with enough pretentious answers and cocky innuendo to ensure no woman with even the slightest bit of common sense would want to have anything to do with him. It was a giant waste of time.

He should delete this crap.

"Dude!" Ray's voice echoed from the toilet. "Help."

Devin slammed the laptop cover closed and went to help his friend. He'd worry about dating millionaires another day.

Chapter 2

Kayla stood, tapping her finger on the notebook in front of her. "Thank you, everyone. I think we're set to move forward with this, but we'll revisit the supply chain issue next month." Everyone stood, as the buzz of chatter quickly rushed to fill the silence that had preceded it moments before.

The board meeting had gone on far longer than Kayla had expected, leaving her back aching and her head pounding. There'd been a great deal of discussion on the need to outsource additional manufacturing of their new spring line, something she hadn't been convinced they needed. Not that her opinion entirely mattered to some of the board members. Despite Fashion Finds being her brainchild, and her having been part of the board since the company went public seven years earlier, many of the board still saw her as a young child who didn't have a clue as to what she was doing.

Typical crap-all-over-the-millennial bullshit. Kayla knew what she was doing, having learned what she needed once she'd decided to take the company public. She had a fantastic mentor who still accepted her calls when self-doubt crept in. Those days were few and far between, even if her board did all that they could to question her ability to drive the company where it needed to go.

Still, there was a part of her that was getting tired of hearing about profit margins and stock prices despite knowing she was responsible to the shareholders. Money, not her love of fashion and design, was the thrust of her existence these days, and it was killing her by inches.

That was the price she'd paid for taking her business to the next step: losing control of what she'd once done—everything from website creation, to sewing and promotion—so she could become rich.

It was strange how privilege worked. When she was nineteen and had an idea, she'd had to work and fight for every inch of progress. The more successful she'd become, the more comfortable things had gotten, the more detached from reality Kayla felt. Before she'd question every purchase, debating between buying that new fabric she prayed would make the perfect new shirt, or helping to chip in to buy groceries for the family. But as the money started to roll in, groceries became less of a concern and where the family should go for their latest vacation was suddenly up for debate. Now, she hardly saw her parents, mostly because she was too busy working to enjoy the finer things, but also partially because the thought of them not liking the woman she'd become in the pursuit of their combined happiness, terrified her.

She often wondered if she had to do it over again, would she walk away from it? Would she go back to the person she was to avoid the pressures of success?

Probably not.

It's hard to walk away from boatloads of cash, especially when her family didn't have a lot growing up. And while she'd like to think she'd do the right thing, she knew damn well she'd take the money every time. Not because she was greedy, or materialistic, but because she was a human being who wanted more from life, wanted more for her family. The money helped, and only a fool would think otherwise.

She smiled until the last board members left the room, handing out handshakes and nods as though she were bestowing a benediction upon them all. But the moment she was alone, she dropped the facade and allowed the tension to seep from her body.

This sucked.

Kayla was tired, and despite what she'd said to Simone at lunch the other day, it turned out she really was lonely. Packing up her notes and her tablet, her mind kept drifting back to Vince and his girlfriend. She couldn't imagine signing up for something like that, a website that was primarily rich people looking for sex. But from the bit she knew about Vince, he wasn't exactly the type of man to do that either. Something must have appealed to him about such a thing.

Because really, a sugar daddy site? That wasn't exactly normal.

Was it?

Walking through the halls heading to her office, Kayla made a point of acknowledging every person she passed. It was vital for her to remember the names and faces of everyone on her floor, which she felt was the very least she should be expected to do. It built loyalty, comradery, and a positive environment. While she might not be able to control certain aspects of her company entirely, this was something she could influence.

"Ms. Arnold?" Her assistant, Rhianna, stood up as soon as she got to her office. "I was about to head out, but I wanted to make sure you didn't need anything before I left."

"You should have left thirty minutes ago." Kayla picked up Rhianna's coat and handed it to her. "Doesn't Tyler have his concert tonight?"

The relief on her face was palpable. "Yeah, but I knew you were going to get stuck in there, so I had Malcolm pick him up."

"I'm fine. Go, go, go." She shooed at her. "I can't wait to hear how he made out. I'd love to see a video if you can get one."

"We have front row seats." There was no mistaking the pride in her voice. "Thank you. Oh, a registered letter arrived for you. They let me sign for it, and I put it on your desk."

"Thank you."

She waited until Rhianna jogged away in the direction she'd only just come, before disappearing into her office to hide. The moment the door was closed, she kicked off her high heels and padded over to her desk. The sun was still high, as the early summer days were growing longer, which tended to keep her in the office longer than she should be.

No wonder she was lonely. She never gave herself the opportunity to meet other people, let alone go out on dates. Yes, Christoph had been painfully clear that he'd only been with her for her money, but that didn't mean all men were that way. Sure, the few dates she'd gone on after that had turned weird the moment some of them learned that she was quite well off, that there was no way in hell they'd ever earn as much money as she did. That didn't mean that every man out there would react badly to dating her.

She was an attractive, smart and ambitious woman. And while she might not have a ton of close friends, the ones who she did have considered her to be loyal and loving. At least, that's what Simone always said to her.

Christoph had said that too. At first.

Falling into her office chair, Kayla looked out over the Toronto skyline. There was no sense in worrying about finding someone to date, not when she had so much else on her plate. While she might not want to worry about supply chains and ensuring her company was working with third parties who paid their employees fairly, that was what she had to do. If that meant staying late on a Friday night when she'd rather be out with Simone having a few drinks and going to a movie, then so be it.

With a sigh, she turned away from the world outside and turned to the letter sitting in the middle of her desk. It was from the Meadow Lake High School Alumni Committee, and just seeing the name brought dread rising in her chest.

Her old high school had been the recipient of some of her charitable endeavors since Fashion Finds hit the big league. But other than attending one reunion, she'd avoided returning. After opening the letter, she quickly read its contents once, then a second time to make sure she understood it correctly.

They wanted to name the library after her, and they wanted the ceremony to happen during homecoming week.

Shit.

Shortly after she realized that her money and success weren't a fluke and that she was set for life, Kayla had reached out to her old school and established a scholarship for young women who were interested in pursuing post-secondary studies in business. She wanted to help girls like her, who had dreams and ambitions but lacked the money to make things a reality. So, with the knowledge of only a few people, she anonymously setup the fund.

And that was supposed to be that.

She'd never wanted the attention, and certainly didn't want a library named after her, even if she'd also sent in more than a few donations to make sure the kids had every advantage they could get. She certainly didn't want a repeat of her fifth reunion.

"Sorry folks." She tossed the letter aside and focused her attention on her emails. It didn't take long for her to get lost in the screens of texts, and before she realized it, her office had grown dark. It wasn't until her phone rang that she realized exactly how late it had gotten.

"Shit." She picked up her cell, to see Simone's name flash. "Hey, you."

"Are you still at work? Tell me you're not still at work."

"Okay, I'm not still at work." Pinching the bridge of her nose, she leaned back into her seat. "I'll be heading home soon. I just need to finish up this one email and—"

"Stop," Simone growled softly. "I'm in an Uber, and I'll be there in five minutes. Come downstairs right now."

"Darling, I can't."

"Yes, you can. You need to have a break. You...you looked awful the other day. If you don't start taking care of yourself, you're going to have a serious health problem. Five minutes. Meter is running."

Kayla stared at the phone after Simone hung up, fighting the sudden urge to cry. She didn't even know why she was upset, not really. Maybe it was as simple as having someone there to care for her. Someone who made sure she was looking out for herself. Simone was right that she'd done enough for tonight. Grabbing her things, Kayla waved goodnight to the cleaning staff and headed for the lobby.

Simone and her Uber were there waiting for her. "I knew you'd still be there. It's nearly ten o'clock." There was no misreading her disapproving glare. "I bet you haven't even eaten."

"I had a board meeting. I wanted to make sure I got caught up on a few things before I left for the weekend." Of course, her stomach chose that moment to growl. "I am a bit hungry."

Like a light being switched on, Simone broke out into a grin. "Awesome! I have wine, and I've already ordered takeout. We're going back to your place, and we're having a late girls' night."

"It's nearly ten."

Simone shrugged. "I don't have anywhere to be tomorrow."

Kayla frowned.

"Oh come on. When was the last time you had any fun?" When Kayla didn't answer her right away, she laughed. "See, it's been way too long. Tonight we're going to drink wine, eat Thai food and watch movies. I saw that Netflix has a bunch of new shows out."

That sounded far better than what Kayla would have done on her own. She smiled and dropped her head to Simone's shoulder. "That sounds great."

They rode the rest of the way in silence, and Kayla handed Simone cash for the Uber, despite Simone's protests. "This was supposed to be my treat."

"I can cover the fare." She waved Simone out of the car before she could protest further.

The driver smiled. "She seems like a good friend."

"The very best." Kayla made sure to hand the driver an extra generous tip. "Have a great night."

One of the first things Kayla had done when she realized that her financial future was secured was to buy a house. Not a small row house like her parents had managed to scrimp and save for when she was a kid, but a large home with a pool in a gated community. Corporate giants, politicians and the occasional actor were her neighbors, making for exciting evening walks.

Kayla opened the door, and Simone bounded straight for the kitchen, pulling a bottle of wine from her tote bag. "So, I've been working all night and finally had enough. My editor wanted me to do a bit of fact-checking when it came to my interview with Vince Taylor. He suspected that there was more to their story than what I put in my article, but there was no way I was going to go to print with the whole sugar daddy site. I mean, could you imagine how awful they would feel if that got out." Simone snorted and pushed her glasses up her nose. "Though I was about to sign up for it myself."

Kayla put the wineglasses on the counter just as Simone popped the cork. "If you want to meet some rich guys, I'd be more than happy to set you up. I can think of at least five men off the top of my head who would be perfect for you."

"If you can think of five, then they can't all be perfect."

"You're too cute for your own good. You make everyone fall in love with you." It was Kayla herself who was the one constantly unlucky in love. "I can't believe you're still going on about that website."

Simone turned around and pulled her laptop out of the tote bag. "I ordered the food before I came, so it will be here soon. And yes, I am. We're going to drink wine and look at it."

"I thought we were going to watch Netflix." Kayla crossed her arms. "Is this a bait and switch?"

"No." Simone giggled. "Maybe a little. We can still watch shows. But I want you to humor me."

There was no point in arguing, not when Simone was this determined. "Fine. But let's go to the living room. I want to be comfortable."

It took them a few minutes to get organized: sweaters, blankets, wine, and food had to be procured, paid for and arranged. But thirty minutes later, Kayla found herself on the couch with her second glass of wine, Simone and her laptop pressed against her.

"There aren't a lot of men on here." Maybe she'd get out of this simply by lack of options.

"What about this one?" Simone stopped on a guy who barely looked legal. He was skinny with long brown hair that flopped over to cover his eyes. "Says he's twenty. Goes to Seneca in the business program."

Kayla tried to picture herself going out with him to a movie or dinner. "He looks like he could be my kid brother."

"You're right. We want younger, but not too young." She held out her now empty glass, which Kayla quickly filled. "I'll change the preference settings."

"This is stupid. I'm not going to find anyone who I'd want to do anything with."

"Keep an open mind."

"This feels like some weird online shopping thing."

"It totally is. Except with all consenting adults." Simone whistled as she clicked the image of a man. "Hello, sexy."

The picture quickly filled the screen, and Kayla's breath caught in the back of her throat. Looking up at her was the handsome face of a man, with brown eyes that seemed to warm her even through the screen. In the picture he wore a dress shirt that was unbuttoned at the neck, with the shirt sleeves rolled up, exposing firm forearms. His wild brown hair contrasted the neatly trimmed light beard he sported. His headshot could have been on the cover of *GQ*, rather than buried on a sugar daddy site.

Simone leaned in closer to the laptop. "His name is Devin F., and he's a PhD graduate student. Wow, dude's brilliant. And hot."

Kayla fought against the urge to squirm in her seat. "Why would a man like that be on a site like this?"

"If he's a grad student, I'm sure he's got a pile of bills stacked up. Probably looking for some financial aid."

"At least he'd be upfront about what he wanted." There was something almost too good about Devin, too perfect. "Keep going."

"Really?" Simone's eyes were wide, even as she took a large sip of wine. "You're passing on hot, smart guy?"

She rolled her eyes. "Next."

"Fine. Here's another one. Ah...eighteen and in his first year of engineering."

They continued to go through the list, laughing more and more as they got deeper into the wine. After about an hour, Simone tipped her head back and fell asleep. Kayla smiled, before getting up and rearranging her friend for a night on the couch. Only once she'd draped her with a warm blanket, did Kayla gather the laptop and the wineglasses, and take them both to the kitchen.

She'd had a surprising amount of fun looking at the various profiles, even if none of them reached out to her. Well, almost none. Despite having said to the contrary, Kayla had been more than a little intrigued about Devin, the hot math guy. And there was a sentence that went against most of her unspoken stereotypes. Taking one last look at Simone snoring away on her couch, Kayla set the laptop on the counter and flicked back through the profile pages until she found Devin.

He really was hot. And the fact that he had a PhD was attractive unto itself. Not that there was anything necessarily wrong with the other guys on the site. They were all sexy in their ways. But if Kayla was even going to consider this—and really, she *wasn't* thinking about doing this—then there was no sense in compromising. If she reached out to a man with an offer of being his sugar mama—and fuck that sounded just weird—then Kayla wanted it all.

Devin certainly fit the bill.

Pouring herself another glass, she drew a figure eight on the laptop's trackpad, moving the cursor on the screen. It would take next to no effort to click on the *email me* button, to see if he was even someone she might have an interest in. Not that she was going to. Nope. What kind of person did that make her, reaching out to someone who was in a far less advantageous position than her, to offer to pay for sex?

Though, according to the site rules, sex wasn't something that had to be on the table. This wasn't about prostitution. It was supposed to be a way for people to connect. She had something that Devin wanted—money. Devin also had something she needed—no strings attached companionship. They would both have clear expectations as to what would be going on. There'd be no surprises, no leaving her the way Christoph had.

The cursor flicked closer to the *email me* button. Kayla paused, staring at the small pixilated gatekeeper.

This was a horrible idea.

There was no knowing what kind of person would be on the other side, what he'd want from her. Despite being the one with the power in this situation, she felt surprisingly vulnerable.

God, she was acting stupid. It was just an email through a system. It wasn't as though she was making a life-altering decision here. She could always say no if she didn't like what she heard.

Besides, she *was* the one with the power here.

She couldn't let Christoph continue to control her outlook on life, dating, and men.

Gulping her wine, she pressed the button and typed out a quick message before hitting send.

There. The ball was no longer in her court.

"You're up, Devin." She smiled as she closed the laptop and went to bed.

Chapter 3

The smell of soup filled the air as Devin gave the giant pot another stir. It was the third Saturday of the month, and he was once again helping out at the soup kitchen. He'd started volunteering here during the second year of his undergrad program, having known a few students who'd needed the extra help when life got to be a bit too much. While his finances had always ridden quite close to the line, he so far hadn't needed to visit here himself. Devin counted himself lucky.

Still, others weren't so fortunate as himself, and it was the least he could do to give back to his community.

Angela Cote was busy sliding another batch of biscuits into the oven. Everyone loved Angela and her baking, and the kitchen was always a tad bit fuller when people knew she was working.

"God, I need to get that recipe from you." He looked over his shoulder at her, taking a long and dramatic whiff. "Seriously, teach me how to make those because I need to win a woman over, and I think that's going to be the way."

"Your handsome face is more than enough to win a woman." She punched his arm as she passed. "Did you add the bay leaves this time?"

"Yes, ma'am." He held up the bottle and gave it a shake. "Eight, as directed."

"Good." She shoved him gently to the side and took over. "Salt?"

"Yup."

"Tomato paste? Not the crushed ones."

"Four cans." Devin leaned over and placed his chin on her shoulder. "Did I do good, Mom?"

Angela snorted, before reaching up to pat his cheek. "Only took you eight years, but yes. You did well."

"Yes!" Devin raised both hands and walked around the kitchen as though he'd just won a boxing match. "I'm the soup king."

"Eight years. To learn to make soup properly." She grabbed the dish towel and snapped his ass with it. "My sons learned that before they were ten."

"Angela, please." He pressed his hand to his heart and gave her his best smile. "Give me this one."

She shook her head, but there was no hiding her smile. "Fine. But I expect you to learn how to make my biscuits perfectly far faster."

"I promise I'll perfect it in six years."

"I'll give you six months. Not a moment longer." She patted his shoulder before moving to the other counter.

They fell into the routine of moving the food from the kitchen to the front where it was available to those who needed it. Devin always enjoyed the days he came here, helping out any way that was required. It was one of the few times he felt as though his life had some purpose, a direction that it didn't otherwise have. Sure, he was smart, could do complex math problems quickly, but that never felt as though it would leave any impact.

Someday, he'd figure his life out.

Maybe.

Only once the supper rush had died down did Devin grab a Coke and head for the back door. "I'm going to take my break."

The staff had set up a small lounge area that was only good in the warm months. Even in early June, some nights were far too cold for them to be out for too long. But the past few weeks had welcomed warmer weather, making it the perfect spot to sit out and enjoy a drink. He fell into the wooden Adirondack chair and fished his cell phone from his pocket.

There was a notification icon at the top of the phone that had been there since last night, but he hadn't had a chance to see what it was for. Probably from a game or something that he'd tried out and thought he'd deleted but hadn't. Still, when he swiped down, he didn't recognize the link.

"What'd I do?" He clicked it, surprised when it took him to millionairesugardaddy.com and asked for his login credentials.

"Shit."

He'd completely forgotten about his profile on the site, and someone had sent him a message. Ray would laugh his balls off if he found out that someone had contacted him. God, he'd never live it down.

The best course of action was to delete his account, uninstall the app and never, ever think about this again. That was the logical, sane thing to do.

And yet.

It was a Saturday night, and he was taking a break from his shift at the soup kitchen, instead of hitting the bars or hanging out with his friends. Why not live a fantasy for a few minutes while he gave his feet a rest? Clicking the button, he immediately sat up a bit straighter.

There were a message and a picture of the woman—the incredibly attractive woman—who'd written it. Her skin was so white, contrasting her black hair that was pulled back into a ponytail at the base of her neck. Her lips were painted red, and her makeup was flawless.

But it was her eyes that took Devin's breath away. Everything about her image projected cool confidence that should have unnerved him. But her eyes, there was a vulnerability to them; in the way she looked at the camera as if to say, I'm here if you can see me. This was the woman who reached out to him, wanting to connect?

"Wow." He ran his thumb across the screen just below her chin.

And if her eyes weren't enough to lure him in, then her message pushed him over the top.

> *Devin,*
> *I wasn't planning on actually connecting to*
> *anyone on this site. The entire thing, well, it isn't*
> *me. But here I am.*
>
> *I'm looking for a man who is upfront about what*
> *he wants. No misleading or flattering statements.*
> *Simple transactions. My money for your time.*
> *I'm not looking for sex, though I'm not opposed.*
> *What I want...no what I need, is to make sure that*
> *I can move forward. I find myself spending far*
> *too much time in the past, and that needs to stop.*
>
> *So, are you a man who can do that?*
>
> *No expectations. Everything agreed upon,*
> *contracted, ahead of time.*
>
> *Kayla*

"Who broke your heart, pretty lady?" Devin couldn't imagine what could have happened to a woman who apparently seemed to be in control of her life, but it couldn't have been good.

He knew guys who were like that, were selfish enough to harm a lover with their careless words and actions. He tried to be kind to the women in his life, even if they eventually got frustrated with his aimlessness and left him. Maybe spending time with someone like Kayla would be good for him as well.

She didn't want a long-term relationship. There'd be no pressure on him to think about marriage, houses, whether or not he wanted kids when he got older. God, he didn't even know what profession he wanted to be a part of, let alone if he was husband and father material. If she was spending too much time in the past, his crime was living in a future with a crippling number of possibilities.

Yeah, having something like this might give him a bit of a lift, might help settle him down so he could think about what he wanted. Plus, having someone pay to spend time with him wasn't exactly a horrible idea. Especially someone as beautiful as Kayla. And if she turned out to have a horrific personality, well, he could cut ties, no harm, no foul. Plus, it would make paying rent for the next few months a bit easier.

He thumbed out a response. Smiling as he did. She might as well know what she was getting herself into before they got too far.

> *Hello Kayla,*
> *A while ago, a bunch of us were drunk, and we were teasing a friend. She turned things around, and I somehow ended up the one with the profile. I'd been intending on deleting it, but then I got your message.*
>
> *It sounds like you've had some troubles in your past. Me? My last girlfriend left me when I wasn't ready to commit to getting married. We'd been dating for three years at that point, and she felt it was time to either take the next step or end things.*
>
> *I'm not looking for love. But I'll be more than up for anything else you want to throw my way. I'll warn you now, I'm a gamer, I don't know what I want to be when I grow up, and I'm not overly fancy. Best for you to understand what you're getting yourself into before we take another step.*

Let me know.

D

There. It wasn't a lot, but if she were going to get scared off, it would probably do the trick.

"Devin?" Angela's voice drifted out from the kitchen. "I need your muscles."

"Yes, ma'am."

He shoved his phone into his back pocket and went to do his Italian mama's bidding. He was in the middle of transferring three pots of soup from the kitchen to the front when he felt his phone buzz against his ass. His heart beat a tiny bit faster. That couldn't be her already, could it?

He had to wait another fifteen minutes before he was able to sneak a look. The icon was back, and this time he didn't hesitate to click it. He smiled as he read Kayla's response.

D? Not even a whole name?

Well, D, I think you and I might be on the same page. Why don't we meet for dinner, to see if this is something we both want to try?

Worst case, you'll eat well, and I'll know for certain that this entire thing was a horrible mistake. Seems like a small price to pay.

You in?

K

Hell yes, he was in. If for no other reason than he wanted to meet Kayla and see if those eyes could speak to him in person the way they did through her photograph.

I'm at your service.

D

A man at my beck and call? This will prove interesting. I'm busy with meetings for a few days. Thursday night work?

K

I'm free when you need me.

D

*Give me your address, and I'll come by with the
car to pick you up.*

K

God, this was weird. He was arranging a dinner date with a millionaire, and she was the one who was going to pick him up. This was a role reversal Devin never thought in a million years he'd ever be a part of. He sent her his address and one final message before turning his attention back to his job.

*I don't know what's going to happen, but just
know that no matter what, I won't do anything to
hurt you. See you Thursday.*

D.

Chapter 4

Devin's body still ached even as he inched his way out of sleep. He'd spent a good chunk of Sunday at the school's gym, and probably pushed himself a bit too hard given how much lifting he'd done at the soup kitchen the night before.

Still, it was Monday, and he had to get his ass in gear. His PhD defense was over, but that didn't mean he had the luxury of sitting on his ass and doing nothing. He had to figure out his next steps: if there were any future academic positions he should be applying for or was there something in the private sector that might be better suited for his skills.

His mind spun as an endless number of possibilities rolled through his head. He was a smart, well-educated man who had taken on various supporting academic roles over the years. There was no reason he couldn't find a job, any job, and move on to the next step of his life.

So why the hell was the mere thought of leaving his apartment to go to the university and look at the academic postings, to talk to his advisors and see what their ideas were on where he should be looking, so goddammed terrifying?

"Get your shit together." He grabbed a T-shirt and went to get cleaned up and ready for the day.

Ray was at the kitchen table, his books and laptop opened, a coffee in his hand and a frown on his face as he stared off into space. Devin paused long enough to realize Ray hadn't noticed him. "Dude, you okay?"

Ray sat back, giving his head a shake. "Hey. Yeah, yeah, I'm good."

"You don't look good." He went over and poured himself a cup of coffee.

"Just have things on my mind."

"What's got you stressed?" Devin knew Ray's summer courses had been a bit harder than he'd expected, but it wasn't exactly like his friend to be this distracted. Usually, Ray was an unending ray of sunshine. It was annoying to no end.

"Nothing." He set his coffee down and pinched the bridge of his nose. "Well, not school."

"Your mom?"

Ray closed his eyes.

For the briefest of seconds, Devin thought his friend was going to cry. He quickly put his mug down and crossed over to Ray, squatted down and put a hand on his shoulder. "Dude, what's going on?"

Ray shook his head.

"You can't keep this shit inside, whatever it is. It will kill you."

Ray let out a strangled laugh. "That would be ironic."

Shit. He knew Ray and his family well enough to know what was going on. "The cancer is back?"

This time the tears slid down Ray's cheeks, and Devin's heart broke for his friend. "She got the results from her five-year checkup. She's been clear of cancer for so long that I'd just assumed she'd beaten it."

"She did once, that doesn't mean she can't beat it again." He didn't know a hell of a lot about breast cancer, but he knew Ray. This was going to be hell on his friend. "Look, I'm finished with school. If you or your family need anything at all, I'm here for you."

"Thanks, man."

"Seriously. I can drive your mom to the hospital or drop things off. Hell, I can sit with her during chemo, if that's what you need."

The tension was still there, but Ray looked to be able to breathe a bit better. "She'd like that. And it would help dad out too."

Devin got to his feet, ignoring the screaming muscles as the blood raced back to where it belonged. "I'm sorry that you guys are going through this again."

"Me too." Ray sat up straighter. "But you're right, Mom's tough. She'll probably knock this out of the park the way she did last time."

"She will." Devin reclaimed his mug, his thoughts having now latched on to Ray's problem. Despite Ray trying to push past what was still upsetting him, Devin knew a distraction would help set his mind at ease. Lucky for him, Devin had the perfect thing. "Remember that sugar daddy site we signed up for?"

"Yes." Ray stretched the word out as he got up from his seat and came into the kitchen. "Tell me you've been talking to a hot, rich girl."

"I've...been talking to a hot, rich girl."

"No fucking way!" Joy lit Ray's face, and Devin smiled. "You asshole. When did this happen?"

"Saturday when I was at the soup kitchen." It didn't take him long to relay the extent of his conversations with Kayla. "We're meeting for dinner Thursday night."

"Of course, you're the one who gets the hot, rich chick." But the smile on Ray's face didn't betray any jealousy. "I want to know all the things."

"You got it."

He waited until Ray refocused on his work before pulling out his phone. There was no new notification from the sugar daddy app, which meant nothing new from Kayla herself. He shouldn't exactly expect anything from her—this wasn't a conventional dating situation—but he couldn't help but be disappointed in the lack of communication. Not that there'd been much conversation between them, but he couldn't help but crave a bit more. A few more scraps of their discussion to see if there had been a spark between them, or if it was something he'd imagined.

Turning his phone over and over in his hand, Devin debated the benefits of texting her again. She might think that he's being pushy and cut her losses before things went too far. On the other hand, she might enjoy getting to know him a bit more before Thursday.

I'm looking for a man who is upfront about what he wants. No misleading or flattering statements. Simple transactions. My money for your time.

Well, if she wanted a man who was upfront about what he wanted, then that was exactly who she was going to get. Casting another quick look at Ray, Devin grabbed his coffee and slipped his phone into his back pocket. "I'm going out on the deck for a few. Want the door open?"

"Closed, please. I'm having a hard-enough time focusing without the nice weather causing me grief."

Sounds from the street outside blasted Devin the moment he stepped out onto the balcony. The small space was jammed tight with the things they couldn't find room for in the actual apartment. Bikes, two plastic containers filled with God only knew what, two cheap plastic chairs and a small plastic table filled the small concrete confinement. Three empty beer bottles were still on the table from when they'd been out a few days ago.

Ignoring the mess, he pulled his phone back out and looked at the app. Maybe this wasn't a good idea? She said she was going to be busy with meetings for the next few days, and the last thing he wanted to do was cause her grief. Not that she had to respond to him…

Fuck it.

She wanted honest and open. Well, that's what she was about to get.

* * * *

After having been on her feet in six-inch heels for over eight hours, Kayla was ready to find the nearest bathtub and soak until the pain eased from her muscles. That relief was still another three hours away at the very earliest. She continued to follow the floor chief down the factory floor, forcing her attention to stay fixed on what he was telling her.

The last board meeting had gotten her thinking about innovations in manufacturing. It was important to her to ensure Fashion Finds was always on the cutting edge while maintaining a safe and positive work environment for her employees. Today, she'd managed to wrangle a tour of a new, state of the art shoe manufacturing facility in Germany. Between the time change and the length of time they walked through the plant, Kayla was ready to collapse.

Instead, she leaned over to where her tour guide was currently pointing. "And after they're done here, they go over to our sewing machines, which are run by our staff."

"That's fascinating." She pulled out her phone to make a note of the production line and blinked for a moment when she realized that there was a new message from the sugar daddy app. The only person she was communicating with was Devin, and as far as she knew, he was still on for Thursday night. Pushing all thoughts of her upcoming date aside, she opened her note app. "How many staff do you have?"

For the rest of the tour, the thought of Devin's message and what it might be, poked at the back of her brain. Was he canceling? She couldn't imagine he'd back out on her, but then again, what did she know about him or his life. Every time she'd pull her phone out to take a note or check her email, a renewed bout of curiosity washed over her. It wasn't until she was finally slipping into the limo, ready to take her to the Frankfurt airport, that she was able to look finally.

Her face flushed as an unexpected wave of embarrassment washed over her. Why the hell was she bothered by this? The dozens of men who'd set up profiles on the millionairesugardaddy.com site didn't care about what others thought about them buying companionship. Why the hell should she?

Because everyone knows that women are treated differently, sweetheart.

She could only imagine what her parents, the board, or anyone else would think of her if they discovered she was buying the time of a handsome young grad student. Her parents would be devastated and chalk the whole thing to little more than prostitution. The board...she could only imagine what they'd say, most likely with it ending in her being fired from running her own company.

Simone would probably give her a high-five and tell her to keep at it. But Simone didn't count. She didn't have control over Kayla's reputation, despite the few fluff pieces Simone had done on her over the years.

No, if she was going to go forward with this, meet up with Devin, then she had to accept that if this ever got out, it might be the end of her professional life as she knew it. Because as much as she might not want to accept the double standard that existed out there, she wasn't a fool.

She could continue to live her life as is, to be Kayla Arnold, the face of Fashion Finds and one of the youngest female CEOs in Canadian history. Or she could be Kayla Arnold, a thirty-one-year-old woman who took a chance on a unique means to find someone who could give her what she needed on her terms.

Pay to play, or some such thing.

Taking a breath and chancing a look at the back of the driver's head, she pressed the notification link and logged into the app. There was Devin's laid-back text, his easygoing nature coming through once again.

Hey, pretty lady,

I know you said you were busy this week. I don't want to get in your way. But I was thinking about you. Thinking about the kind of person you are. Should I look you up online, or go with the flow?

D

That wasn't exactly what she was expecting. She'd just assumed that Devin had done that already, googled her the moment he'd seen her name listed. That's what she would have done, had their positions been reversed. Then again, guys tended to be more trusting of women than the other way around.

Everyone knew who she was in the business world, but he was an academic and probably not up on the world of women's fashion. It was nice to have a shroud of anonymity, even if it was only temporary. But she'd never tell someone else to go into a situation blind.

She pressed the reply button, taking her time as she tried to find the right words.

> *I'm in Germany at the moment for work. I'll*
> *be back in the country tomorrow morning.*
> *If you haven't looked me up yet, go to www.*
> *fashionfinds.com and look at the CEO. That's me.*
>
> K

There. He'd either be scared off, or not, but at least he would know what he was getting into. Her nerves chewed at her, sending her scurrying for a distraction that she could do in the back of the limo. Emails, yes, there were always emails.

She managed to get through the first dozen or so before she stopped short. The email heading screamed at her, making her wish she'd remained blissfully ignorant.

To: Arnold, Kayla
From: Meadow Lake Alumni Association
Subject: Library Dedication Homecoming Week.

Dear Ms. Arnold,

We hope this email finds you well. As per our earlier letter, the Meadow Lake Alumni Committee is greatly appreciative of your continued financial support over the years. As a result, the committee has voted to rename our high school library the Kayla Arnold Library.

While we understand that your schedule is full, we are hopeful that you will be able to attend not only the ceremony but our entire homecoming week. It would be an excellent opportunity for some of the recipients of your scholarship to meet with you and express their appreciation in person. We've had a significant number of requests from the girls and their families to meet you, and it would be wonderful if they could see someone as successful as you are having come from our small community.

Anything we can do to accommodate you, even if only for a

short period, we would love to have you.

Please contact me, and we can finalize the details.

Best regards,
Maureen Toomey

Shit.

Kayla hated the thought of having a library named after her but knowing that the girls wanted to meet her was a whole other matter. She knew how insulated Meadow Lake was, how much it would have meant to her to have met Bill Gates, Oprah Winfrey, or Margaret Atwood when she was in high school. She might have been able to blow off the honor, but not the obligation.

Closing her eyes, she leaned her head back against the seat, ignoring the sharp leather smell and artificial air freshener. It was too much in a way, having to plot and calculate the possible outcomes of every decision she made. What would happen if she went with her gut, stayed home to avoid the inevitable mix and mingle with her high school acquaintances, the fake smiles, and jealous glances?

She'd feel guilty. Those girls needed someone to look up to, someone who was just like them to prove that they didn't have to accept the lives that their high school guidance counselor indicated was the best, the safest for them. They could aspire to be businesswomen, doctors, lawyers, mothers, secretaries, anything at all. They didn't need to follow a particular pattern because they did or didn't do well in certain classes. Their family backgrounds were only a starting place and not a defining moment.

But if she went, she knew damn well she'd be opening herself up to questions.

Where's Christoph? Did you two break up?
I can't imagine she walked away from him? He's so hot.
I heard she didn't give him a dime. They were together forever.

Her phone pinged again, and she looked down without thinking. It was another message from Devin.

Germany? I haven't been further than Buffalo.

CEO? I'm a grad student with massive student loans. That's impressive. For the record, you're so far out of my league you might as well live in

Germany permanently. Are you sure you want to
keep our dinner date?

D

Devin.

She'd only thought so far as going out to dinner with Devin, to have a fun night to prove that she could still do that. But he was perfect: smart, handsome, and clearly, he had no problems talking to strangers. And the best part was that she could buy his time, and not have to worry about emotions getting in the way. He could be her social buffer, to keep the awkward questions about Christoph at bay.

Devin. Lifting her phone, she smiled as she thumbed her response.

And I have a proposal. One that will help with
those loans. We'll talk more Thursday.

K

All she had to do was convince him to come with her for a week to the middle of nowhere Ontario.

Easy.

Chapter 5

Kayla ran her hands down the front of her dress, smoothing out the nonexistent wrinkle on the midnight-blue material. It was a prototype from her fall line, one of the few that she'd designed personally. She'd hoped to launch a new signature collection, ones that were hers alone, but the board wasn't quite ready to agree. Strange, given how broad her social media reach was, and how many of the women who reached out to her said they wanted something that was more like the clothing she'd put out years ago.

It had been a long time since she'd gone through the process of designing something start to finish, and standing there, wearing one of her creations, sent a thrill through her she hadn't felt in ages. Not to mention that she looked damn good in it.

"Eat your heart out, Devin."

The past week had been enjoyable. Since their initial conversation Saturday night, Kayla had continued to text him randomly. Their conversations never went deep, only skirting the surface of topics that fell squarely into the category of small talk. Movies, the weather, annoying traffic in patterns in the city—pretty much everything all of the go-to topics that she'd hit on a first date.

Which meant their actual first date was going to be interesting.

What the hell do you talk about when you can't discuss movies, television or the weather?

A knock on her door pulled her back to reality. She grabbed her wrap and her purse before heading out. "Hello, Mark."

"Good evening, Ms. Arnold. All ready to go?"

"I am."

He opened the back door to the car, offering his hand to help her in. He'd been her driver for two years now, and she always felt relaxed around him. Maybe because he was older and acted more like a protective second father than a driver. Regardless, it was lovely spending time with him. When he climbed into the front, he adjusted his mirror. "You look beautiful. Business meeting?"

"Believe it or not, I'm going on a date." She smiled at his reflection. "It should be interesting."

"That's wonderful to hear. I've often mentioned to my husband that you're far too beautiful to be single."

"Beauty and compatibility as a partner are not exactly related." She hadn't realized she was the topic of supper-hour conversation between spouses. Though, it made sense. "How's Alex doing?"

"Neck deep in grading final papers. You'd think it would get easier after all these years, but apparently, his students have a way of being insanely creative in their research."

"Creative good, or bad?"

"Let's just say the references are lacking or consist of 'I found this on Buzzfeed.'"

"Oh dear. Well, he only has two more years before he retires. Then he won't have to worry about it."

Mark sighed. "True. But then he'll probably go nuts being home all day. Knowing him, he'll last a month and will put his name on the substitute teaching list."

Kayla chuckled and found herself relaxing.

"You shouldn't be nervous. Any young man would appreciate spending time with you."

"I'm not nervous." Nauseous, panicked, more than a little terrified—yes. "I just haven't done this in a while."

"Blind date?"

"No. We've been texting for a week."

She flipped her phone around in her hand and brought up the last message she'd received from Devin.

> *Just tried on my suit and pleased to announce*
> *that it still mostly fits. I'll be the tall brunet dude*
> *in the suit jacket an inch and a half too short in*
> *the sleeves.*

Despite having seen his picture, she didn't exactly know what to expect from him. People tended to put photo number one hundred up when it came to dating sites, only the best angle, best lighting, that didn't much resemble the actual person. Even the one that Simone insisted on uploading didn't exactly look like Kayla. She appeared cold, untouchable, even to her own eyes. Why Devin didn't run for the hills the moment he laid eyes on that, was beyond her.

"Mark?"

"Yes, ma'am?"

"How do you describe me to others? I mean, when Alex asks what kind of person I am, what do you say?"

The car rolled to a stop at a light, and he looked at her over his shoulder. "Are you okay?"

"Of course." She pulled her shoulders back, and her practiced mask slipped into place. "Maybe I *am* nervous."

The light changed, and Mark returned his attention back to the road. They didn't say anything until they reached the apartment building address that Devin had provided.

"We're here. I'll get the door for him." Mark undid his seatbelt but stopped before opening his door. "And I've always told Alex that you're a beautiful woman, who tries to do right by everyone she meets. I've also said that you're one of the saddest people I've ever met. And that breaks my heart."

And with that, he left the car.

Oh.

Tears threatened, and it took an act of sheer willpower to keep them from coming and ruining her makeup. The last thing she wanted was to meet Devin with raccoon eyes and a red nose.

"Damn you, Mark." She was going to have to give him a raise.

Distraction. *Come on, girl. Hot date's about to happen.*

Taking a deep breath, she turned her attention to the building, hoping to catch a glimpse of Devin before he came out. Mark stood inside the doors waiting for Devin to come down. One moment he was standing all stiff and professional, and the next she saw his entire body relax as he shook hands with someone she couldn't quite see.

The moment they opened the doors and stepped out into the evening sun, Kayla's breath caught in her chest. Standing a half-head taller than Mark was Devin. Devin wasn't wearing a suit jacket, which gave her a clear view of his body. His hair appeared the same as it was in the photo, but his beard was a bit darker and fuller. His plum-colored dress shirt fit him perfectly, and he'd rolled up the sleeves enough to show off the muscles of his forearms, which was completely unexpected.

And freaking hot.

Mark opened the door to the car, and Devin leaned down to look in. Kayla fought to keep her face schooled, devoid of the surprise she felt at the unexpectedly potent charm that flowed from him.

"When you said pick me up in a car, I was thinking *a car*." And then he smiled.

Kayla's heart fluttered. Pressing her lips together a bit tighter than necessary, she beckoned him to join her. "I guess I didn't think anything of it."

Devin slid into the seat beside her, his gaze bouncing around the back of the limo. "This is a bit of an upgrade from my Kia."

"I had a Kia once. It was my first car out of high school." She'd loved that little thing and the independence that came along with it. "It was awesome on gas."

"I know, right?" He folded his long legs in as he secured his seatbelt. "It's the only thing that saves me some days. I drive for Uber when I get bored."

Mark climbed into the front, gave Kayla a wink before sliding up the privacy window, leaving her and Devin alone. Well, that must mean that he approves, because if her driver had any trepidations about Devin, there was no way he'd do that. That little bit of confidence was enough to relax her a tiny bit more. Maybe this wasn't going to be the disaster she'd anticipated.

Devin turned in his seat, flashing her a smile. "Are you okay?"

"Yes, of course." She ran her hands across her thighs. "I'm glad you agreed to come out tonight. I have to admit the whole website thing is a bit much."

"I did it in a drunken attempt to find a friend a date." He ran his hand along the back of his head. "Not that I remember much. As I said, I was going to take my profile down, but then life got in the way." He turned his face toward the window for a moment, before giving his head a shake. "So, pretty lady. Where are we going tonight?"

She wasn't typically one for compliments, but she had to admit, she loved the way he called her that. "Something fun. Top of the CN Tower for dinner."

"I haven't been up there since junior high." His smile lit his entire face. "And I've never gone to the restaurant. What made you choose there?"

Kayla couldn't contain her surprise. "I don't know. I thought it would be...fun."

"Fun is the very best reason to do something." He cocked his head. "I get the impression you don't do much simply for fun these days."

It was her turn to look away. "Why would you say that?"

"Just based on our texts." He reached out and gave her hand on her lap a light squeeze. "But tonight, we're going to have a good time."

"We are?" This time she didn't hold back her smile. If this was who Devin was, an easygoing guy who wanted to have a fun night out, then things were going to be fine.

"Of course." He leaned back in his seat and looked around the limo again. "Man, Ray is going to be pissed that I got to ride in a limo."

"That's your roommate?"

"Yeah. He's working on his master's degree. We had a few classes together during our first year, and both needed a roommate. It worked out. He's good people, even if he makes me do stupid things when I've been drinking."

"He's not working on his PhD as well?"

Something changed on Devin's face. "His mom got sick. Breast cancer. He dropped out for a few years to help his dad out."

God, she couldn't imagine. "That's awful. I'm sure his parents appreciated it. Is she okay now?"

"He just found out that the cancer is back."

Without thinking, she reached out and gave his thigh a gentle squeeze. "I'm sorry."

Every trace of the jovial man she'd met only moments ago had vanished. "Mind if we don't talk about this?"

"Of course. Why don't you tell me about your thesis?"

Kayla was surprised how quickly they slipped into conversation on their way to dinner. It wasn't exactly something she'd expected but was wholly relieved as they chatted. She certainly wasn't used to talking to someone who wasn't either out to prove her wrong or looking to get something from her. And Devin didn't seem to want anything from anyone. In fact, he didn't seem to be overly passionate about any particular thing. *Strange.*

The limo pulled up in front of Ripley's Aquarium, where a large crowd of Blue Jays fans was heading to Rogers Centre for a game. Mark jogged around and opened Devin's door, from which they both climbed out.

Devin shook his hand, grinning. "Thanks, man."

"No problem at all." Mark turned to her, barely able to contain a grin. "Just text me when you're finished, and I'll be here waiting for you."

"Thank you, Mark." She nodded and turned her attention back to Devin. "Shall we?"

No one looked twice at them as they crossed to the entrance where an attendant was gathering the next group to go up to the observation deck. Kayla gave the young woman her name, and before she knew it, they were being ushered into the glass elevator, heading up to the restaurant.

Ironically, Kayla hated heights. She'd do everything in her power to avoid having to go up ladders, look over balconies, pretty much anything that could potentially give her that nauseous, nervous panic that started in her feet and raced up her legs until she couldn't move. Yet, when she was trying to figure out a place to take Devin, the idea of going up the tower kept coming back every time she'd dismissed it.

Just like this date, the thought of eating on top of Toronto seemed crazy, a bit scary, and entirely something she needed to do. Old Kayla had always tried to confront her fears, whenever possible. It was one of the reasons Fashion Finds had been so successful out of the gate.

New Kayla not so much. The weight of her corporate responsibilities had consumed her. She'd been too terrified of a misstep that would see the board try to remove her, or worse, impact her employees who depended on her. It was one thing to be fearless when she was on her own; it was another when she was the boss.

"Wow. I forgot how cool things look up here." Devin pressed his hands to the glass wall and looked down as the elevator continued to climb.

Kayla wanted to barf. "I'm glad you're enjoying yourself."

He looked at her, but she couldn't move her gaze from the fly that had buzzed in with them and was now resting on the glass. It wouldn't take a genius to realize that she wasn't overly keen on the ride, but thankfully, Devin didn't call her on it. Instead, he moved away from the glass to stand directly beside her.

The doors dinged open, and she marched quickly from the elevator to the restaurant, with Devin sauntering behind her. She approached the hostess and gave their names.

"Yes, Ms. Arnold. We've been expecting you. Please come this way."

When they didn't go out to the 360 Restaurant, Devin took her by the hand. "I thought we were eating?"

"We are. But I thought a more private setting would be appropriate."

The hostess led them to the LookOut level, where a private table had been set up. "Your waiter will be along shortly. We've already set up the wine you requested." And with that, she left them.

Devin whistled as he walked into the room. "This is...you booked this for us?"

"I've had a few corporate events here over the years. Though I don't think they've had it booked for one couple before." What was the point of being rich if she couldn't show off every now and again? "I wasn't sure if you liked red or white wine, so I asked for both. But if you don't like either, they can always get you something else."

It might not have been some people's first choice for a fancy restaurant, but you couldn't beat the view. Devin walked up to the window, staring out. "Pretty lady, you're amazing. Don't let anyone tell you otherwise."

Her cheeks hurt from trying to fight back the smile, so she didn't. "You're quite the smooth talker."

"I'm just calling it as I see it. And I like red wine."

Wanting to give him time to enjoy the entire reason she'd booked this place, Kayla went and poured them each a glass of wine. "I also figured it was better to have some privacy so we can talk about...the website."

She still couldn't quite bring herself to say sugar daddy—sugar mama, whatever—despite them both knowing the truth. It somehow made things feel awkward, despite them both understanding precisely the reason they were here. Devin turned his back to the view, and the setting sun cast a pink light across him, giving him a heavenly glow.

Girl, you're losing it.

"Why don't we have a seat and discuss possible terms?" She held out the glass, doing her best to avoid touching his fingers as he took it.

"Sounds good." He moved around the table and pulled her chair out for her. In anyone else, she would have assumed he was playing the part of a suitor, but with Devin, she assumed it was simply good manners. He took his seat, claimed his glass of wine and held it out. "Best start the night with a toast. To chance encounters."

"To chance encounters."

Their conversation halted temporarily when their waiter came to take their orders. Only once they were alone again, did Kayla let out a breath and say the words she'd been practicing in her mind for a week now.

"I'd like to make you an offer. If after tonight we're both in agreement, I'd like to pay you to pretend to be my boyfriend."

Devin swallowed the wine he had in his mouth, letting out a small cough. "Pardon?"

It was strange vocalizing the things she'd been considering since this entire sugar daddy thing started. But knowing what she had on the horizon, and how people would respond, this was the best option for her. "I have some events coming up soon. Some are related to my company, but a number of them are personal. It would be a great help to me if I had a boyfriend with me. Seeing as I have no desire to enter into an actual relationship, this seems like the most practical thing to do."

Devin gave his head a small shake, before giving her a pained smile. "Dare I ask what things?"

"My high school reunion."

She'd read and reread the email from the committee, not wanting to answer until she knew if she was flying solo, or if Devin would be there for support. While she wanted to be there, she didn't think she could do it alone.

Devin was staring at her, which was more than a little unnerving. Kayla straightened, and reflexively tucked her hair behind her ear. "I'm willing to pay you for all of your time. We can negotiate a flat fee plus perks if that will help."

He was spared from answering when the waiter brought their meal. Despite the aroma of perfectly cooked salmon making her stomach rumble, she couldn't bear to take a bite, not until she knew what he was thinking.

As Devin cut into his steak, he seemed to be trying to find the right words. He finally put his knife and fork down, placed his elbows on the table and rested his chin on his joined hands. "Why do you need to bring a pretend boyfriend? Why not go alone, or bring an actual friend?"

"I did that for my five-year reunion. My best friend Simone came with me. It was shortly after Fashion Finds started to take off and the money was starting to flow."

"How'd that go?"

"About as you'd expect. My family wasn't exactly poor, but we didn't have very much. When I went back and financially I was well above most of my peers, they treated me differently."

In high school, she'd been considered average. Nothing special about her grades, her ambitions, or even her circle of friends. But coming to her reunion, everything had changed. She'd been inundated with requests to have some alone time to discuss *this awesome business idea I have. You'll get rich. I just need some startup money.* The first time, she'd been flattered. The fifth time, gutted. No one wanted to spend time with her because she was Kayla Arnold, friend and fellow grad. They only wanted to be near her for what she could do for them.

And that didn't even touch on the men who tried to woo her.

She reached for her wineglass but didn't take a drink. "When I wasn't dogging requests to provide free business advice, I was sidestepping more than a few unwanted advances. Apparently, the only thing better than being friends with someone super rich is marrying someone super rich."

"Then why go at all?" His eyes wrinkled as he frowned, which was more than a little cute. "If you don't want the attention, there's a straightforward solution."

Reaching into her purse, she pulled out the letter she'd received from the committee. "I'm apparently the guest of honor this year. And while I'd like to go, I don't want to be put in the same situation that I was the last time I went."

He took the letter and with a questioning glance, read it. "A library? I take it you threw some cash their way?"

"I helped pay for some of the books. A lot of the books. And a few computers for the kids to use." She reached down and ran her finger along the edge of her plate. "I also set up a scholarship."

Devin rolled his eyes. "Can't imagine why they'd want to put you on the spot like that. The nerve."

"I never asked for it."

"That doesn't mean you don't deserve it." He set the letter down on the table between them. "You're deciding if you should go or not, and if you do, you'd like to have a pretend boyfriend to deflect any unwanted suitors."

"Basically. Yes."

"And you don't think you can simply say no to these guys?"

Sometimes, men didn't get it. "I don't want you to think that the people of Meadow Lake are a bunch of jerks. They're not. But the last time I went there…" She'd met Christoph there. It was at the reunion that he'd come on to her, hard and fast. She'd been flattered, but also felt more than a little steamrolled. Considering how that relationship had ended, the last thing she wanted was a repeat performance. "Did I mention I'm willing to pay you?"

"Yeah, that came up." He shook his head and went back to his steak. "I guess that's the whole point of the sugar daddy site."

"It's a business transaction. I'm paying for your help. Think of it as a temporary job. I'd even find a way to give you a reference if you think that would help."

If Devin were having a crisis of conscience, then Kayla would have to come up with a plan B. One that didn't involve her going to the event at all.

"I hate to see a woman in need. I'll have to check with Ray to see if he or his mom might need me. Other than that, I don't exactly have any specific plans for the next little while, so I'm sure I can fit you into my schedule."

Joy flared brightly in her chest. "Really?"

"Sure. Why not." His smile radiated from him.

"Excellent." Maybe this was going to work out far better than she'd anticipated. "As long as we establish some rules, we'll be all set."

"What kind of rules?"

This was the simple part—the rules that had kept her safe since Christoph broke her heart.

"No dancing at all. No public displays of affection. And no matter what, there will be no kissing."

Chapter 6

Devin stood in his bedroom trying to shove as much clothing as he could manage into his suitcase while pondering his Kayla problem. Since their dinner at the tower two weeks ago, he'd done some reading on her; mostly because the woman he'd spent several hours with was nothing like the woman he'd been texting the week before.

She hadn't changed her personality, but without the shield of anonymity, her words took on an entirely different meaning. It wasn't that she lacked self-confidence, or that he doubted she could handle herself in any situation that she found herself in. But there was something hidden. A barrier that she'd erected to protect herself from harm, one that rarely if ever, came down.

He'd seen that same shield on more than one occasion at the soup kitchen. People who did what they had to do to survive and refused to let emotions get in the way. Those tended to be the people who'd been hurt the most in life. Which meant someone had hurt Kayla badly enough that she was asking him to act as a buffer. That was more than a little fucked up. It also pissed him off. Who would hurt someone else that badly?

Not that she'd admit to him that there was a problem. Despite everything that had passed between them, Kayla didn't know him well enough to share her personal history with him. He didn't exactly blame her either. He was the slacker smart guy who didn't know what he wanted from life. People like Kayla, who appeared to have their shit together, they were supposed to be the ones who looked down on people like him, to scold them for not knowing what step to take next.

She hadn't done that. But she might if he chose to share his challenges with her.

Balling up the T-shirt he'd been holding, he squeezed it before tossing it into his suitcase.

"Dude!" Ray called out from the kitchen. "Are you going somewhere?"

Shit.

He had told Ray about his trip with Kayla, and the fact he was going to be out of town for a week. Between classes and staying with his mom when she wasn't feeling well, Ray had become more than a little forgetful. "I'm in my room."

Ray burst into the room, the same way he always burst into any room. "You're not moving out, right? Like, I can't afford this place on my own, and you just defended, and I know you're graduating and stuff. But don't leave me."

Devin couldn't help but laugh. "I'm not moving out. Remember, I'm going away for a week."

"Yeah, right. Sorry about that. Mom's been needing a lot of help."

Reaching out, Devin squeezed Ray's shoulder. "Dude, it's fine. Family first, right?"

"Yup." Ray smiled, but it was no way reflected in his eyes. "So, where are you going? Please tell me it's somewhere awesome."

"Meadow Lake."

"That's...not awesome? I've never heard of it."

He hadn't either, which was why he'd spent time reading up on the small town. Apparently, he couldn't break his research habit even now that he'd graduated. "Cottage country. I'm going with Kayla as her date for her high school homecoming week."

"Kayla?" Ray's eyes widened. "Oh shit. Is this the sugar mama?"

"My first job." It felt strange thinking of it that way, but it was the only thing that made sense to him.

Ray leaned in closer. "So...what's part of the job? Will you have to be proficient in undoing buttons? Will she time your panty removing techniques?"

"It's nothing like that. She doesn't even want me to touch her." The whole idea of sex had of course been in the back of his head, but he wasn't exactly surprised when she hadn't indicated that was on the table. The no kissing thing was more than a little strange. "I'm the pretend boyfriend to keep her safe from unwanted advances."

"That's disappointing. I figured a sugar mama would want a bit of fun. Isn't that the whole point of the site?"

"I think it's whatever we negotiate."

"Well, it will be fun for you." Ray crossed his arms and sat on Devin's bed. "When you get back are you going to start looking for work?"

"Yeah. Probably." He refolded his dress pants, focusing his entire attention on his hands.

He hadn't wanted to admit it to anyone but defending his PhD hadn't been stressful because he didn't feel prepared or didn't think he'd be able to answer the questions regarding his research. He'd been freaking out because it was over. He'd walked his educational road as far as it would go, completing each of his degrees in succession until his only option was to graduate or defer. And while he might not know what he wanted to do with his life post-school, he also didn't want to incur any more student loans.

Indecision shouldn't be expensive.

He could feel Ray staring at him, but Devin didn't give him the satisfaction of looking. "What?"

"You cool?"

"Yeah, of course." He snorted, tossed the dress shirt into the bag, and reached back in to fold it. "Why wouldn't I be?"

"You're a horrible liar."

"I'm not lying." He gave up on folding his shirt and tossed it back in. "The idea of jobs freaks me out."

"What do you mean? Your advisor loves you. She said she'd give you a glowing reference, right?"

"She did." Tessa had even pulled together a list of teaching positions at a few universities and colleges around the country. Every time he went to look and apply for one of them, something inside him panicked, and he'd close the application half finished.

"Then what's the problem?"

"I mean, I can probably find a job at a college or university teaching math. Or go out into the business world and do corporate research. Or... something." He laughed, but it lacked the joy he normally felt. "Maybe I'll go back and do a different degree."

Ray shook his head. "You'll be the most educated gamer in the world."

"I should go into computer programming. I could build a game that would kick ass."

"Yeah, right." Ray slapped his thighs with his hands. "So, I get this place for a whole week?"

And that was apparently the end of that. "Give or take a day. I might come back early. It will depend on what Kayla needs."

"Kayla, eh?" He pushed away from the door. "You didn't mention her last name."

"Nope. I want to maintain a bit of her privacy if I can."

"Is she hot? Like, if she changes her mind about the sex thing you'd be all over it? Or were you relieved she was not into the sexy-fun-times?"

"Hot. Like, I'm not even in the same universe, let alone her league."

Ray sighed. "Does she have a friend? Doesn't even have to be rich."

Leave it to Ray to make him smile. "I'll ask her."

"Maybe I should check out my profile on the sugar daddy site. I have the whole place to myself for a week. I should take advantage and do a little entertaining."

Devin slammed his suitcase closed and looked long and hard at Ray. "I know you're kidding, but you should consider that. With everything that's been going on with your family, you should make sure you take some time for yourself."

"Maybe." But Devin could tell from the tone of Ray's voice that wasn't going to happen.

Ray's cell phone rang, and he quickly pulled it from his pocket. "That's dad. They're at the doctor's this morning."

"Go. I'll see you when I get back."

Kayla wasn't going to have the limo come to get him for at least another two hours, but from the sound of Ray's voice there might be tears, and he wouldn't want Devin to hear that. Poking his head out of his bedroom, he waved at Ray. "Hey. I'm going to head out. So you have some privacy."

Ray nodded but wouldn't meet his gaze. "Thanks. Have a great time."

Shit, maybe he should stay. He opened his mouth to ask if that's what Ray wanted but stopped when Ray turned his back to him. No, his gut reaction was the right one. "I'll text you later."

Devin left the apartment as quickly as he could. Now that he'd painted himself into this particularly exciting corner, he needed to find something to do for two hours while dragging around his suitcase. He stepped into the elevator and pulled out his phone to text Kayla.

Hey pretty lady. Where are you?

It took until he reached the sidewalk for her to respond. *At work. Why?*

He knew exactly where her office was from the research he'd done the night before. While he wasn't crazy enough to merely show up at her office unannounced, a part of him wanted to see her sooner rather than later.

Is Mark there with the car? Got ready too early and was going to head over. If that's okay. And when he realized how that sounded, he quickly added. *I can wait outside in the car. Or at a coffee shop if that's easier. Don't want to cause problems.*

He started walking down the sidewalk, the rattle and bang of his suitcase tripping over the ruts in the sidewalk setting a steady beat as he went. Normally, he wouldn't approach a woman at her work unless asked to. He knew it could cause problems for some women, and others wanted to keep work and private life separated. His dad had drilled into him the need to respect the women in his life, to follow their lead and let them set the boundaries.

Given that Kayla was paying him, the boundaries should have been clear cut, obvious. Yet, here he was, unsure of if he should even be texting the woman who was hiring him to play her boyfriend for a week.

The situation was more than a little fucked.

Though the moment his phone beeped, and he saw Kayla's message, he couldn't help but smile.

> Sure. Mark will meet you in the lobby to take
> your bag. I'm on the twenty-third floor.

He was going to see where the magic happened. Devin hailed a cab and threw his stuff into the backseat.

* * * *

Kayla hadn't been able to concentrate since she'd agreed to let Devin come to the office. It had been impulsive, not precisely the sort of decision she'd usually make. She hardly knew him and couldn't imagine what he'd think of Fashion Finds. In her experience, most men didn't particularly care about the fashion aspects of her company, and only cared about her bank account.

Christoph used to show up unannounced all the time, and Rhianna would have to run interference whenever he did. He'd had this strange sixth sense when it came to picking the worst possible time for Kayla, typically when she was up to her eyes in paperwork that required her immediate attention. God forbid, she didn't drop everything for him the moment he graced her with his presence. Despite the fact she worked hard, that the company was essential to her, and her attention necessary, Christoph always assumed she owed him her time.

We're dating, and you're the boss. Just get someone else to do it and come to lunch with me.

That had been his favorite quip—you're the boss. As though she could shirk her responsibilities just because it was her name at the top of the org chart. But Christoph didn't care, and always got angry when she didn't give in.

At the very least, Devin asked. It meant a lot, even if he was doing this because she was paying him.

She tossed her pen aside and leaned back in her chair.

How had she'd gotten to this point, paying a man for his time? It wasn't exactly the sort of thing she'd ever thought she'd do, and yet, after having spent one evening with Devin, she knew, in the end, it was the best way to handle the reunion.

He was charming, funny and one of the most laid-back men she'd ever been with. Not to mention he was freaking gorgeous. She'd never dated an academic, not because she wasn't interested, but mostly because she wasn't dating anyone, smart, talented, handy...breathing.

Even this thing with Devin wasn't dating. It was a practical solution to her problem of wanting to avoid anyone else trying to make a move on her. Because a woman who merely said no tended not to be enough of a deterrent for some men. But if she was in a relationship, whoa there, sorry, didn't mean to step on another man's toes.

Jackasses.

Her phone buzzed on her desk. Mark let her know that Devin was here and was on his way up. The rush of excitement was unexpected, but it got her moving enough to finish answering the email that had been in front of her for ten minutes. Still, when Rhianna knocked on her door, Kayla couldn't help but smile. "Yes?"

Rhianna poked her head in, her face a blank. "There's a Mr. Ford here for you. He says he's expected?" There was enough skepticism in her voice that Kayla knew she'd get rid of Devin if she gave even the slightest indication he wasn't welcome.

"You can send him in. Thanks."

She was able to take a breath before Devin sauntered in, giving Rhianna a wink and a smile. "Thank you, beautiful."

The moment the door closed behind them, Kayla leaned back in her seat and crossed her arms. "You're a terrible flirt."

"I don't know. I think I'm pretty good at it."

"And you're corny too."

Devin shrugged as he came entirely into the office. "I'm a math geek. I had to learn long ago not to take things too seriously or else I'd go nuts."

"There's nothing wrong with taking things seriously. It's better than the opposite."

Christoph had always told her she was too stiff and needed to smile more. But unlike Devin's easygoing charm, Christoph seemed ever to have an edge to him. He was trying to change her for his reasons, rather than showing any genuine concern. At least, she could now assume that given how things had gone between them.

No, her hesitations about transactional dealings with Devin were long gone. It was best if they both knew where they stood. Knew exact expectations from each of them and how things would eventually end— with a handshake and a nod before they both parted ways.

Devin made his way to the guest chair opposite her desk, though he chose to lean his hands against the back of it, rather than sit. "So, this week. What should I expect?"

Kayla took a small breath, giving herself a moment before answering. "I just received the agenda, and it looks like it's going to be a lot of full days. Originally, I was only planning on attending the library dedication, but once they learned I was available, they booked me for several events. Meeting with students, talking to the Junior Achievement groups. You don't have to be there for all of those, but the more you're around, the more I'll pay."

She got to her feet and came around her desk to stand before him. The last thing she wanted to do was give him the impression that she was hiding or scared of any of this. "I'll pay you ten thousand for the week, plus I'll cover all accommodations and food. If there's anything you need at all, please let me know, and I'll have Mark get it for you."

Devin's mouth fell open. "Ten grand?"

"We can negotiate if you want, but I think the offer is rather generous."

"No, no. That's...wow. Yeah, we're good."

Kayla's heart warmed at the shock and pleasure on his face. "We'll have to share a room, but I've made sure to ask for two double beds, so you don't have to worry about sleeping with me."

"I wasn't worried." There was a sparkle in his eyes that told her all she needed to know about his thoughts on sharing a bed. "But that's good to know. Anything else I need to be prepared to handle? Any old lovers you want me to keep my eyes open for, or former teachers who tried to fail you?"

She knew he was only kidding about the old lover, but the genuine fear that Christoph might be there gnawed at her. "I'll make up a list."

"Okay." Devin relaxed, as though being her protector was an easier concept to grasp than that of a sugar baby. "When do we leave?"

It was a four-hour drive in traffic to Meadow Lake if they managed to avoid any accidents. But with the regular exodus from Toronto to cottage country that happened Friday nights in the summer, she wouldn't be surprised if it took them longer. "We can go now, though we'll stop about halfway so we can get something to eat. We'll get there after dark."

"I trust your man Mark to get us there in one piece." Then he straightened to his full height and offered her his arm. "Madam."

She hesitated for a moment before she reached out and slid her hand over the crook of his arm. The heat that came from Devin warmed her cold fingers, as she gave his firm muscles a gentle squeeze.

Yeah, he was opposite of Christoph in every way possible. While she'd always considered her ex an attractive man, she knew that every moment he'd spent in the gym was calculated to turn his body into something that gave him a very particular look. She'd asked him once why he spent so much time on his abs, but not his legs, and he'd snorted.

"No one looks at my legs. I'm in suits all day, so I have to make sure I can fit into the right size dress pants."

It hadn't made a whole hell of a lot of sense to her, but then again, neither did most things Christoph did.

As they stepped out of her office, Kayla became immediately aware of the curious glances she and Devin were getting. She dropped his arm and stepped close to Rhianna. "I need to head out now. You have my numbers, so if there's a problem, please don't hesitate to call me."

"Unless the building is on fire, I'm not going to interrupt your reunion for anything." Rhianna's gaze slid to Devin for the briefest of moments, before she grinned at Kayla. "Don't do anything I wouldn't do."

Kayla widened her eyes in silent warning. "Have a great weekend." She spun and walked past a waiting Devin. "We better head out."

If he was upset by her change in demeanor, he didn't show it. With three long strides, he quickly caught up to her, falling into step easily. Neither of them said anything else until the elevator doors dinged and she stepped into the underground parking lot, where Mark had already pulled the car around.

He opened the door for them with a grin. "I've stocked the back with your favorite travel snacks. There's also drinks and water. If you need anything at all, please let me know."

"Thank you, Mark." She didn't wait for Devin and quickly slid into her usual spot.

Mark shut the door, giving her a few precious seconds to steady herself before she was locked in the back of a limo with a man she barely knew, heading home to an event she didn't want to attend. God, this wasn't something she'd typically do. It was so far out of character she was half ready to tell Mark to check her temperature to make sure she wasn't delirious with a fever.

The other door opened and as quickly as she had her peace, it was gone as Devin crawled in to join her. He turned and grinned at her, the look of joy melting away her tension. "I'm never going to get used to riding in the back of a limo."

"You'd be surprised." Though as she looked around this time, it was easy to see things through his eyes: exciting, lavish and new. "I have good snacks though."

"I bet it's something fancy, like caviar and crackers. Or chicken pâté." He stretched his legs out and rested his hands on his belly. "I'm prepared to be amazed."

Kayla leaned forward and opened the compartment Mark filled for her before every trip. The crinkle of the plastic gave away her guilty pleasure. She used her teeth to open the package and held it out for him to take one.

Devin looked at her briefly before letting loose a soul-melting laugh. "Twizzlers?"

"They're my favorite. Ever since I was a kid, Mom always got them for me whenever we were going on a road trip. The habit stuck."

She couldn't quite place the look he was giving her, but a small part of her was relieved when he reached out to snag three of the treats. "I think we're going to have a fun week, Ms. Arnold."

Settling back beside him, she took a bite of her strawberry strand. "I hope so."

She really did. Because the alternative wasn't something she wanted to consider.

Chapter 7

By the time the limo pulled into the bed and breakfast where they were staying, Devin's back was screaming at him. The seats in the limo were comfortable enough, but he'd tried his best to keep a small physical distance between them. Kayla had been sitting rigidly in her seat for the first twenty minutes of the ride, looking more than a little on guard. The moment he shifted his weight and leaned against the door, she'd relaxed.

So, he continued to lean, keeping that boundary and giving her the space she apparently needed. He couldn't imagine what happened to her to cause her not to trust men. At least, he assumed it was a trust thing. It could simply be that they didn't know one another well enough yet.

Looking out the window, he read the sign of the B&B. "Maple Hall? That sounds formal."

"The Babineau family has owned this place for as long as I've known. They have maple trees on the property, and every spring tap them as part of the syrup festival. I used to love coming here as a kid."

The way she'd said it made him look back at her. "When was the last time you were here?"

"I moved my parents to Toronto seven years ago, so I don't get to visit very often. The last time I was here was the last reunion I attended." She sighed as the car rolled to a stop. "Here we go."

Before she moved, Devin reached out and gave her hand a squeeze. "You're not in this alone."

Her shoulders relaxed, and she smiled. "Thanks. I'm not used to having a man at my side."

God, he wanted to beat the shit out of whoever had hurt her. "You do now. Whatever you need, no matter how big or small, I'm here to give it to you."

"I know. That's why I'm paying you."

He squeezed her hand again. "I'm not doing that for money. You look like, more than anything, you need a friend this week. Let me be that for you."

Kayla blinked once, then twice before nodding. Before either of them could say anything else, Mark opened Kayla's door and offered his hand to help her out.

Yeah, this was going to be a strange fucking week.

Devin collected himself before letting himself out of the limo. Mark frowned, no doubt annoyed that Devin didn't wait. Well, he'd really hate him in a moment. Walking around to the trunk, he took their bags out of Mark's hands. "Let me get those for you."

"You can't...this is my job."

"I know. But there's no reason I can't step up. My mama would kick my ass if I didn't pull my weight."

Kayla stood there, hands clutched neatly in front of her and smiled. "You're going to spoil Mark if you keep that up."

"I get the feeling Mark deserves to be spoiled a bit." He chuckled at the incredulous look the driver gave him.

"My husband would disagree."

Kayla reached into her purse and pulled out her phone. "Devin's right. You do deserve to be spoiled. There's a wonderful winery a few kilometers from here." She pressed a few buttons and turned the phone around. "I can get you tickets for a tour and tasting. It will be better than having to sit around while I'm in functions all week."

"I can't do that. Who's going to drive you?"

She shrugged. "We'll figure out the timing. Interested?" There was something in her tone that told Devin that Kayla knew Mark was more than interested. "If you find wine you like, I'll make sure to have a case of it shipped to Alex. Get you in his good books for having to be away this week."

Mark sighed and ran his hand through his white hair. "You know I can't say no to you."

"Or to getting treats for Alex."

"That either." He smiled before nodding. "That would be wonderful."

"I'll make the arrangements." Turning, Kayla nodded at Devin. "Ready to head in?"

Right, he was going to have to shift into pretend boyfriend mode. Giving himself a quick pat-down to make sure his dress shirt and pants weren't too wrinkled, he gave her the best smile he could and held out his arm. "Ma'am. Might I be your escort?"

Kayla blinked up at him before gracing him with a smile of her own. "Of course, Mr. Ford."

Mark cleared his throat. "That should be *Doctor* Ford. He's got his PhD after all."

Shit, that's right. Considering how hard he'd worked to earn his degree, one would think he'd be all over making sure everyone used his shiny, brand-new title. In a way, it was like a new shirt that hadn't been washed and didn't quite fit right. Someday he wouldn't think twice about it, but for now, it was a bit awkward. "Why don't you just call me Devin?"

"Sounds good." She turned and together they walked up the steps to the bed and breakfast.

Devin had never stayed in a B&B before. He'd always assumed they were essentially someone's home who'd opened their doors to travelers and used the proceeds to pay down their mortgage. Walking into Maple Hall chased away every single preconceived notion he'd had. The building was old. High ceilings gave the room a sense of space that he hadn't anticipated. The scent of old wood hit him immediately, though it was quickly swallowed up by the fresh scent of maple.

Kayla led him to a small registration desk, where an older man had been sitting. The second his gaze landed on them, he set down his tablet and stood. "Ms. Arnold. I'm so happy to have you staying with us again."

"It's Kayla, Mr. Babineau. You know that."

"You're my most prestigious customer, Ms. Arnold. And I will always treat you as such." His eyes shifted to Devin, and for a moment, Devin knew he was being assessed. "This is your companion?"

Best to make nice and prevent any problems. "Devin Ford." He stuck out his hand and gave Mr. Babineau a firm shake. "Kayla's told me so much about this place. I have to say I'm super excited to have a chance to stay here." There. That was good. Friendly and kissing up just enough to ensure their towels got changed.

And from the smile on Mr. Babineau's face, he agreed with Devin's mental assessment. "I remember when this one was a kid. She'd try to sneak extra maple candies when she thought no one was looking."

Kayla blushed, the sight of which nearly took Devin's breath away. "I'm still so sorry about that."

"Aaah." Babineau waved it away. "You were a child. And have repaid us many times over. Now." He turned and picked a key from the wall. "Marie cleaned everything in the suite this morning. If you need anything at all, please call down, and we'll get it for you."

"Thank you so much." She smiled as she took the key. "I know everything will be perfect."

Devin trailed behind her up the stairs to the room, like a dutiful fake boyfriend. He'd successfully jumped the first hurdle, though he suspected the rest of the challenges would be far more difficult.

The lodge was far bigger than he would have assumed from seeing it on the outside. There were at least six rooms on the top floor, and he had to guess there were a few more downstairs. "So, do the Babineaus live here too?"

"They have a small cottage on the property just behind the lodge. It gives them some privacy, but they're close enough to the main house to be here quickly if there's a problem." She stopped in front of the furthest door down the hallway. "This is us."

Devin wasn't into things like fancy houses and frilly things. Which was why when Kayla opened the door, and he stepped into a room that wouldn't have looked out of place in the early 20th century, he found it to be beautiful. "Wow."

As promised, there were two beds in the room, another reminder that this week wasn't about him. He closed the door behind them and waited to see which bed Kayla took, before putting his suitcase on the remaining one. "Does Mark have a room here as well?"

"Yup." Her lips made a small popping sound on the word. "He and Mr. Babineau will play crib when he's not carting me around. They've had a bit of a rivalry going on for a little while now."

He sat on his bed and watched as Kayla unpacked her suitcase, putting everything away into the dresser provided. He'd stayed at a few hotels over the years, but he never unpacked. It was strange being with someone whose entire approach to life was different from his own. "What's on the agenda for the rest of today?"

Kayla stood and smoothed down her long, black hair that already looked perfectly situated in her low ponytail. "Tonight, we're having dinner with the Alumni Selection Committee." There was something in her tone that told him she was less than looking forward to that. "The winery I mentioned earlier? They also cater private functions."

"Sweet. I love wineries. I did a bus tour of Niagara-on-the-Lake back in my second year..." The words died in his mouth when he realized her entire body had gone rigid. "What's wrong?"

"I used to work there when I was in high school. I was too young to serve wine, but I was the hostess. It wasn't the best of jobs."

God, he wanted to hear more of that particular story, but he could tell she wasn't interested in sharing. Okay, so this was also going to be part of his role as pretend boyfriend—emotional support for past trauma.

He wasn't typically the most observant of men when it came to emotional moments with women—it was one of the reasons he was still single at twenty-nine—but there was something about Kayla that he could read easily. She was used to being the one in charge, the one who everyone else relied on. It was also apparent that she didn't have someone to help her shoulder the load when things got to be too much.

Well, okay then. He could do that.

At least for the week.

He stood up and walked over to her. She stiffened when he got close, so he stopped. "This week is going to be hard for you, isn't it?"

"I've done this before."

"That doesn't answer my question, but that's okay." There was a large bouquet of freshly cut flowers in the middle of the dresser. He reached out and plucked a carnation from the middle of the bunch and held it out to her. "So, I'm not good with the feelings side of things. I mean, I'm a good listener and stuff, but I don't know what to say all the time. Numbers, I know. The rest of the stuff takes work. But I'm here for you this week. I don't care about anyone else, or their motives, or anything. Just you. If you need anything, need me to step in, or back off. Hell, if you want me to leave, just say the word, and I'm doing it. Promise."

Holding out the carnation, he waited for her to take it. She stared at the flower for several long moments, before finally accepting it. "Thank you."

"You're welcome."

He held his breath as she lifted the carnation and took a sniff. "These are my favorite."

"My mom loves them too. Dad couldn't afford to buy her roses, so he always got these for her instead. The one year he got a big bonus from the car dealership that he worked at, and he went out and bought her a dozen roses, she told him never to do that again. Carnations always made her think of him, and roses die too quickly."

His throat had unexpectedly tightened at the memory of his father. He coughed once and strode past Kayla to look out the window that faced the main grounds. "Man, this place is amazing."

Kayla didn't say anything for a while, but she went back to unpacking her things. It wasn't until she disappeared into the bathroom that he was finally able to get his sudden wave of emotions under control. He needed to toughen up if he was going to be there for Kayla. Everything else in his life—his family, friends, his inability to figure out what he wanted to do with his life—everything was on hold for this single week.

Still, he took a moment to pull out his phone and text his mom. *It's your baby. Been thinking about you. All good?*

He knew she was on days at the hospital this week, so chances were, she wouldn't get back to him for a while. Still, he knew having a note from him always made her smile, and that eased the ache in his heart.

It was also nearly time to buy her another bouquet of carnations.

Kayla emerged from the bathroom, and she'd changed her clothing without him realizing that's what she'd been doing. Instead of her buttoned-up business attire, she'd changed into a floral printed dress, that somehow both clung to her waist, hips, and breasts perfectly, but was also flowy. Flowy? That was a word he was reasonably certain that he'd never once thought before now.

Apparently, changes abounded around Kayla.

"You look amazing." He quickly sat down on the chair closest to the window, when he realized he was getting hard. "You're going to leave quite the impression."

"Thanks." She cocked her head, her gaze traveling down his body. "So you approve?"

Don't tease me, woman. "Oh yeah."

"Need a moment?"

He couldn't stop his groan. "I'm a healthy man with an appreciation for the female form. Be kind."

"You better get cleaned up. We'll need to head out soon."

Devin knew he should wait a bit longer to encourage his erection to recede, but no way was it going to happen with Kayla standing there looking hot, and smirking at him. "Alright, alright. But this is on you, pretty lady."

Standing, he strode past her as quickly as he could, but not before he saw her look down at his crotch. Well, if she was curious what he had below the belt, then she could look her fill. He was only here at her request, and while sex wasn't something they'd talked about, she was the one who could change the rules if she wanted.

He wasn't about to say no.

Grabbing his bag with his toiletries on the way, he found solace in the massive bathroom. The moment he closed the door, he rested his body against it, as though Kayla and her tiny frame could burst into the room with super-human strength. Letting out a shuddering breath, he reached down and gave his cock a hard squeeze. He couldn't jerk off to relieve the pressure with her standing on the other side of the door. And there was no way he'd be able to do anything in bed later tonight with her sleeping beside him.

Shit. He gave himself another squeeze.

This was going to be one long, painful week.

Chapter 8

Kayla took another sip of wine, making sure to smile and make direct eye contact with each of the Alumni Committee members who sat across from her. They'd only been at supper for thirty minutes, but she was already more than ready to head back to the lodge and soak in the tub.

That wasn't going to happen anytime soon, so she kept her back straight and played the part of the benevolent benefactor.

Devin was beside her, deep in conversation with the high school principal. The woman was old enough to be Kayla's mom, but that didn't seem to matter to Devin. She envied the way he could jump into a conversation with anyone he met, immediately putting them at ease. She'd taken on an edge early in her business dealings, and the attitude stuck. Frosty was her default setting and had worked for her to this point.

Still, a small part of her was jealous. Yes, she could walk into a room and talk to people, and she was pretty damn good at it too. But internally, she'd always struggled with conversations. The words she said were calculated to create the most significant impact, to get the results she wanted from the situation. It wasn't that she was manipulative, more than she knew what people wanted to hear, how they liked their egos stroked. It took forethought and planning.

Devin could just sit down, look at a person and connect with a few words.

She was convinced he wasn't even aware that he was doing it, which made her all the more jealous. Currently, he was explaining the benefits of a new school math program. Kayla did her best not to eavesdrop, but his deep bass and rich laughter were a siren song to her. She didn't care the first thing about math, but the way Devin spoke about it pulled her in.

"Isn't that right, Ms. Arnold?"

Kayla snapped her attention back to Mike Mallory, one of the superintendents of the district who sat across from her. The trio of people was staring at her expectantly.

Shit.

Giving them a little smile, she wiped the corner of her mouth with her napkin. "I'm sorry. I zoned out there for a moment."

Devin spun in his seat toward her, draping his arm along the back of her chair. "I told you we should have waited an extra day to come." He then looked over at the trio and pointed at Kayla. "She's been pushing herself too hard again. She was in Germany on Monday, and back in the office Tuesday morning. I mean, who doesn't at least take a day to deal with the effects of the time change?" He then leaned in, placed a kiss on her cheek and turned his attention back to the principal.

Kayla knew she was blushing, more from the unexpected rescue than the kiss. Other than Simone, hardly anyone stuck up for her. Most people knew she could handle herself in just about any situation—and she could—but it was nice to know that not only was Devin paying attention to her, that he was willing to offer a small hand without her asking.

That was a pleasant change.

And more than a bit unnerving.

Mike sat back and looked far more impressed with her than he should have been. "Germany? That's not exactly a quick trip."

"I was investigating several innovations in clothing manufacturing. They are on the cutting edge in several areas." She pressed her hand to her chest and lowered her chin a bit. "Still, I shouldn't have zoned out. What was the question?"

"We were saying that a lot of the challenge with teens and education in this day and age is lack of focus. They're so concerned with their phones and social media that they can't seem to do anything that doesn't involve a selfie."

Kayla blinked. That wasn't her experience with teens at all. "I think that might be a bit unfair. While I agree that social media and cell phones have certainly changed their perspective on the world, it's certainly not lack of focus. More likely, overwhelmed with the sheer volume of information that they're bombarded with on a daily basis."

"Yes, but that doesn't mean that they aren't self-absorbed—"

Kayla held up her hand. "I've had some students from the Shad Valley Business Program come work with my company over the summer, and every one of them has proven to be focused, capable and incredibly in tune with the world around them. What was your reality, even my reality as a high school student, has changed. Rather than try to force the kids into a mold that no longer reflects society today, we should be accommodating them, preparing them for the world that will face them once they graduate. The education system is failing them."

Everyone at the table had stopped talking and were now staring at Kayla. Nothing better than insulting a bunch of people who'd spent their entire lives educating children at a dinner in her honor. She should apologize, or at the very least, reword her comments. She might have even done so if it wasn't for Devin once again.

He cleared his throat and smiled. "You know, I have to agree. As a recent graduate myself, one of the hardest things I've had to learn to deal with is the dichotomy of what we were told life was like after school, and what the reality is. The stress these kids are under, the pressures of having to live up to unrealistic expectations, the illusion of perfection that they're shown daily…is crazy. And too much."

Kayla couldn't take her eyes from him as he spoke. Her throat and chest tightened, making it difficult to breathe. He understood her, and the point she was trying to make. Someone on her side, who didn't know that here in Meadow Lake she was either Kayla Arnold, super rich woman who they could try to use for their benefit, or Kayla Arnold formerly poor kid from the wrong side of town.

Devin knew none of that. He merely heard what she was saying, saw her point, and agreed with it.

Mike nodded, though he was now looking down at his half-full glass of wine. "Good point. We're playing catchup with them while trying to balance provincial education requirements. It's a fine line we have to walk." He straightened, lifted his glass and gave Kayla a bright smile. "But with you as an example of what our students can accomplish when they put their minds to it, we'll be able to continue to inspire our youth for a long time. To Kayla."

"To Kayla!"

Lifting her glass, she took a sip without really tasting the wine. This was why she hadn't wanted to come to the reunion in the first place. These people didn't care about her, not really. They only cared about what she could do for them, what she represented. She was a showpiece, not a person.

Even Christoph had treated her like that.

The rest of dinner went smoother, as the conversation drifted back to safe topics, such as the homecoming events and the dance planned on the last night. Devin kept the conversation going, which gave her a chance to sit back and relax. Maybe he was right that things were catching up to her a bit. It was only nine thirty, but she was more than ready for bed.

Shortly after they finished dessert, and she'd emptied her wineglass, Kayla yawned. She'd tried to hide it behind her napkin, but Devin noticed. Because of course, he did.

Pushing back from the table, Devin got to his feet and softly clapped his hands. "I hate to cut our wonderful evening short, but I have to get this pretty lady to bed before she falls asleep at the table."

There were a few protests, but Devin gave his head a shake. "I'm telling you, Germany and back in two days. It's a killer."

"While I'm not quite that done in, I am a bit tired." She stood and shook hands with everyone, promising to be at the school first thing in the morning for the student breakfast.

On their way out the door, she stopped at the hostess station, shook the young girl's hand, while quietly slipping her a hundred-dollar bill. "I remember not being included in the tip share when I worked here. Thank you for your hard work."

They left the girl gasping and smiling.

Mark was already waiting for them as soon as they stepped out of the winery. He only smiled and opened the door for her, which meant she looked more tired than she realized. Once she was safely hidden in the back of the limo, she sighed and relaxed against her seat. "Thank God, that's over."

Devin grinned, leaning over, so his head rested on her shoulder, and he was forced to look up at her backwards. "It wasn't that bad. Anne-Marie is a pretty awesome principal, from what she said about her school. And after I corrected some of her misconceptions about their new grade ten math curriculum, I think she wanted to hire me."

The intimacy of their connection, the feel of this handsome man pressed against her, the ease in which he could tease her and ease her tensions, sent Kayla's heart racing just a tiny bit more.

Without thinking, she reached up and cupped his cheek with her hand. His skin was warm and smooth, with no hint of any stubble. The scent of his aftershave was something that reminded her of outside, without being artificial. It stuck in her head, and she was tempted to ask him what it was. Not that she had any intention of letting things get personal between them, but after all he'd done for her in such a short period, she knew it was going to be harder than she realized to keep him at arm's length.

Devin didn't move, didn't try to press himself on her in any way. He waited until she dropped her hand before slowly sitting back up. She folded her hands in her lap and forced her eyes forward. "Have you thought about that?"

He cleared his throat and frowned. "Thought about what?"

"Being a teacher. You're personable and clearly, love what you do. Students would be lucky to have you."

In the short time they'd been together, she'd seen him only ever in what she'd mentally dubbed *awesome-happy* mode. But that one simple question seemed to wipe out his happy mood in a heartbeat.

"Yeah, I thought about it. I was a teaching assistant at the university during my PhD. But it's not my thing."

"I find that hard to believe." If anything, she would have pegged him as a natural.

"Do you mind if we don't talk about that? I'm enjoying my little escape from reality."

"Sure." It was weird thinking about Devin having any problems at all, given his personality. She looked out the window, suddenly unsure of everything she'd assumed this week would be about. "We're almost back."

Devin didn't say anything at first. He turned, adjusting his seatbelt so it didn't get in his way. "I think we might have a problem."

"We do?" She frowned. "What's that?"

"I'm about to break one of your rules."

Her mind raced through the possible list of what she'd told him the night of their dinner. Well, they weren't anywhere near a dance floor, and the public was as far away as it could be. Kayla's mouth suddenly watered at the thought of what a kiss with Devin might be like. "You don't think you can restrain yourself?" She chuckled.

"No, I don't think I can." He moved closer, and it was his turn to reach out and cup her cheek. "If you'd like me to stop, you should probably say something."

Would she? When she'd made those silly rules, it had been with the intention of keeping things professional, of not making the same mistakes with Devin that she had with Christoph. But it didn't take a genius to realize that no matter what she did or didn't do with him, Devin was a completely different animal from her ex. Christoph had been calculating with his words. Gaslighting wasn't a thing she'd been familiar with until she'd been on the receiving end with him. She'd questioned her words, her actions, even the way she'd dressed because of one or two well-placed words that had slowly whittled away her self-confidence.

Devin didn't seem to be like that. At first, Christoph hadn't either. Neither had the other men she'd tried to date before. Somehow, she'd always gotten it wrong, always saw something different from what was there.

Even now, sitting in the backseat of her limo driving back to the room they shared as a pretend couple, him waiting for her to permit him to kiss her, she questioned if this was yet another horrible mistake. One little kiss. A step on the road to heartache.

Yet, why not? It had been so very long since she'd been with someone. To feel the touch of a man's hand on her naked skin. At least with Devin, she was the one in charge, the one calling the shots and putting boundaries on what could and couldn't happen.

It was only a kiss. A little intimacy that in the grand scheme of things wouldn't mean very much to either of them. Right?

Devin hadn't moved, his gaze flicking from her mouth to her eyes, waiting for the silent signal to proceed. She instinctively knew that he wouldn't do anything without her consent, and that was a power rush all unto itself.

Finally, she shifted in her seat to move closer. She was painfully close to him, her eyes protesting under the strain, even as her body wanted to close that final short distance between them. A breath away, Kayla let her body press against his, her breasts rubbing gently against his arm. She shifted again, avoiding the temptation of his mouth, to brush her lips against his cheek until she reached his ear.

"No kissing was one of the rules." She flicked her tongue against his earlobe, thrilled at his sharp intake of breath. "But I didn't say anything about sex."

She felt him swallow hard. His hands shifted to cup her hips. "No, that wasn't on the list."

"Nope. It wasn't."

"But kissing?"

"That's…intimate. Something I want to keep…special."

His fingers flexed against her, holding her tight against him. "Yeah. I get that."

Kayla tilted her head, giving her better access to the side of his throat just below his ear. Gently, she nipped at his skin with her teeth, relishing the taste of him. "But sex. That's about fun."

Devin chuckled. "I like fun."

"That's good. Would you like to have fun with me?" She slid her hand down his stomach, only to stop just above his belt. God, she wanted nothing more than to reach down and touch him, to see the cock that she'd only glimpsed an outline of earlier. "You can say no."

"Are you insane? Like I'd say no to you. How could anyone?" Devin turned his face, bringing his mouth dangerously close to hers. "But are you okay with this? I want to be sure."

God, he was too fucking precious. "I'm sure."

The limo came to a stop, which meant that their time alone was about to be interrupted. Mark wouldn't have a clue what was going on back there, which meant he would open the door without a second thought.

Sighing, she pulled back. "Guess we'll have to wait until we get to the room."

Devin groaned as he covered his tented fly with his hands. "You're going to kill me. You know that, right?"

The rush of fresh outside air washed over her as Mark dutifully opened her door. "Home again."

"Thank you, Mark." She took his hand and slid out of the limo, leaving Devin to catch his breath.

Her body shook as she walked toward the B&B, lust pumping her blood faster than she'd ever anticipated it could. She knew her face was flushed, her nipples hard, and all she wanted to do was to strip out of her dress and feel Devin press against her.

Speaking of him...

It only took a few moments before he fell into step beside her. "Mark knows something's up. He gave me the weirdest look."

"He's not a fool." She snuck a glance at Devin as they started up the stairs. "Though he's probably a bit surprised. I'm not normally one for getting hot and heavy in the car."

"Lucky me."

That was the last thing he said to her until they reached the room. Kayla slid the key into the lock far easier than she'd expected and stepped into the room to the sight of two beds and the scent of flowers. She kicked her shoes off and crossed to the bed she'd claimed as her own, before turning to face him.

"The rules are still in effect. No kissing." It was strange, she wasn't opposed to kissing him in theory, but the reality of their situation called for some boundaries. So, no kissing was it.

Devin had closed the door and pulled off his tie as he toed off his dress shoes. "I can do that. Everything else is fair game?"

The way he asked his question sent a shiver through her. "Within reason."

"Good." He crossed the distance between them and encouraged her to sit on the edge of the bed. "Let's have some fun."

Chapter 9

Devin's cock was so hard he was genuinely terrified that he was going to do damage to himself. He'd had casual sex with women several times over the past year and jerked off on a regular basis to the point where it could be considered an aerobic activity. But it had been a very long time since he'd been this aroused by a woman.

His brain was fucking short-circuiting, he wanted her so badly. Wanted to taste and feel her. Wanted to know the sounds she made just before she came. Wanted to smell her pussy, to memorize the scent that was uniquely her.

He helped her shift back to the middle of her bed, watching intently as her dress slid its way up her legs, exposing inch after inch of creamy white skin. She looked like a china doll, something that would break if he squeezed her too hard. So far from the actual woman Kayla was.

She was fire and steel, wrapped up in a beautiful package that served to lull others into a sense of wonder. Devin had been fooled, but not anymore. With his gaze locked onto hers, he slid his hands up her long legs, finally being able to touch her the way he'd been fantasying about since nearly the moment they'd met.

"Lay all the way back." He watched as she shivered but did as he'd asked. "You're beautiful. I'm sure people tell you that all the time, but you are."

It wasn't simply her physical attributes that drew him in. Her keen intelligence, her insights on the world, business, what other people seem to need; he'd never met anyone like her.

When his hands disappeared beneath her dress, he watched as her breathing increased. The gentlest of touches against the edge of her panties sent another painful pulse of blood through his cock. If he didn't come soon, he really might die. Like for real.

Not before she does.

"I want to see you." He took hold of the band of her panties, waiting until she nodded, before slowly peeling them from her legs.

Her dress still covered her pussy, leaving what lay beneath to his imagination. She watched him as he slid the silk from her, the scent of her arousal potent. If he knew her better, he might press them to his nose, make a show of smelling her, of how much it turned him on. Instead, he let the tiny scrap of fabric dangle from his finger for a moment, at which he cocked an eyebrow.

"You dress sexy, even when no one will see it."

"Maybe I was hedging my bets?" She gave him a sly smile of her own.

Yeah, this was going to be fucking wild.

He let them drop to the floor, no longer able to hold himself back from seeing the one thing he'd been fantasizing about for weeks now. Slowly, he pushed her dress up, exposing her pussy for him to look on.

Fuck.

A bed of brown curls couldn't conceal her swollen clit. It peeked out from beneath its hiding spot, a prize for his eyes only. Gently, he parted her thighs, his gaze unwavering from the glistening nest that beckoned him to lean down for a taste. "Look at you."

Kayla hesitated for a brief moment before she spread her thighs further apart. "Less looking would be good."

He was never one to deny a woman what she wanted. "Yes, ma'am."

The bed dipped under his weight as he eased forward, his upper body sliding into position between her thighs. Devin might not be able to kiss Kayla the way he wanted, but at the very least, she couldn't argue with the trail of kisses along the inside of her knee, up along her inner thighs. As much as he wanted to press his mouth to her pussy, he continued plying her body with small kisses and licks, wanting to make sure that he worshiped her body the way she deserved.

When he reached the bend between her thigh and her body, he paused to lick a long swipe across the sensitive spot. Kayla gasped, and her hands flew to the back of his head even as she squirmed beneath him. Oh yeah, that was precisely what he'd hoped for. With his hands, he squeezed her hips before sliding them beneath her to cup her ass. Every bit of her was a contradiction of soft and firm. Taut muscles and smooth skin, her steel control and gooey center that had her tipping a high school student a hundred bucks because the girl was underpaid.

He could only hope that her calm and reserved exterior would give way to a passionate and emotional woman, writhing beneath him as they came.

Devin moved slowly, with deliberate purpose, placing kisses along her belly just above her pubic mound. With each brush of his mouth against her, she shuddered and squirmed. Her hands never left the back of his head, and her fingers encouraged him on, lower.

Not yet.

Pressing his nose to the soft curls, he sucked in a deep breath, groaning low as the scent of her arousal stuck somewhere high in his nose, and tickled the back of his brain. No matter what happened beyond this week, he knew there was no way he'd ever forget Kayla. Using his nose, he pressed down, teasing the small bump above her clit. He'd been told once by a girlfriend that she loved the pressure there almost as much as she loved him sucking on her. He'd made a point to remember that, to see if any of his other lovers enjoyed it as much as she did.

Kayla gasped and flexed her fingers against his scalp.

Yup. Another winner.

Devin lifted himself up on his elbows so he could use his fingers to part her folds and smooth down the dew-slicked hair, that hid his prize. When he finally got to see her clit, unimpeded, he sighed. "You're just as beautiful as I'd imagined."

"You're a big fucking tease." She lightly tapped the top of his head.

Devin was many things, but thick wasn't one of them. The woman wanted to come, and he was just the man for the job.

Without another word, he lowered his mouth and flicked his tongue across her clit. The taste of her juices filled his mouth, making it water. Another lick and she sighed, her thighs falling all the way open. It didn't take long for him to fall into a rhythm, licking and sucking her, lapping up her essence as Kayla writhed beneath him.

God, he could die here doing this. The smell, taste, and sounds coming from her were enough to make his heart—and his cock—explode from joy. He needed to feel her come, wanted to know that he'd been the one to give her that pleasure, to push her to the edge and over. Devin adjusted himself so he could use his hand. Sliding first one, then a second finger into her pussy, he started with short, gentle thrusts until she began to buck against him, then he increased the pace.

Yes, this was what he wanted. There was nothing better in the world than having a woman come apart, to know that he was the one who'd been able to take her there. Sex was pure, primal, and all about forming a connection with the other person. This was something he didn't have to think about or worry about doing right.

Kayla began to squirm and buck her hips, making it hard to keep up with her. He curled his fingers inside her and did his best to press against the spot that he hoped would give her the ultimate pleasure. "Come on, baby. You can do it."

She moaned, her hands falling away from him to grip the duvet cover. "Faster."

The lady knew what she wanted, and who was he to deny her. Increasing the pace, he made sure to match the rhythm of his tongue against her clit with the thrusts of his fingers. The moment her body began to vibrate around him, he knew she was just about there. He held everything steady, not wanting to change things at the last second and ruin this for her. The seconds started ticking off in his head before finally, Kayla sucked in a deep breath and cried out as she came.

Devin continued to devour her until she fell limp on the bed. Only then did he pull back, taking a moment to wipe her juices from his mouth against the side of her thigh. His cock throbbed as it pressed hard against his pants and the mattress, but he wasn't going to do a thing about it until he knew for sure Kayla was good.

Thankfully, she reached down to him, tugging him up. "Tell me you have condoms."

"I do, though I wasn't expecting to use them." He was simply an eternal optimist and liked to plan for all best eventualities. "Don't move."

She cocked an elegant eyebrow, spreading her legs even further apart. Devin stood up and stared down at her. There was something exotic and dangerous about seeing her half-naked with her dress still on. It was as though he was partaking in some strange forbidden fruit, something that would irrevocably change his life forever.

He pointed at her and tried to say something, but the words refused to come. Shit. Instead, he spun on his heel and raced to the bathroom and his shaving kit, to find the condoms he'd hopefully stashed there when he'd packed. The tile floor was cold against his feet, even though he still had his socks on. He was still entirely dressed, and so far, this was turning out to be some of the best sex he'd had in years.

Condoms, condoms...I know they're here somewhere.

"Ah ha!" He'd thrown three into his kit, and they'd fallen to the bottom, covered by his shaving gel bottle.

Looking at himself in the mirror, he couldn't help but grin. Okay, this was happening, and it was going to be the best. He splashed some water on his face, wiping it down before turning and marching back out to where Kayla was waiting.

Undoing the buttons of his shirt, he smiled at her. "Found them."

Kayla hadn't moved, her legs still spread wide and the flush from her orgasm still covered her cheeks. "Excellent."

God, this was mental and amazing all at once. Devin should try to make a show of removing his shirt, do a little striptease or something. But while he knew he had a certain amount of sex appeal, he was also painfully aware of his awkwardness when it came to certain bedroom moves. Things tended just to go weird when he tried hard to be sexy. Simple and straightforward, that's how things needed to be.

If Kayla minded, she didn't show it. Her gaze lingered on his chest, as she tilted her head against the pillow, her finger brushing against her lips. "Looking good, Mr. Ford."

"Thank you, Ms. Arnold." He let his shirt slip down his arms to fall in a silent heap on the floor. He hooked his thumbs into the waistband of his pants and posed.

Okay, maybe a little bit of showing off was healthy.

Kayla made a low humming noise in the back of her throat. "There's something wrong when you have less clothing on than I do."

"Really?" He then went for his belt and as quickly as he could manage, pulled it open. "You mean you don't enjoy having a little show? I'd think that as a woman you might enjoy being entertained in the bedroom, rather than expecting to get pawed at a moment's notice."

"Pawed?" She snorted. "Maybe I like getting pawed?"

"Do you?"

She shrugged. "Sometimes. It depends on who my partner is."

Devin held her gaze as he tugged open the front of his pants, exposing his black briefs beneath. This was way more teasing that he was used to when he was about to have sex, but he liked it. Hell, he liked her, and they hadn't spent much time together. Making sure he gave her one of his best smiles, he pushed his pants down.

Now clad in only his briefs and his socks, Devin held out his hands. "Ta-da."

"Very sexy." Kayla reached between her legs and carded her fingers through her pubic hair. "And very fit for a math guy."

"Even math guys know where the gym is."

"True. But in my experience, math guys don't often visit them."

Knowing the roster of his fellow graduates, Devin couldn't argue with her. "You really are overdressed now."

"I am." She shifted on the bed, her dress riding higher on her belly. "You should come help me do something about that."

Oh yeah.

Yanking off his socks as he went, Devin climbed back onto the bed between Kayla's legs. He set the condoms on the bed as he helped her sit up, immediately reaching for the zipper on the back of her dress. Working together, they pulled the thin fabric from her body, exposing her pale skin for him to see. He dropped the dress and reached for her bra, gently unfastening the hooks and freeing her breasts.

With that final barrier between them now gone, he was able to look his fill at the woman who leaned back on the bed, stretched out beneath him. "God, look at you."

"I'd rather you do something more than look."

"Yes, ma'am." He should have removed his briefs when he was still standing, but it was a bit late for that now. Carefully, he pushed them down to his knees, revealing his hard cock to her.

Kayla whistled. "Impressive."

"I take pride in my attributes." *And once again, thank you God for all you've given me.*

Kayla reached out and pulled one of the condom packets from the roll. "Mind if I suit you up for action."

His cock twitched at the thought of her touching him. If he didn't get a hold of himself, this was going to be a very short ride. "Be gentle with me. I'm...ah...well, close to the edge."

She sat up, ripping the condom packet open with her mouth. It was both primal and elegant in a way that he couldn't imagine any other woman pulling it off precisely that way. Devin had to hold his breath as she reached down and with deft fingers, rolled the condom down his shaft. She even reached down and gave his balls a gentle tug, before she stretched back down on the mattress.

Okay then. Time for a little action.

Reaching for her knees, he lined himself up and gently sunk into her warmth. Not only had it been a little while since he'd been with a woman, but the teasing that had brought them to this moment had pushed him close to the edge. Closing his eyes, he took a breath and did his best to calm his furiously pounding heart. Then, just as slowly as he pressed in, he leaned forward and kissed the side of her throat.

Kayla sucked in a breath, but she didn't protest. He knew her rules, and the last thing he wanted to do was to fuck this up and break them, even if he didn't fully understand her reasoning. So, mentally he found a compromise between what he wished he could do and what she wanted him to do. He continued to kiss her throat, down across her collarbone, and over to her shoulder. With each kiss, he thrust into her slowly, methodically, knowing that if he went too fast, everything would be over sooner than he wanted.

And he didn't want this moment to end.

Kayla sighed as she raked her nails lightly down his back. She hooked her legs around his waist, the heels of her feet resting against his buttocks as he moved. Her pussy was wet, making each movement inside her comfortable; her muscles were still twitching from her earlier orgasm. There was nothing he wanted more than to make her come again. Some women he'd been with in the past couldn't go more than once, but there was something about how her body was responding to him that made him think he had a chance to feel her glorious release once again.

He began to thrust harder but didn't increase the pace. Turning his head, he sucked her earlobe into his mouth, flicking the sensitive skin with his tongue, before nipping at it. "You're so fucking beautiful. I want to hear you come again. Feel your pussy squeeze my cock. Your nails on my back."

Kayla groaned, granting him his wish. "Harder."

He did as she asked, even as he pulled back to gain access to her breasts. The pink nipples were hard, just begging him to suck on them. Despite the awkward angle, he cupped her left breast as he lowered his head and flicked the bud with his tongue.

"Fuck." She arched her back, moving her breast closer still. "Like that. Yeah."

She started to meet his thrusts with some of her own, which made it challenging to continue to suck on her. Still, he wasn't about to lose their rhythm if he could help it. Pulling back, he captured her nipple between his fingers and squeezed it as he pounded into her.

Shit, if she didn't come soon, then there was no way he'd be able to hold back. But the longer he thrust into her, the more her body shook, the closer to his orgasm he got. Devin tried to hold back, but when she swiveled her hips in a particular way, that was all it took to push him over the edge.

"Shit!" His eyes slammed closed as his orgasm rolled over him.

Kayla moaned, thrashing beneath him as he continued to come. She was close. Even as his pleasure subsided, and his body protested the continued movement, Devin didn't stop. "That's it. Come for me."

She turned her head and pressed the side of her face to the mattress, once again exposing her long neck. As tempting as it was to reach down and kiss her there once again, Devin didn't dare move. He could tell that she was close and didn't want to fuck this up. Instead, he pinched her nipple again, rolling it with each thrust.

"Yes!" She arched her back as she cried out, her body going stiff as she came.

Her pussy clenched around his cock, squeezing him to the point where for a fleeting moment he thought maybe he could come a second time himself. Or die trying.

Finally, Kayla fell back, a sheen of sweat coating her skin as she swallowed down great gulps of air. With that, he was able to stop and fell forward on to his elbows, his body covering hers.

For several long minutes, neither of them said anything. Devin did his best to get his heartbeat under control by taking long, slow breaths. It's why he didn't immediately notice her squirming. "You okay?"

"Bathroom."

"Shit, sorry." He should have known that he would be heavy on her. Reaching down, he held the condom in place as he slid from her body, letting her get up. "You okay?"

"Yeah, I'm good." But she didn't meet his gaze and even moved away from his touch. "Excuse me."

He could only watch her retreating as she strode to the bathroom, closing the door behind her.

Huh.

Was that a brush-off? He wasn't sure, but it felt a bit like one. Not that she owed him anything. The sex had been mutual, but not part of the entire sugar mama deal. If she didn't want any post-sex cuddles, then that was up to her. It was weird, though; he'd forgotten that they weren't a couple. That there wasn't an actual relationship between them, and chances were there would never be.

This had been about sex, comfort and having a fun time.

Still, when he got up and tied the condom off before tossing it in the garbage can, he couldn't help but be disappointed. There'd been... something between them. Hadn't there? Maybe, but then again, maybe he'd read more into their time together than there was. He would need to keep a distance between them if he didn't want to fall into the trap of making her uncomfortable. He gathered his clothing, slipped back on his briefs and moved over to his bed.

When Kayla came out of the bathroom, she'd slipped a bathrobe on.

"Are you okay?" He tried to keep his voice light, not wanting her to think he was bothered.

"I'm good. Tired." She looked at him for only a moment before moving around to the side of her bed to turn down the blankets. "I'm going to get some sleep."

"Good idea." He moved to do the same, climbing into his bed, shivering as his heated skin connected with the cool sheets. "Sleep well, pretty lady."

Then he rolled to his side, with his back to her. He didn't fall asleep for hours wondering what the hell he was going to do.

Chapter 10

Kayla's phone alarm went off, dragging her from the depths of a dream that vanished the moment she opened her eyes. A glance over at the other bed revealed it empty. She sat up, frowning as she looked around.

"Hello?"

Devin wasn't in the room. It was eight-thirty, which only gave her an hour to get dressed and find him so that they could make their way to the school for the graduate breakfast.

She'd slept surprisingly well, considering her brain had shot into overdrive after their previous night's hot sex. The moment he'd relaxed against her, the reality of what she'd just done came crashing down, and the pleasure and ease that she'd felt during the act evaporated faster than rain on hot asphalt.

While they technically hadn't broken a single one of her rules, having sex was undoubtedly an intimacy that went further than she'd ever intended.

Lord, don't kiss the man, but sure, he can go down on you. Why not? Makes total sense.

Idiot.

Sliding from the warmth of the sheets, she paused to look at his empty and haphazardly made bed. He'd done his best not to wake her, but also took the time to straighten things up before he left. Devin was her polar opposite in every way possible, which only served to confuse her emotions further. He was kind, observant, but in a casual way that relayed the genuine affection he seemed to have for everyone he met. And while she had no problems getting along with most people she met, it was taxing always to have to be *on.*

It didn't take her long to get cleaned up and slip into the navy-blue dress pants and white top she'd selected explicitly for breakfast. She wanted to ensure that she looked professional and maintained her sense of style, but still look approachable enough that any of the students who might want to talk to her would.

Her next challenge was finding Devin.

Which turned out to be surprisingly easy. The moment she set foot on the stairs, she was met with the sound of male laughter.

"That's a double run, man. You're screwed now."

"I'm not getting skunked by a novice."

"Crib's a math game. That's kind of my jam."

Devin was standing at the registration desk opposite Mr. Babineau, with Mark flanking the end. The trio were fixated on the crib board that she couldn't see but knew was there. Based on everyone's body language, Devin was winning, and Mark was enjoying seeing his rival losing.

She walked as quietly as she could toward them, not wanting to ruin the moment. It gave her the opportunity to look at Devin, to take in his firm body and easy gestures. His back was to her, showing off his sculpted ass, and how perfectly the fabric of his dress pants clung to him. He turned his head to smile at Mark and held up his cards. "This round should do it."

Mark caught sight of her first, straightening up as he grinned. "There she is. You need to see how much of a crib shark your boyfriend is."

Boyfriend.

She shivered at the word, even though she knew everything between them was completely fake. She couldn't imagine being Devin's partner. Not because he was horrid or that they were incompatible—just the opposite. There was a small part of her who was terrified that if she let someone else into her life, she'd eventually find herself back where she was when Christoph left—broken and alone. There was no way she could ever put herself through that ever again.

As she moved to stand beside him Devin didn't give any indication that he was awkward or upset about what had happened between them. "I've never been a fan of cards."

Mr. Babineau gave her a small glare before returning his attention to his cards. "Crib is more than cards."

"It's about ego." Mark chuckled as he crossed his arms. "And it's Devin's kitty, so Matthew here is screwed."

"Not yet." He placed some of his cards down. "Eight."

"Fifteen for two."

Mr. Babineau growled as Devin moved his peg. Kayla put her hand on Devin's shoulder. "What's that little line on the board that his peg is behind?" She knew damn well what the skunk line was, but she couldn't help but get into some of the teasing action as well.

"Behave, or else I'll forget to change your towels today."

Kayla grinned. "I was only asking."

In a flurry of card placements, she watched as Devin's peg reached the end of the board, but only after Mr. Babineau cleared the skunk line. The innkeeper sat down in his chair, wiping his forehead. "That would have been humiliating. Good game, son." They shook hands, and Mr. Babineau quickly packed up the board. "I won't make that mistake again."

"Aw come on, it was fun." Devin smiled, the light in his eyes doing funny things to Kayla's insides. "I doubt I'll get that lucky again."

"That wasn't luck, that was talent." Mark picked up his coffee mug and stepped back. "Though right now, I need to get the two of you to the breakfast."

Devin turned and stuck out his arm for her to take, though he didn't meet her gaze. "Madam. Your chariot awaits."

"Thank you."

They walked silently behind Mark to the limo. Kayla hated that she was the source of the awkwardness between them. She waited until they were safely hiding in the back of the limo before she turned to face Devin.

"I'm sorry."

She'd expected him to brush her apology away. *It's all good, pretty lady. It was just sex, right?* But instead of that, he shifted away from her, his gaze locked on the floor. "Did I do something to upset you? Did I hurt you, or did you feel forced in any way?"

Wait, what? "No. Why would you think that?"

Only then did he look at her, and Kayla hated what she saw. Pain and confusion were etched on his face, both directed her way. "I like to pride myself on taking care of my lovers. Making sure that they receive the pleasure they want and deserve. I've never had anyone run away from me like that and I wanted to make sure I hadn't hurt you."

God, what had she done to stumble upon a man like him? Christoph, even some of her other lovers, had never cared about her feelings the way Devin did. And they weren't in an actual relationship. In a vain attempt to protect herself, she'd ended up hurting a man who'd done nothing but gone out of his way to help her.

She was the current asshole in his pseudo-relationship.

Reaching out, she took his hand closest to her and held it. "I'm sorry. You did nothing wrong, and I enjoyed what we did. I…" How to explain this without sounding like a fool? "I was married for a while. Five years. I told you it didn't end well."

"That's the Christoph guy?"

She nodded. "I thought I'd gotten over him, what he'd done to me, years ago. But when I'd tried dating afterwards, things never went well. It wasn't necessarily anything the men had done, but I couldn't get over it. I guess my old issues got the better of me again. So, as I said, I'm sorry."

Devin's gaze lifted from the floor to her eyes as she spoke. Strangely, she couldn't read his emotions the way she usually could with him. "You deserve better than what he gave you. I hope you find a man who can make you happy. Until then, I'm here to help you." He squeezed her hand back, and that simple gesture was enough to assure her that things were okay. For the time being at least.

* * * *

They were greeted at the school by a contingency of graduates. A short blond girl strode out from the small pack and stuck her hand out half a second after Kayla climbed out from the limo. "Hi I'm Stephanie Lukas, I'm one of the school's co-prime ministers. This is Anton Burke, my partner." A tall reed of a young man stepped up beside her, though Stephanie didn't look his way. "Welcome back to Meadow Lake High, Ms. Arnold."

Stephanie spoke the words in a rush, but she'd obviously practiced. Kayla beamed at her, remembering when she'd run for student council herself, though she'd never been lucky enough to win the vote. "Very nice to meet you Stephanie, Anton. Thank you so much for inviting me back."

They fell into step beside the students and Kayla listened to Stephanie as she relayed the schedule for the morning. "The parents and faculty are here as well. We've set up breakfast in the gym, which is across the hall from your library. And thank you so much for everything you've given us. I've spent so much time there it feels like a second home."

Stepping through the door and onto the beige tile that comprised the school foyer, brought back a rush of emotions that Kayla hadn't anticipated. The place hadn't changed much from the last time she'd been here. There were some new student-painted murals on the wall, the word welcome painted in different languages along the top wall that led to the office, which were new to her. Several more trophies lined the case that was the pride and joy of the small school. But mostly, everything looked the same. Familiar in a way a comfortable pair of old jeans were.

The entire wave of nostalgia was ironic, given how much she'd hated the school when she'd been a student. Devin pressed his hand against the small of her back, reminding her of his presence. He looked around and whistled. "That's an impressive number of awards."

Anton, his hands shoved deep into his pockets, grinned. "Our girls' softball team won provincials this year. And our senior football guys came second. We had a good run."

"Sure did." Devin gave him a fist-bump. "I can smell the food from here. This is going to be amazing."

"Oh yeah, grad breakfast always rocks. This way." Anton led them toward the gym, and Devin followed along beside him.

Stephanie fell alongside Kayla, giving her head a small shake. "Boys."

Kayla stared at the back of Devin's head. "They have their moments."

"I'm glad we have a minute before we walk in there. I wanted to say thank you." Stephanie stopped walking. "I'm not supposed to say anything to you about the money or the donations. The teachers didn't want to embarrass you, but I had to. I spent a lot of time in the library, since day one of me coming here. It meant a lot to have a safe space and all those resources. I just wanted you to know that."

Shit, Kayla was going to cry. "It was my pleasure. We didn't have a lot here when I was a student, so I wanted to try to make things better for the people coming behind me."

"You did." Stephanie was blushing now and shifted her gaze to where the boys had disappeared. "Your boyfriend is hot."

Kayla burst out laughing. "Don't tell him that I said so, but yes, he is." And a far kinder man than she deserved. Even as a friend. "We better get in there and get some food before they eat it all."

"They can't start until you arrive. That was the rule." Stephanie beamed. "We can stand out here all morning, and they'd all have to starve."

This was a girl who enjoyed her limited power. Unfortunately for Stephanie, Anton marched back out into the hallway. "Come on, guys. People are going to start a fight here if we don't feed them soon."

Stephanie rolled her eyes, before leading Kayla into the gym.

After singing *Oh Canada*, and a few words from the principal, breakfast was served. Kayla and Devin were in the seat of honor at the front of the gym, which meant they had students serving them. She remembered being on the other end of this event, being a student helper and then a graduate.

Back then, she'd been so fixated on getting out of the school, out of Meadow Lake in general, she hadn't enjoyed the moment.

This was a second chance for her to relive a time in her life that had been painful but rewrite some of that angst. She could see things with fresh eyes, and maybe she'd hit a time where she'd come to find a softer place in her memories for the school and town that had shaped her.

Devin shoved a croissant into his mouth and moaned. "I like your school."

Looking around, she smiled. "Yeah. Me too."

She picked up her coffee and got it halfway to her mouth when movement at the door caught her attention. Every second of peace and comfort she'd felt *poofed* as her gaze landed on the one person she'd been dreading to see.

Christoph.

Chapter 11

Devin had been doing his best impression of someone who didn't have a care in the world. He'd been sure to keep his smile firmly in place and his cache of pseudo-dad jokes flowing. It had been easy to get the teens to smile, and even a few of the teachers as they'd engaged him in conversation.

The reality though, was that he was ready to leap across the table to pound the crap out of the man who'd walked into the gym a half hour prior. Not that Devin knew who he was, or what he'd done, but based on the complete and utter change in Kayla's entire demeanor, none of it could be good.

It would have been great to have had the chance to talk to Kayla about who the new arrival was, but the morning had kicked into gear, and the speeches had begun. With his attention split, he did his best to watch Anton and Stephanie continue to showcase the very best of the school's graduates while ensuring that the new guy remained in his seat on the opposite side of the gym.

The guy was good-looking, dressed in a suit that put Devin's clothing to shame. There was a chance he was a teacher, someone on the board of education, or maybe a town official, based on the smiles and quiet handshakes people gave him as they'd slip past.

Kayla had only looked at the man once when he'd initially arrived and had made a point of staring straight ahead at the student speakers ever since. That level of avoidance was impressive, considering the new guy was staring at *her* at a near constant level. Except when he was staring at Devin. The guy didn't precisely glare at him, but instead stared intently, as though he was trying to solve the puzzle that Devin comprised.

Feedback from the microphone screeched through the gym, sending a ripple of shivers and cringes through the crowd as Anton took the microphone from Stephanie. "We, the grad class of 2018 will always have a home here in Meadow Lake, though our paths will take us far and wide. But like our past graduates, we know that we will always be welcome back. Stephanie and I would like to thank our special guest Kayla Arnold, for attending our breakfast. We'd also like her to know that the students of Meadow Lake High are thankful for all that you've given us over the years."

Every eye in the room turned toward them, and he felt Kayla stiffen even more than she had before. But her smile and small wave at everyone as they applauded her didn't give away her discomfort to anyone but him. It was weird how quickly he'd become attuned to her moods, despite the short time they'd been together. She'd never craved the approval of her hometown, but she'd achieved it nonetheless. That she had, didn't surprise Devin in the least.

Stephanie quickly snatched the mic from Anton. "We'd also like to thank Mayor Arnold for taking time out of his busy schedule to attend our breakfast." The applause picked up and was even punctuated by the occasional *whoop* and whistle, as the new guy—Mayor Arnold—stood up to wave.

Wait a second...

Arnold was the same name as hers. Her reaction made complete sense if this was Christoph Arnold, her ex-husband.

It's bad form to kick the mayor's ass. Probably end up in jail. Keep your cool, dude.

Devin turned to Kayla, who'd gone white. She squeezed the cloth napkin in her hands as though her life depended on it. Under the table, he reached out and placed his hand over hers. "You okay?"

She nodded once, stiffly. He could feel the vibrations rolling through her body as she stared at Christoph. Either she wasn't expecting him at the breakfast, or there was something else going on. The crowd settled down once again as Christoph took his seat, and the attention returned to the students. Thankfully, the rest of the speeches went quickly and smoothly, and before he knew it, they were standing up and getting ready to leave.

It took him several long, deep breaths to ensure that he kept his cool when he saw Christoph start to come their way. The older locals knew the history between them, and Devin couldn't help but notice people lingering around them, trying not to be obvious about their eavesdropping.

"Kayla." Christoph leaned in and placed a kiss on her cheek, completely ignoring the way she physically stiffened from the contact. "I have to admit I didn't believe Carmine when she told me you'd agreed to attend the school's dedication event."

She straightened, clasped her hands in front of her and smiled. "I never wanted it to be a big deal. But it's important for the kids to see that the sky's the limit for them."

Christoph looked at her; the smile plastered on his face wasn't reflected in his eyes. "Yes, some of our students have been luckier than others in that regard."

"Yes. I have to admit that I'm surprised to see you here. I didn't know that you'd moved home after the divorce." There wasn't any bitterness in her voice, not even when she said *divorce*. "And mayor? When did that happen? Did your dad retire?"

Devin's jaw ached, he was clenching it so hard. He wanted nothing more than to step in and say something, deflect what was apparently a painful conversation for her. But he wasn't an idiot and knew that while he might want to play the knight in shining armor, Kayla was the one in control. If she needed his assistance, she'd let him know.

Right?

Right.

Instead of saying anything, he glowered. At least, that's what he hoped he was doing. Devin didn't exactly have much in the way of experience when it came to looking intimidating. If anything, Kayla was far more likely to put the fear of God into someone than he was.

Christoph stepped closer to her, and for a moment, Devin wasn't sure if he was going to try to lead Kayla away from him or not. "He retired two years ago. I ran in the last election and won by a landslide."

"I'm surprised you moved back. The last time we spoke, you were less than interested in living a simple life." She crossed her arms and looked up at the ceiling in dramatic fashion. "What did you say? *Cruises, five-star dining, and parties with celebrities.* You wanted every bit of luxury that I could afford."

Christoph's gaze finally shifted to Devin, but only for the briefest of moments. "Why don't we go somewhere we can talk. Privately."

That was Devin's cue—or as close to one as he was likely to get. He held out his arm for Kayla, who slipped her arm around it without looking. "I'd love to, but Devin and I have a previous engagement."

Maybe he was secretly like Beetlejuice because now that he'd been named, Christoph turned the full force of his displeasure on him. "And who are you supposed to be?"

"Devin. Her boyfriend." And then he grinned as big and wide as he could manage. "It's a pleasure to meet you, Mr. Mayor. As a representative of your town, you must be so proud of Kayla and the wonderful benefits she offers the community as a successful former resident." Then he winked at Christoph, before turning back to Kayla. "I know you were hoping to catch up, but we really should go. If we're not in the car soon, Mark will come hunt us down and throw us into the limo."

Kayla relaxed her grip on his arm, looked up at him and smiled. "You're right. I'm sure we'll see you again before the end of the graduation and homecoming activities. Have a wonderful day, Mr. Mayor."

Before Christoph could say anything else to them, they stepped past him and headed straight for the limo. Devin continued to smile and nod at the people they passed, knowing full well that each and every one of them would be bending their heads to discuss the drama that had unfolded. Hell, it was something he would have done himself if he hadn't been smack-dab in the middle of it.

"Ms. Arnold!" Stephanie, ever perky yet serious, bounded over to them. "I hope you didn't mind being called out like that." She glanced over to where Christoph was now talking to someone else. "The teachers said you weren't too keen on the publicity, but Anton and I wanted people to know what you did for the school."

Kayla released Devin's arm, leaned in and hugged Stephanie. "Thank you. I don't do these things for the accolades, but knowing the students are enjoying the improvements to the library means a lot to me."

"It means more to us." Stephanie was blushing, as she looked around. "Well, me. Anton was supposed to come over too, but he's talking to—"

Devin looked over to where Stephanie was looking, seeing Anton talking with a pretty blond girl who was nearly his height. God, he'd forgotten how stupid high school boys could be—how dumb he'd been when he was seventeen and full of hormones, happy when any pretty girl even looked his way. Instead of letting Stephanie think…whatever it was that in-love and ignored teenage girls thought, he reached out and gave her shoulder a light squeeze.

"Speaking from experience, you have to be painfully obvious with guys. I found out seven months after I graduated that Angie Masters had a crush on me all through high school. She never said a word, and despite being book smart, I was an idiot when it came to girls."

Stephanie's blush deepened, but she nodded. "Thanks."

Kayla reclaimed his arm. "We better go."

"Stay strong, Stephanie." He winked at her as they finally left the gym.

Kayla waited until they were nearly to the school doors before she spoke. "That was nice of you. Saying what you did to Stephanie."

"No nicer than you. Boys are dumb. Typically. I was, at least. It's good for certain girls to know that."

"What kind of girls?"

"The smart ones. I remember being dismissive of half the girls in my class because they were quiet, or better at certain things that I was. Our egos are fragile at that age. Well, mine was. I'm, like, old and stuff now, and maybe dudes are better equipped to handle those things now."

She snorted. "I doubt it. But you never know."

"More importantly, are you okay? Your ex is the mayor? That's a bit fucked up."

"You have no idea. I'd been dreading seeing him, but I thought it would have been at the Alumni Homecoming. Had I known that he was living here now, I would never have come."

Mark had the limo parked in the lot a few feet away. He waved at them and got into the car to drive over. Kayla hardly moved, her body stiff and her face a mask. He couldn't imagine how she felt, seeing someone who'd hurt her so unexpectedly. It made the awkwardness between them about their sex seem irrelevant.

There was a burst of laughter behind them, the loudest voice being that of Christoph. Mark and the limo were now sitting behind a car, waiting for his turn to pull into the driveway for the school. Shit, they were going to have another encounter, whether they wanted to or not.

Now, he was a smart guy and knew that Kayla had been serious when it came to her rules about their pretend relationship this week. But she hadn't anticipated her ex's presence, nor what that would do to her. It was up to him to protect both her mood and her reputation.

Kissing, while ideal, might be too much after everything that she'd been through today.

But a little PDA would go a long way to put her ex on his heels.

Devin waited a heartbeat as Mark pulled the limo in front of the school, before he wrapped his arm around Kayla's waist, picked her up and spun her around with a laugh. She gasped before laughing herself as he placed her down in front of the car door.

"Your chariot, m'lady." He then opened the door with a flourish and ended it with a bow.

The mask had cracked, as Kayla smiled brightly and took his hand to help get into the back of the limo. "Thank you."

Closing the door, he saw the small group of people that included Christoph, standing there watching him. He gave them another little bow before making his way around the other side of the limo and climbing in as well.

Kayla was looking out the window at the group when he joined her. Shit, maybe he'd misread the situation. "I know PDAs were on your list of things that I wasn't supposed to do with you while we were here, but I thought your ex needed to see that you weren't the least bit bothered by his presence. I'm sorry if I overstepped."

When she turned to look at him, he was surprised to see that her smile was gone, and there were unshed tears in her eyes.

"Shit, I didn't mean to upset you. I'm so sorry—"

She held up her hand. "It's not that at all."

"What then?" He slid his hand across the seat until he could brush her fingers.

"Except for my best friend Simone, I can't think of anyone else who would have done that for me."

He knew what she was implying, but that didn't make it any easier to accept. "Except for your best friend Simone, you need to get better people in your life."

He expected her to deny the sentiment and was more than a little surprised when she didn't. Instead, she undid her seatbelt and slid beside him. Devin didn't say a word as she rested her head on his shoulder.

Oh.

That was unexpected.

"So…you're not mad at me?"

"For what?"

"Breaking one of your three rules." He took a deep breath and decided also to ask the other question that had prevented him from getting much sleep last night. "Or for having seduced you. Based on how you reacted, you weren't happy with how things had gone."

"Is that what you thought?" She didn't pull away from him, but she did move both her hands to her lap. "I was surprised by what we did. It wasn't unwanted or even unpleasant."

But there had been something. Devin might not be the most observant when it came to women, but even he could hear that she'd left something unspoken.

Fine, she wasn't obligated to talk about it. And he had to remember that this entire week was for show and not the prelude to a fantastic relationship with a millionaire. This was a show, and he was little more than the dutiful actor hired to do his best to convince the audience that Kayla Arnold was as happy as she was successful.

The longer Devin spent with her, the more he realized that Kayla was as far from happy as someone could be. *Don't worry, pretty lady. I'll do my best to make things better for you.*

The limo started to move, and Kayla was forced to sit back and do up her seatbelt. "I appreciate your help. It was wonderful to see Christoph look so annoyed."

"So, PDAs are okay now?"

"As long as they annoy my ex, absolutely."

Well then, that was something. And if things continued to improve, maybe he'd even convince her to dance with him at the alumni dance. Or let him kiss her. Purely for the sake of making her ex jealous. Because that's what this week was about, right.

It had nothing to do with the fact that he might be becoming a tad bit infatuated with her. Or maybe even the tiniest bit in love.

Nope. Not at all.

Sitting up, he squashed that thought and gave her one of his best smiles. "I'll make it my mission to annoy your ex every chance I get."

And if his actions began to win Kayla over as well, then all the better.

Chapter 12

The afternoon event was the one Kayla had been looking forward to the least—mini golf. It had become a tradition that the Alumni Committee always held two events for returning graduates. The golfing tournament was held annually at the Lake's Edge Golf and Country Club. She'd been invited in the past but had vowed when she'd been a student that she'd never attend. The club members were the town's elite, many of whom were wealthy retirees who had few ties to the community. She wasn't the only former grad who felt the same way, so it was easy enough to beg off attending.

But there was no way she'd be able to avoid mini golf.

The tradition had been started five years after the Lake's Edge tournament had started, by a group of students who weren't invited to the adult golfing event. Those students graduated, but they continued holding it as a fundraiser for the alumni. Mocking Lake's Edge, their awards, even their dress code, had become a point of pride.

The Bucket Club, a low budget driving range and mini golf park held the distinction of hosting the event. It had the added benefit of being on the road on the way to Lake's Edge, which meant all the club members would have to drive past on their way to their event.

As a teen of few means, Kayla had dreamed of being able to attend the mini golf tournament so she could thumb her nose at all the well-to-dos.

Now, it felt a bit disingenuous.

She was the rich one. She could have walked through the front door of Lake's Edge Lodge, smiled and received a membership without having to show her bank account. She would have had more in common with the stockbrokers, lawyers, and venture capitalists on the membership roster than she did with Jason McTavish who owned the bike store on King Street.

Yet, here she was in a pair of golf shorts from her 2013 summer collection, accepting a putter and two balls from Jason as he checked her off the list.

"I was shocked when I saw your name on the list, Kay. Sandy and I took bets as to whether you'd show up or not."

Jason and Sandy had started dating just before graduation, and Kayla had been thrilled to hear that they were still going strong. They'd been *that couple*, the one that had overcome a few unexpected ups and downs, and somehow ended up together, stronger as a unit.

Once upon a time, Kayla had assumed she and Christoph were that couple as well. That while yes, he was older than her and hadn't paid her any attention until she'd hit it big with Fashion Finds, that they had shared roots and that would be enough for them to live happily ever after.

Instead, they were divorced, Christoph was now the mayor of Meadow Lake, and she was mini golfing with a pretend boyfriend she met on a sugar daddy site.

Speaking of Devin...

He was currently over at the sponge toss, throwing large orange sponges through oversized holes in a wooden wall meant to look like the high school mascot. She stopped to watch him, the joy he always seemed to have in any given situation. Whether it was eating overcooked bacon and dry pancakes at breakfast, or playing card games with strangers, Devin loved life and all of its various forms.

"Your boyfriend is quite the man."

Kayla started at the sound of Ms. Simon, the school principal, suddenly beside her. "He is."

"We had a great talk about the new mathematics program that the province is implementing next year. It was refreshing to hear the opinion of someone who knew the topic but wasn't a teacher or parent. He made some interesting points."

Devin burst out laughing and ducked as several of the student organizers threw soaking wet sponges at him. "He tends to do that."

Ms. Simon smiled. "He's also really good with the kids. At supper last night he said he didn't know what he wanted to do with himself now that he's finally out of school. If you want my unsolicited opinion, he should go back to school and get his teaching degree. The world can always use another teacher who loves what he does."

"I'll be sure to mention that to him." Kayla also thought Devin would be a great educator. It was too bad he didn't seem interested. The world could use another person out there encouraging young people to do their best. She couldn't help but wonder what he would end up doing with his life beyond this week. Maybe he'd travel or spend it on personal items—though what those might be, she wasn't sure. For all she knew, he would take her money, and she'd never see him again. No harm, no foul.

Except, there was a part of her that would be sad to see him go. To know that he was out there in the world and that she'd never get to see him. And that was a revelation that she didn't know how to process.

Devin laughed when one of the students landed a hit with a sponge, square in the middle of his back. His white polo shirt darkened as water dripped down to the ground. With a sigh, she lifted the two putters and rested them against her shoulder. "I better go save him."

"Probably wise." Ms. Simon faced her, holding out her hand. "I know you're probably getting tired of hearing this but thank you. I haven't told many people about all of the extras that you do for our school. Including the ones that the board doesn't know about."

Not for the first time since her return, Kayla felt like her old student self, getting in trouble for something she'd done. "I don't know what you mean?"

"The bundle of tickets that arrive annually for musicals in Toronto. Tickets to Blue Jays and Raptor games for the sports teams. All anonymously delivered for the students with a hand-signed thank you card. There aren't many people who would do that, and I can't think of another one of our benefactors who would be so secretive. Local businesses will let us know that they've donated, even if they don't want things public. So, I put two and two together."

Shit. She hadn't even told Simone about doing that. A fierce blush heated her skin, and she knew she was busted. "Please don't mention it to anyone."

"I would never do anything to jeopardize your gifts. It's nice to know that there's someone out there who wants these kids to succeed as much as I do." With a smile and nod, Ms. Simon left her alone.

Well. That had been unexpected. She seemed to be having more than a few of those moments since coming back to Meadow Lake.

Devin caught sight of her and frowned. Her confusion must be showing, so she waved him off but made her way over to him. The moment she got within range, she smiled and held out his putter. "Ready for a round?"

His grin was all the approval she needed. Taking the putter, he moved back a bit and extended it. "Toss me the ball."

"Okay." She did but gasped when he caught it on the flat edge of the putter. "How'd you do that?"

"Not only am I a math genius, but I also love mini golf. when I was a kid, I used to play with my dad every Saturday he wasn't working." His smile dampened for the briefest of moments before it returned. "I would practice bouncing balls on the putter every time we went." He hit the ball high up into the air, spun around and caught it again. "I got pretty good."

The kids around them whistled and applauded, as Devin caught the ball, stopped and bowed. Kayla loved how playful he was, how there was nothing malicious in anything he did. No hidden agenda in any of his actions.

"We better get in line to start our game." She nodded toward the beginning of the course and they headed off to more claps and a few whistles. Devin looked back over his shoulder and gave the kids two thumbs up.

Being around Devin was a unique experience. It was as though she'd been holding her breath for years, and with him, she was finally able to exhale, only to suck in a fresh breath that got her synapsis firing. She'd never been so aware of another person before, his moods and thoughts as transparent as an announcer with a bullhorn. He lived his world outwardly, engaging with everyone and everything around him.

Kayla still couldn't wrap her brain around what it was like to be like that. To have the ability to take whatever the world threw your way with a smile on your face. She'd fought for everything so long, that it was her default setting. But maybe on that next big exhale, she'd be able to reset herself, her outlook on life and live a little less aggressively.

For the first time since they'd met, Kayla had to fight through her unexpected awkwardness and scattered thoughts to talk to him. "You and your dad are close, I take it?"

Devin looked down at the putter in his hand, before nodding. "Were close. He died when I was eleven."

Her stomach flipped as she reached out for his arm. "I'm sorry."

When he met her gaze, she could see that despite the passage of time, the pain was still simmering below the surface for him. "Thanks. He died a hero, so while I miss him every day, it's hard not to be proud of him. Of what he did."

"Next group please." The attendant beckoned them forward, putting a temporary pause on their conversation.

There was no way she could have known about his dad, but deep-down Kayla felt as though she should have. No one could be as free and happy as Devin was without there having been something in their past to make them appreciate the value of life. If it had been anyone else, if she'd had the typical bit of distance between them that she'd insisted upon, she might have realized sooner. With Devin, it was easy to become blinded by his sunny nature. Something that she'd have to continue to remind herself of.

They stepped onto the first green and Kayla set her ball down on the well-worn spot on the green felt. Devin bumped his hip into hers. "Hey now. What makes you think you're going first?"

"Does it matter?"

"Does it *matter*?" He rolled his eyes and held his hands up to the sky. "Does it matter, she asks. Of course, it does. It can completely impact a golfer's mojo. We need to decide who gets the honors."

Okay, he was cute when he was competitive. "Flip a coin?"

"Please, nothing so pedestrian." He held out his hand in a fist between them. "Rock, paper, scissors."

"You're serious?" The question was completely irrelevant because of course, Devin would be completely serious about mini golf and rock, paper, scissors. "Fine. Let's do this."

"Awesome. We go on three. One, two, three, go!"

A tie—paper.

Devin growled. "One, two, three, go!"

Another tie—rock.

Kayla couldn't hold back her grin. "If we don't break the tie this time, I'm just going to go first."

"We'll break." Devin leaned forward, as though he was about to take off in a sprint. "Here we go. One, two...three..."

"Devin!"

"Go!"

Kayla went with rock, as Devin made the scissor motion. "Woot!"

He groaned, doubling over. "My mojo."

The crowd behind them laughed, dragging Kayla's attention to the fact that they'd been the center of attention. Rather than her standard response—turning away so she wouldn't have to be seen—she smiled and gave a small bow of her own. She then rolled Devin's golf ball away with her toe, lined up and took her first shot.

She was having a surprisingly good time. Playing mini golf at her school reunion.

So weird.

Despite his concern for his mojo, it became quickly apparent that Devin was the far better golfer of the two of them. For every shot he made, Kayla would somehow get stuck and need to make three. She groaned when her ball got sucked behind the windmill on the sixth hole. "God, I'm never going to finish the course, let alone win a prize at this rate."

"Prize?" Devin stuck his head around the windmill to see her. "You didn't say anything about prizes."

"Well, they're nothing special. The top five winners get gift cards or wine. Sometimes maple syrup. The five worst scores get wooden spoons."

He frowned. "Spoons?"

"Don't ask. It has a long tradition."

"Ah, I'm asking. Spoons?"

"It had to do with someone a long time ago saying that the losers were getting their asses spanked. And then that somehow transformed into them getting wooden spoons and posing for pictures." Devin stared. "We haven't been allowed to actually spank people for years."

He laughed. "Because rules."

"Exactly." She took another swing, which sent her ball ricocheting through the windmill and finally into the hole. "There we go."

They'd caught up to the group at the hole ahead of them and had to wait. Devin stood beside her, but his gaze was bouncing around, taking in everything around them. The Bucket Club was run down but in a well-used, well-loved kind of way. She'd always thought of it as a bit of a dive when she was younger, but even though it wasn't as fancy as some other places she'd been over the years, there was a certain warmth to coming back. Probably because her parents would bring her here at least once a month in the summer, one of the few family outings that they could afford.

"You and your dad," the question popped from her without thought, "did you used to come to places like this? Or were you more into the crazy fancy mini golf adventures?"

It was probably not the best idea to be asking about his dad, but she couldn't help but be curious. He died a hero? What could that possibly mean? Was he a cop, or firefighter? Something completely different? It explained a lot about Devin's personality, and still posed more questions.

Devin's body appeared to relax as he smiled. "Naw, we were pretty much restricted to whatever location we could find. We went to a place close to where I grew up most weekends. He used to call it our bonding time, but really, I think it was to make sure that I wasn't loud on the weekends. Mom's a nurse and worked a lot of overnights. I had a hard time keeping quiet when she was sleeping in the day."

"Your dad sounds like a pretty awesome man."

"He was." Devin's smile didn't waver, but his eyes grew sad. "I know you want to know what happened to him. It's hard when someone drops a bombshell like that and then doesn't fill in the blanks. I don't normally talk about him with anyone. I honestly didn't expect to talk about him with you at all."

"Why not?" She wasn't that unapproachable, was she?

"Well, our arrangement doesn't exactly lend to heart to heart conversations."

Right. Their arrangement. She licked her lips and shrugged. "Maybe not. But as you said, we need to make sure that we can fill in the blanks when we're talking to someone."

He leaned in. "And you're curious?"

And there was her blush. "Yes, I'm curious. How was your dad a hero?"

"It's probably not the first five things that came to your mind. He and his friends always went ice fishing in the winter. I'm not exactly sure how much fishing they did, but he always had a great time. He and two of his friends went out late in the spring, thought they could squeeze out one more weekend, even though there was a warning of thin ice. When they were out there, a teen on a snowmobile went through the ice. Dad and his buddy ran to help, but in the process of saving the kid, Dad slipped into the water himself. His friend and the kid couldn't get him out, and he went under. He drowned."

"We're done finally." The kids ahead of them waved, and Devin moved up to take his spot on the tee.

Kayla could only stand and stare at him, his words echoing in her head. She couldn't imagine how she'd feel knowing that her dad died to save someone else. Pride, for sure. But she'd probably be furious that he'd done something that ended up taking him away from her.

She needed to call her parents later and tell them how much she loved them.

"I'm going to take your shot if you don't hurry up." Devin made a dramatic move, pretending to swing.

"Go for it." Her voice wavered, forcing her to clear her throat. "You're whooping my butt anyway."

The second he finished, Kayla leaned in and placed a kiss on his cheek. Devin frowned. "What was that for?"

"For your dad. The world needs more heroes like him. Thank you."

At that moment, something passed between them, an emotion that Kayla couldn't name, nor did she want to take the chance and try.

Devin's gaze slipped to her lips. "You better take your turn. Quickly."

"Why?"

"Because I'm about to break two of your rules if you don't stop looking at me like that."

"Like what?"

Devin growled. "Please."

She did as he said, but she knew that whatever this was between them was something more than him pretending to be her fake boyfriend. If she wasn't careful, she might end up breaking a few rules herself.

Chapter 13

The rest of the day, Devin hadn't been able to take his eyes off Kayla. It was entirely her fault with the coy looks and small smiles wherever he'd do something funny. That only had him trying harder to make her smile, to laugh out loud, anything to see the darkness that had been hovering over her since the moment the limo had pulled into Meadow Lake, evaporate.

The only problem with his grand plan was the more she smiled, the more he wanted to throw her over his shoulder and haul her back to the B&B like a caveman bent on female domination. As much as his lizard brain wanted to do that *right the fuck now come on*, the rest of him knew better.

Or at least he assumed it was better. Though the way his cock was throbbing in his pants, even his intellectual self was beginning to reconsider that analysis.

Once everyone had completed their mini golf rounds, the next step was the awards. He'd come in second and played it up to the crowd when he'd gone up to accept his prize. Stephanie had been the one to hand him the gift certificate to a local diner—a romantic dinner for two—which he'd turned around and given back to her.

"I think the smartest of the two co-primes should get to have a night of fun. Besides, I don't live here and won't have a chance to get to enjoy it."

He also made sure to nudge Anton as he walked by and nodded toward Stephanie. "Take the chance, man."

Kayla also had one—a spoon. She was blushing madly as she went up to receive her award, and he could tell she wanted nothing more than to disappear into the woodwork. But when Stephanie handed it to her, Kayla surprised him by turning around and bowing as she waved the spoon above her head. The crowd ate it up, clapping and cheering for her as she came back to join him.

"Well played, Ms. Arnold."

"Thank you."

Stephanie took the mic once more. "Ms. Simon wanted me to let everyone know, that between registration and donations, this year's event has raised one thousand and seventeen dollars! All proceeds go toward the school's lunch program for in-need students. Thank you to everyone who came out today. I hope we'll see you all at the library dedication event that's being held tomorrow at noon."

Several people around them turned to look at Kayla, smiling and nodding as they applauded. He'd expected her to tense or somehow brush off the attention or the honor. Instead, she straightened and gave everyone another little wave.

Well, good for her.

It was a significant honor and based on everything he'd heard since arriving, she more than deserved it. He slipped his arm around her waist and tugged her a bit closer to him. Sure, it might be a bit close to the whole PDA thing, but at this point, it wasn't anything more than what he'd done with her already.

Even if the proximity made him want to kiss her.

For a really long time.

His cock twitched again, and this time he didn't quite stop from groaning.

"You okay?" She turned against him, placing both her hands on his shoulder. Her hip was dangerously close to his groin. "Sore from the golfing?"

Yup, she's trying to kill me. "You're a tease."

"I've never once been told that."

There was no way he was going to let that go unanswered, so he pressed his hard-on against her. "You keep smiling. And looking at my chest. And the look on your face is something that I'd see in a movie where there was some seduction going on. Only I'm the one being seduced, and that's not something I'm used to being on the receiving end of."

"I can't imagine why not? You're an attractive man." She leaned against his cock, increasing the pressure. "Both inside and out."

Dear God, she was trying to kill him. The people around them didn't even realize that there was an attempted murder going on. *Wake up, everyone!! I'm dying from lust!*

He managed not to tear her clothing off, right there and then. "I hope Mark has the limo close by. I don't want to have to walk too far with a massive boner for everyone to see."

"I'll cover you." She took his hand and led him in the direction of the parking lot but stayed close enough in front of him to help block everyone's view.

They only got stopped twice on their way back by people offering their regrets of not being able to make the dedication tomorrow. Kayla was generous and spoke to them, all while Devin stood there dying a little bit more with each passing second. It wasn't as though he could do anything about his arousal, but at least he wouldn't have to worry about hiding it from the world.

He could see the limo pull up, gravel spitting and flying beneath the weight of the wheels. Mark got out and stood by the back door waiting for them. He must be used to being her rescue in situations like this because the moment she saw him she made her excuses and they were on their way once more.

Devin sighed when they climbed into the backseat, and the door was finally shut on them. "Thank God."

Then he nearly flew out of the seat as Kayla pressed her hand to his groin and squeezed. "Poor baby."

"What are you doing?" His heart pounded with each movement of her fingers against him. Shit, if she did that for very long, he was going to come in his pants.

She paused, and he had to bite his tongue not to beg her to keep going. Shit, she was going to drive him mad. Instead, she turned in her seat and looked at him with that strange expression he hadn't exactly been able to put a label on earlier. "You're a good man, Devin. You deserve to have happiness in your life."

"I'm happy." *I'll be even more so if you squeeze my cock again.*

"You like to show the world that you are, but I'm not as convinced as I once was." She pulled his button, popping it open. "And I know we have some guidelines that we're working within. That this isn't a relationship. That in a few days' time we'll be back to Toronto and reality. But while we are here, and the world isn't quite so overwhelming, I thought we might be able to have some fun."

The limo began to move, as Kayla pushed her hand into his pants and cupped his balls. He moaned as he pressed his head back against the seat. "Fuck."

"We don't have a condom, or else I might be willing to try that." She gave his shaft a stroke, taking her time to run her thumb across the slit across the head. "But that doesn't mean there aren't other things we can do."

He wanted nothing more than to see her on her knees between his thighs, sucking him off. He might have even suggested it if there wasn't something else, a little kink of his that he wanted more. Forcing his eyes open to look at her, he hoped this didn't make him sound weird. "Can you talk dirty to me? While you jerk me off?"

Kayla pulled back a tiny bit, but he could tell it was out of amusement rather than thinking he was strange. It might not be the most extreme kink out there, but Devin always felt a bit exposed when he asked a woman to do it for him. Because gentlemen should always put their lady first.

She reached down and pulled the front of his pants farther open. "Just promise me that you won't laugh. I'm not exactly known for my blue vernacular."

The way his cock pulsed as she said *vernacular*, the content of her little talk might not matter. "You're fine. Trust me."

He knew she didn't know initially what to say, but she at least began to fist him with precise movements that would be more than enough. When she leaned in so her lips brushed his ear, he nearly came then and there. "I keep picturing you with your head between my legs."

Oh. Shit.

He sucked in air with great gulps, trying to cool, or at the very least slow, down his libido. There was no way he was going to last long at this rate. Not that it mattered. He closed his eyes and let his mind pull up images as she continued to speak.

"The way your tongue caressed me, and the way you fucked me with your hand...I haven't had a man do that for me before. Not like that."

Why wouldn't another man go down on her? That was the second thing he'd wanted to do to her from the moment he saw her. The first was to kiss her senseless.

Soon. He hoped.

Kayla gave him a hard squeeze as she flicked his earlobe with her tongue. "Do you know what I'd like to do with you?"

Every dirty thought he could imagine raced through his head. "What?"

"I wish we had a condom. Do you know how many times I've been in the back of this limo? Thousands. I've never once wanted to have sex here before I'd met you. I don't know if I could, knowing Mark was up front and might see, but I've been wondering what it would be like."

Yeah, sex in a limo was totally on his bucket list. "What else do you want?"

She chuckled, and the sound of her rich voice sent a shiver through him. "I'd like to dress in one of my latest designs, something light and sexy. I wouldn't put anything on underneath, and then we'd go out to dinner. You'd know that I was naked the whole time. And when we got back home, you'd fuck me hard in the foyer while I still had that dress on."

Devin felt his balls tighten and for a moment he thought he was going to come. Not only was the idea of fucking her clothed after a night of teasing something he wanted to do *right the hell now*, but she'd also said home. A future between them wasn't something that he'd contemplated, but the ideas were arousing.

Waking up to Kayla in the morning. Seeing her black hair spilt across the white sheets as she breathed softly, her lips parted as she dreamed. Waking her with kisses on her shoulder, down her chest, pausing only long enough to suckle her breasts. They'd make love, coming apart together, to then get up and have breakfast. She'd be his purpose in life, the thing that he got out of bed for every day.

The perfect daydream.

Kayla quickened her strokes as she sucked on his lobe again. "You better come soon. We're almost back."

"Okay." He closed his eyes, pulled in a deep breath of her scent and pushed his cock into her hand.

Clenching his teeth, he hissed as the first waves of pleasure had his body tense. He did his best to keep sounds of his pleasure bottled up, contained as much as possible so Mark wouldn't be any the wiser about what they'd done. Kayla continued to stroke him, catching the spurts of his release with her hand. It should have been longer, but the moment passed quickly. He fell back against the seat and Kayla pulled back.

Her hand was covered in his spunk, and her face flushed. "That was hot."

"The second we get back to the room, I'm going to make you scream." There wasn't a chance in hell that he wouldn't repay her for what she'd just done for him. "The second."

Kayla grabbed a box of tissues that were tucked into the side console and cleaned herself up. Thankfully, they were able to rearrange themselves back to what looked like normal as the limo pulled into the driveway of the B&B.

Devin couldn't wait for Mark to get out and open the door for them and did it himself as he took her by the hand and pulled her behind him. Mark was half standing out of his seat as he called out. "You okay?"

"We're good," Kayla yelled back, trying to turn, but Devin wouldn't let her stop. "Won't need you anymore today."

Devin wasn't sure, but he thought he heard Mark laugh.

Nope, he wasn't even caring right now. All that mattered was getting Kayla back to the room so he could show her exactly how she made him feel.

"This is crazy," she said as they marched up the stairs, but he couldn't tell if she was talking to him or herself.

"You need more crazy in your life. Live on the edge and all that jazz."

"We've only known each other a few days."

"So what? You want this, right?" He stopped walking and faced her in the hallway. If he was being a blind horny fool, he needed to know that right now. "Yes?"

She reached up and cupped his cheek. "Yes."

"Then we're all good. I've said this before, but you deserve every good thing coming your way."

She opened her mouth to speak, but nothing came out. The temptation to cover her lips with his, to give in and kiss her the way he wanted to, was about to overwhelm him, so instead he took her hand in his once more and pulled her the rest of the way to their bedroom.

Time to show her how awesome she is.

There was something refreshing about having already had an orgasm and knowing that he was about to devote his undivided attention on Kayla. That he wouldn't be distracted by his libido and would spend every bit of brain power on making this the best ten minutes of her life.

Hell, maybe even fifteen!

Because as much as he prided himself on his ability to give a woman what she wanted, Devin was also practical.

The second they were through the door, he kicked it shut, picked her up and tossed her on the bed. Someone had come in and tidied up the room since they'd been gone, which gave him a clean area to work with. Setting Kayla in the middle of the bed, he leaned over her, and for a second almost kissed her on impulse.

Nope, don't want to do anything to ruin this moment.

Instead, he leaned close and smiled. "What do you want? I can go down on you or use my hand. I can make love to you, though it might take me a minute to get action ready again. Anything you want." His cock was already on the way to getting hard again. He was on board with anything Kayla wanted as well.

For her part, Kayla looked ready for anything. She pulled herself into a sitting position, leaning her body against the bevy of pillows piled on the bed. "You were talking about things that turned you on in the limo. The dirty talk and stuff."

Oh. If he could do something for her that would fulfil some fantasy, all the better. "Yeah. You have something like that?"

As a rapid blush covered her face, she nodded. "It's not anything radical or weird."

"I don't even care. I'll dress up in a monkey suit and fuck you with a banana if that's what you want."

She laughed, turning her head from him. "No, nothing like that. Could you…I mean, would you mind…shit."

"Anything. I'll agree to anything. Just say it."

She looked him in the eyes, her chin dropping toward her chest. "Can you hold my hands down, so I can't get away. Then fuck me with your other hand?" She rolled her eyes. "That's stupid. Lame."

His cock was full on hard. "That's the hottest fucking thing I've ever heard."

"Really?"

He nodded, before sitting down beside her on the bed. Devin knew himself well enough to realize that saying too much while doing this wasn't going to work for her. He was far too goofy to pretend to be any sort of dominant personality. But he could give a stern look as well as the next teaching assistant. Schooling his expression as best he could, he took both of her hands and lifted and pressed them against the pillows above her head.

"Don't move those."

She nodded and bit down on her bottom lip.

"I'm going to take your pants off now."

It took a bit of maneuvering, but he was able to slide the pants from her long, shapely legs. He decided to leave her panties on; a bit of a tease for both of them. He then got back into position beside her and replaced his hold on her crossed wrists.

God, he should probably say something. Make some attempt at dirty talk while he fingered her to orgasm. But words had never been his strong suit, and he didn't want to risk ruining the mood with her laughing at something that he'd said.

Instead, he held her gaze with his, and slowly caressed her breasts through her shirt. Her nipples were hard as he pressed the palm of his hand against her. Twice they'd had sex, and twice he'd left her partially clothed. He didn't want to distract himself with that particular analysis, so he enjoyed the feel of her body.

As he moved his hand lower, Kayla's breathing grew more rapid. He teased her belly button as he passed by it, taking time to circle it with his fingers. The soft near-invisible hairs that covered her stomach caught on his nails the lower he went. When he finally reached the band of her panties, he paused long enough to give her time to say no, in case she'd changed her mind.

Kayla nodded as she sighed.

Here we go, boys!

She was already wet as he pressed his fingers into the black mound of curls hidden beneath the lace. Her clit was swollen, sensitive. He pressed against it the same way he had last night, knowing she liked his touch there. For good measure, he pressed down a bit harder on her wrists, reinforcing the fantasy of being held down.

"This is going to be quick," she said, little more than a whisper.

"I better make it good then."

If time and arousal were going to be a factor, then he knew he wouldn't have much opportunity for teasing. By-passing her clit, he slipped his forefinger into her pussy, all the way down until his hand stopped him from going farther.

She gasped and tried to twist—closer, away, he wasn't sure—but he held her tight. He fucked her with his hand, steady and strong as she opened her legs as far as she could, given their position and her panties. It didn't take long for him to add a second finger into her pussy. Her moans increased, as did her thrashing.

"That's it," he cooed, "fuck yourself on my hand."

Her hips met his fingers, as she drove herself harder down on him. Her muscles clenched around his digits and he knew she was close. Shifting his angle, Devin increased the pace as he watched her face, wanting to see the moment her orgasm hit.

One second, her face was scrunched up in intense concentration, and the next everything in her expression expanded. Her mouth opened, and a cry slipped from her as she arched her back off the bed, forcing her pussy down hard on him.

He continued to fuck her as long as he could, ignoring the pain in his wrist at the awkward angle as she pressed against him. After a few more thrusts, she finally collapsed, and he knew she was spent.

Giving her time to collect herself, he pulled his hand from her panties and went to the bathroom to wash up. His heart pounded as blood surged through him at warp speed. God, he was lightheaded at the intensity of what they'd done, and he hadn't even fucked her.

This was the type of relationship he'd always dreamed about—one filled with passion with a woman who was intelligent, driven and generous. He didn't care that their coming together had begun by a sugar daddy site, nor did he care that they came from entirely different worlds. They fit together, worked well both sexually and personality-wise, despite only having known one another for a short time.

All he needed to do was convince Kayla that she should give them a chance. That there was no reason why their fake relationship couldn't become a real one.

He looked at himself in the mirror and grinned.

Operation: Win a Millionaire's Heart was on.

Chapter 14

Kayla couldn't quite put her finger on it, but something had changed between her and Devin after their sexual adventure in the limo and room. They weren't worse, or even better for that matter, merely different. They'd gotten cleaned up separately in the bathroom, chatted a bit, but never getting in each other's way. Devin would smile, do his typical silly bows and flourishes when it looked as though he would get too close, then back off.

Except, unlike yesterday after they'd had sex, this time she didn't want him to avoid her. His attentiveness was so unlike anything Christoph had done for her, that it had initially thrown her off guard. But today, after mini golf, after learning about his dad, she couldn't help but be more than a little drawn to him.

And as strange as that was, she couldn't help but like it.

They'd only been in each other's company for a few days, and she was quickly becoming infatuated with him. It was more than a little too close to how her relationship with Christoph had begun. Her urges to stare at him, to try to interpret the meaning behind every move he made. Sexually, Christoph had been excellent in the bedroom, and Kayla had never once complained about him ignoring her desires. Even if once they were done, he was more concerned with other matters, rather than cuddling.

It was his behavior outside their home that had been her point of contention.

Christoph had wanted status, had wanted Kayla to spend her money on a lavish lifestyle that, while undoubtedly sustainable given the success of Fashion Finds, wasn't one that she'd enjoyed. Not to mention, his treatment of her as little more than a walking wallet, didn't help any.

By the time they'd left their room, it was getting close to eight o'clock at night. They were both starving, and Meadow Lake wasn't exactly known for its fancy dining or late-night restaurants. Their current options for food were Kelce's Pub, where they could get a pretty decent plate of fish and chips, or one of the fast food joints. The problem with Kelce's was that it was owned by Christoph's cousin. And with Christoph the current mayor, and Kayla not exactly comfortable being the returning ex with a new boyfriend, it was probably best to avoid the spot.

Stepping out into the warm evening air, she was surprised when Devin reached down and took her hand. When she sent him a questioning glance, he smiled. "We're in public and everyone thinks we're a disgustingly cute couple. It would look weird if we weren't holding hands."

It was tough to argue with that logic, even if it did break one of her rules of conduct. "That's fine. Better not to raise suspicions."

"Exactly." They started to walk toward the downtown core. "So, where do you suggest we eat?"

"There's an A&W about a ten-minute walk from here. If you want to go?"

"Really? I'm surprised a highfalutin woman such as yourself would want to go there."

She rolled her eyes and stepped up their pace. "I love a Teen burger as much as the next person." In reality, it had been more than a few years since she'd had one. Christoph would have made his displeasure clear had she even suggested it. And since he'd left her, she hadn't thought of going to a place like that again.

"That's good. Because I'd kill for a Papa burger right now. I think I even have a two-for-one coupon on my phone app. At the very least we'll be able to get some free fries or something."

It was easy for her to forget that Devin had been a student not that long ago and was still watching every single penny closely. She squeezed his hand, leaning a bit closer to him as they walked. "I think I can afford to buy you what you want without the coupon."

He frowned, looking confused for a moment before the penny dropped. "Right. Shit."

"That's fine. It's nice actually."

"That I forgot that you have more money than I'm likely to make in my lifetime?"

"Yes." They passed a couple on the sidewalk, and Kayla nodded and smiled as they said hello. "That was the main issue between Christoph and myself. He wanted us to live the life that fit my bank account. Cars, vacations, parties. He hated when I'd say no because of work. Or hated when I'd travel to another country for work and would refuse to blow off my obligations to stay longer and party."

"But, he knew you before your company hit the big time, right?"

"Yes. That was one of the reasons why I thought what we had would last. He knew me when I was just Kayla from Meadow Lake, fashion nerd who spent too much time in the Home Ec. room. He was the son of the mayor, older than me and destined for greatness. I was surprised when I came back for my five-year reunion that he was there. That he even knew who I was."

She'd assumed afterwards that he'd found out that the quiet girl who'd made it big was going to be in town and he'd wanted to find his way into her heart, and by extension, her pocketbook. But every time she'd thought about that first night, he'd genuinely appeared to be interested in her.

Maybe he had been. But not anymore.

The A&W was busy; teens filled the place both in front and behind the counter. Devin placed their order, but when she went to pay for it, he waved her off and pulled out his debit card. "I have a coupon as well."

The young man behind the counter barely acknowledged Devin. "Okay. That's fourteen thirty-six." The food was on the tray in a flash, and before she knew it, they were taking a seat at a table in the corner.

Looking around, for the first time in a long while Kayla felt different. And by different, she knew she meant normal. It was nice.

It didn't take either of them long to devour the food in front of them. Devin sat back and burped. "God, that was what I needed."

"I need to ask Mark if the limo can make it through the drive-thru. I'd forgotten how much I loved these."

They started to get up to leave when a group of kids sitting at a table opposite them, waved at Devin. "Hey, you're the mini golf guy, right?"

"That's me. What can I do for you?"

Kayla hung back, obviously not the one they'd want to talk to, given her less than stellar performance on the course.

One of the girls, a brunette with a nose piercing, leaned forward as she batted her eyes at him. "Is it true that you were able to get a hole-in-one on the gnome hole?"

Devin grinned. "Oh yeah. I knew the second I saw the slope of the course that I'd be able to nail that one."

Kayla somehow managed to stop her knee-jerk eye roll.

"But *how*? No one has ever managed to do it, except maybe Jonathon who manages the place. And you don't even live here. It's not like you could have practiced a thousand times."

Devin moved to the table. "It's just physics. Give me your placemat."

For the next five minutes, Devin had the rapt attention of six teenagers as he proceeded to make an impromptu math lesson around mini golf. Kayla even found herself drifting closer so she could see the lines and angles of his diagram. By the time he stood back up, even Kayla thought she might have a chance at making that hole.

"Still, you'll have to practice it. A bunch." Devin stepped back beside her and moved to take her hand in his. "I'm also like, really freaking good at mini golf."

The group thanked him, and they left. Kayla waited until they got back outside before asking the one question that had been eating at her for a while now. "Why are you not a teacher? You're good with kids."

"Kids are easy. But the paperwork, grading, needing to have time for extracurricular activities, meeting parents, all that stuff is a bit terrifying to me."

"But you'd get used to that. Not everyone can make math interesting. You have a knack for doing that and making it relevant to their lives."

He shook his head. "I don't think so."

"Even Ms. Simon thought so. She wanted me to convince you to complete an education degree."

"Sweet of her, but I'll pass." Devin dropped her hand and put his in his pockets. "So, is the library dedication the only thing on the agenda tomorrow?"

She couldn't imagine why the thought of being a teacher was upsetting to him, but she wasn't so self-absorbed not to realize he didn't want to talk about it. "Yes. The homecoming dance is tomorrow night." And Sunday morning, they'd be on their way home, back to reality.

Kayla to her business and Devin to his life. Only he'll be ten thousand dollars richer. Kayla wasn't sure what she would have gained from her week back home.

"That will be fun. Except for our problem of rule number two." He stopped and turned to face her. "It's going to be hard not to dance with you at a dance. Especially when you're the guest of honor and everyone thinks we're a couple. We're probably going to have to get out on the floor at least once if we want to keep up the front."

Kayla had managed to go a significant portion of her life avoiding anything that resembled dancing. She was horrible at it in the worst kind of way. "Trust me when I say that there's an excellent reason that rule exists. No one will question it. They went to school with me and know the horror that is my coordination."

Devin threw his hands up in the air. "But you have to dance. You don't have to be any good."

"It's not happening." She crossed her arms and wanted to laugh at the annoyed look on his face.

But Devin wasn't the least bit dissuaded. "Do you know how to do the step dance thing?"

"The...*what*?"

"You know." He then bent his knees slightly and stepped first his right foot toward his left and out, and then did the reverse with his left. He also added in an awkward bounce that made him look like a crazy fool. "Step-dance thing."

"You're so white."

"Look in the mirror, pretty lady?" He laughed and added a butt wiggle. "Anyone can dance. Come on, try it."

"Hell no."

He took her hands as he continued to dance in the middle of the sidewalk. Cars drove past, and she even caught sight of a few people pointing, but they were gone as quickly as they arrived. God, she didn't want to do this. Except, she kind of did and began to mimic his steps, smiling as they moved.

"See, you've got it." He started humming a song, something that sounded familiar, but that she couldn't name.

She knew they were breaking both rules one and two, but she was having too much fun to care. "I'm horrible."

"No, you're not. But you do worry too much about what other people think." He smiled at her, and something in her chest melted. "You don't have to be perfect all of the time. Just yourself."

Another car came past them, only this time it stopped. Devin couldn't see it, as it had stopped behind him, but Kayla could make out the face of the person looking through the window at them. It was Christoph.

All joy she'd had engaging in their silly public dance, vanished as her eyes met his. "Shit."

Devin stopped moving and turned to see what she was looking at. "Is that your ex?"

"Yes." She didn't want a confrontation, not when everything had been going so well.

"Well, it's too bad he ruined our fun. Let's head back to the lodge." Devin held out his arm for her to take. "M'lady."

It shouldn't be as hard confronting Christoph as it was. Their marriage had ended painfully and far faster than she would have ever imagined. Simone had told her time and again that Kayla hadn't been the one to blame for the breakup, but that also hadn't mattered. She couldn't help but wonder if she'd handled things differently, if she'd given him some concessions, that they might have made it through the hard times.

Not that any of it mattered now. She slipped her hand around Devin's arm. "Let's get back."

She'd only have to worry about Christoph for a few days more. Then she'd be back in Toronto and her life, and he and Meadow Lake would be shoved back in the past where it belonged.

Chapter 15

Devin did his best not to squirm or play with his tie as he sat on a stage listening to Ms. Simon tell the world what an amazing person Kayla was. The last thing he wanted to do was detract from the ceremony, or to give any indication of the turmoil that was currently churning inside him. This was her special moment, the reason she'd asked him to come along in the first place. He owed it to her to make sure everything went off without a hitch.

As much as he wasn't supposed to have any feelings for Kayla, every moment he spent in her company, served to ratchet up his emotions. Even now, sitting beside her saying nothing was enough to make his heart pound and his hands vibrate with excitement. Which was bad and good. Bad, because he'd officially fallen hard for this woman. Good, because he was reasonably sure that she might be falling for him as well.

Operation: Woo Kayla was working.

At least he assumed it was based on the increased number of smiles and glances she threw his way. Not to mention, she would touch his arm more and more. Those little accidental brushes had to mean something, right?

Maybe.

God, he hoped so.

After they'd returned to the B&B last night, Mr. Babineau caught him before they made it to the stairs. When he'd challenged Devin to another round of crib, Kayla pushed him toward the reception desk with a smile. "It's good. Go have a few rounds and kick his butt."

He'd lost the first two games because he'd been wholly preoccupied with trying to figure out if Kayla was putting some distance between them, or if she merely wanted him to have some fun with someone who apparently meant something to her. He would have asked her, but by the time he'd come back upstairs, she'd already crawled into her bed and was asleep.

Ms. Simon's back was currently to him as she continued her speech. "I wasn't a teacher at Meadow Lake High when Ms. Arnold was here. My first meeting with her was at her five-year reunion. This charming young woman took me aside, introduced herself and offered to buy the school a new computer lab. At first, I was sure I misheard her. A computer for the lab had to have been what she'd meant. But no, she, in fact, did mean an entirely new computer lab. Well, as a principal you get excited whenever someone offers something that generous, but you often wonder if reality will get in the way of that happening. Regardless of some bumps in the road, Ms. Arnold made good with her offer. And that was the first of many donations she's made to Meadow Lake High over the years."

Devin couldn't stop from sneaking a glance at Kayla, whose cheeks were a beautiful shade of pink. He reached out and took her hand in his, setting it against the side of his leg as they listened.

"Ms. Arnold is a kind, generous alumni, who never sought the attention or recognition that we're bestowing on her today. Which is why myself and several other board members were so adamant that we wanted to do this for her. She represents the best of who our students are. Of what they can accomplish when given the support and encouragement of our teachers and school."

Kayla jerked, a small motion that Devin only felt because he was holding on to her. It took all of his efforts not to look at her, not to draw any attention. He'd never seen her this nervous and he could only imagine the pressure she was feeling. All he could do was give her hand another squeeze and hope for the best.

Oblivious to Kayla's reaction, Ms. Simon turned toward Kayla and smiled. "It's with great pleasure that I'm able to introduce Kayla Arnold to you all, and to welcome everyone to the new Arnold Library."

The gathered crowd broke out into applause, with the occasional whoop and cheers from the small contingency of students in the back. Kayla let go of his hand and made her way to the podium. He'd known she was going to give a speech, but he hadn't heard her practice at all.

"Thank you, Ms. Simon." Kayla's voice was clear, confident and filled the foyer as she spoke. "It's been many years since I was a student at Meadow Lake, but the same spirit fills these hallways. The same energy and hope. My life has changed dramatically since the days when I used the school lunch program and did my best to find time on the old clunky 486 computers in the back to get my assignments done. I'm thrilled to have been in a position to be able to give back. Thank you for this honor, and I wish all the students of Meadow Lake High, the best and brightest of futures."

She stepped away, and her entire body relaxed.

Everyone then moved into position for the ribbon-cutting ceremony. Devin pulled out his camera and made sure to take some pictures, each candid shot having Kayla front and center. There'd be more than enough official photos, but he knew from experience that it was the unexpected pictures that tended to have the most meaning long after the event was over.

At least, those were the ones of his dad that he treasured the most.

His dad would have loved seeing this, even if he hadn't known Kayla. He'd been an amazing teacher, a natural. It had driven Devin nuts as a student, being the son of a beloved educator. His teachers had crazy-high expectations of him and what he should be able to do in school, based on who his dad was. Even after his dad died, his legacy chased Devin through to graduation.

Every now and again, his mom would ask Devin if he'd reconsidered going into the education field. Hell, every time anyone mentioned that he'd be a great teacher, it ate at him. He might be good, but he'd never be as good as his dad. And fairly or not, he knew that he'd be compared to his dad by anyone who knew him. Given that his father had won numerous teaching awards and was well known throughout the entire Toronto school district, Devin wasn't about to play that game.

He'd figure out something to do with his life. There were so many professions out there, eventually he'd find his niche and succeed.

Eventually.

Kayla was maneuvered to stand in the middle of the group. Ms. Simon and one of the men he'd met at the dinner their first night, flanked her.

"Sorry, I'm late." The crowd parted as Christoph moved through the crowd. "We had a small water main break outside of city hall. I couldn't get my car out."

Christoph slid onto the end of the group, only to have the photographer hold up her hand. "Actually, Mayor Arnold, could you change spots with Ms. Simon? We should have you in the center of the picture."

Shit.

Of course, the mayor would show up for something like this. And watching the dread clearly on Kayla's face as Christoph moved beside her, it must have been something she'd been worried about as well.

It took all of his strength not to rush the group, pick Kayla up and carry her away to freedom. First, she wasn't exactly someone who required rescuing and wouldn't appreciate it. Second, he was scared that if he didn't keep his distance from Christoph, he would do something that would embarrass or upset Kayla. She had more than enough going on that she didn't need him making a spectacle of things.

And he'd absolutely make a spectacle.

Pictures were finished, and handshakes were happening, as Devin did his best to move closer to her. There was a line of well-wishers between him and her, preventing him from being able to do anything when Christoph turned to her and held out his hand. Being too far away to hear anything, he could only watch as she reluctantly shook it, and listened to whatever he was saying. The expression on her face was one that Devin had never seen before. He tried to pierce the crowd but stopped dead when Christoph leaned in and kissed her softly on the cheek. She gasped, her skin flushed red as she watched Christoph disappearing into the crowd.

And in a blink, Devin realized that Operation Seduce Kayla was over.

Because while she'd said she'd wanted nothing to do with her ex, the look of longing and sadness wasn't something he'd expect to see on someone who'd moved on. Devin didn't know the extent of her feelings toward her ex, if she'd been thrilled when her marriage had fallen apart, or if she'd welcome the opportunity to start fresh with Christoph.

Frankly, none of it was Devin's business. He was just the guy she'd met on a sugar daddy site, little more than a rent-a-date for the week. It had been Devin who'd made the mistake of developing feelings for Kayla. He'd been the one to let his imagination run wild with the possibilities of a relationship coming out of this. She'd owed him nothing except the ten thousand dollars she'd offered to pay him for his time. There'd been no misleading promises, only his desire to make the pretty lady in the picture smile.

How utterly arrogant he'd been.

His dad would have given him hell.

The crowd finally cleared enough that Devin was able to make his way unimpeded to her. "That was quite the morning." He did his best to smile and project his sunny nature as much as he could. Even if it was the last thing in the world he felt like doing.

If Kayla was feeling any inner turmoil, she didn't show it. "I hate giving speeches. I always think I'm going to bore everyone."

"You did great." He leaned in and placed a soft kiss on the cheek opposite the one Christoph had touched. "You've done a lot of good here. I know the school was grateful to have the chance to thank you properly."

She blinked up at him. "I know."

"I'm surprised your parents aren't here. I would have thought this being their hometown and you being recognized like this, that they would have wanted to show their support."

Her gaze dropped to the floor. "I sent them on a cruise."

"You what?"

"I know it's probably selfish, but this was going to be hard enough for me to get through without them being here. They never liked the attention that came along when my company took off. So, I took a chance and sent them away for a month. They'll have more fun, and I'll let them know when they get back."

There was something in the way she spoke that didn't quite sit right with him. Another reminder that he didn't know her as well as he'd assumed he had. His mom would have kicked his ass if he'd cut her out of an opportunity to celebrate his accomplishments. Hell, she'd already demanded that he get extra tickets for his PhD graduation so she could hand them out to all her friends.

He looked around, smiling at a few passing people. "Well, only the dance to get through tomorrow night and the week is over. You'll be able to get back to your normal life of being a super-busy CEO of a successful company."

"Are you okay?" She took his hand in hers, lacing their fingers. "You seem off."

"I think I'm tired." Not even a lie. Exhaustion had hit him hard in the past few minutes. "Maybe I'll take a nap when I get back to the lodge."

"You don't want to celebrate?" She nodded toward the door. "I was going to see if Mark would want some company for the wine tour. We could get a few bottles for the road."

It would be for the best if he stuck to his guns and went back to the room. A bit of space between them would be good. But despite everything, Devin couldn't say no to this woman. "If you don't think he'll mind? It would be cool to get out and get some fresh air."

Her grin did crazy things to his insides. "He won't mind. In fact, he's been bugging me to go with him. It will be fun."

"How can I say no to fun?" They had only two more days together before going home. Even if nothing would come of their relationship, Devin knew there was no way he could stay away from her. "Let's go get some wine."

In the end, the chips would fall where they wanted to. Worst case, Devin's life would be the same as it was when Kayla had first messaged him on that stupid app. After all, this was only meant as a bit of good fun. Even he could protect his heart for a few days.

Chapter 16

"We don't normally bring people out to see the actual grapes. But for you, we'll happily make the exception."

Kayla trailed along behind Carlo with Devin and Mark a few steps behind her. Carlo was the owner of Lake's Edge Winery and had come out from the office to give her a personal tour when he'd heard she was on site. "Thank you for doing this. I know how busy you must be."

Carlo waved her away. "My son lives in that school library that you helped pay for. It's the least I can do to show my appreciation."

"I'm glad that so many kids have enjoyed it."

That was more than a little understatement. She'd been more than a little overwhelmed by the volume of people who'd come up to her at the dedication to offer their thanks. She'd had no idea that the money she'd sent had meant that much to so many people in the town. One student had broken down crying when she'd told Kayla about how she was one of the scholarship recipients and that she was excited to be attending school in the fall. The whole day had been a little bit much for Kayla to handle.

And then, there'd been Christoph.

Things had ended so badly between them, she'd been caught completely off guard when he'd spoken to her at the library.

"Kayla, it's been good to see you." Gone was the smugness that usually oozed off him, to be replaced by something that looked more than a little like pride. "I didn't know how much you've done for this place until recently. I'm happy you're getting recognized."

All she could do was take a breath and smile. "Thank you."

He touched the side of her arm for a moment, before letting his hand fall away. "I've always regretted how I acted toward you. I didn't see it

*then, but I do now." He then leaned in and kissed her cheek. "I have to
go. See you tomorrow at the dance?"*

She couldn't speak but managed a nod.

"Good." And without another word, he was gone.

Carlo had launched into an explanation about the types of grapes they
used, the growing process and how the Canadian weather impacted the
wines. "We're obviously farther north than the wineries in Niagara region,
which accounts for the different flavors we're able to produce."

Mark chuckled. "I've appreciated more than a few glasses of your
differences since we've come here. It's amazing."

Devin hadn't said much of anything since they'd left the school. All she
could assume was that he'd seen Christoph and her talking, seen the kiss.
Was he upset? She could ask him, but she doubted Devin would admit to
it even if she did.

The more important question was why was he upset in the first place?
Despite the sex and the connection that they seemed to share, she couldn't
imagine that he had any *feelings* for her. Well, nothing beyond sexual
attraction. They'd been having a good time; eating fast-food burgers and
dancing on the sidewalk last night more than proved that. And sure, the
sex was great, but that was just sex.

Right?

The way they'd met didn't exactly lend to the most solid of relationship
foundations. Even if she couldn't get him out of her head. Or hated that
he'd said so little since leaving the school that she was starting to miss
the sound of his voice.

In fact...

She stopped walking until Devin naturally fell into step with her, and
then linked her arm around his. He raised an eyebrow.

"What?" She smiled and tugged him closer. "He's leading us to the
tasting area. I have a feeling I might need help walking after I get done.
It's been a hell of a day."

Carlo laughed. "And my wife tells me that there's still the dance
tomorrow. Not that she'll go."

Devin pulled Kayla a bit closer. "She's not into going down memory
lane?"

"I'm not from here, so I don't know the whole story, but she wasn't a
big fan of high school or some of the people who attended. But that's not
my story to tell, so I'll leave it at that." Carlo waved them along. "The
good stuff is this way."

They were brought to a small dining room off the side of the main building. The décor was simple—white linen and brushed nickel on tables, flowers and vines placed throughout the room—but added to the sense of elegance of the place. "This is amazing."

Several ideas for a photo shoot popped to mind, her mind's eye placing elegantly dressed women throughout the room in long flowing dresses. God, she'd kill for her sketchbook right now.

Devin leaned in. "I don't know what's going on in your brain right now, but the look on your face is amazing."

When she turned her head to look at him, their mouths were so close she nearly kissed him. Pulling back a bit, she couldn't stop from smiling. "I got inspired by the room. I'd love nothing more than to make some designs that capture the feel of this place."

"I haven't seen this side of you." Devin's gaze flicked from her face toward where Carlo was leading Mark to the tasting bar. "It's easy to forget that you're a designer first, and a rich and powerful CEO second."

Kayla had to admit that was something that she tended sometimes to forget herself. "I have been working on some designs for a new signature line. Usually, I have a team that helps, but this time I wanted to try to do it on my own. Like old times."

"You should. It's important to always stay in touch with your roots, even if you don't always like where they started from." Devin nodded in the direction of the bar. "We should probably join them before Mark drinks all the samples."

"We'll have to get an Uber if he has too much." She smiled, and they headed over, all the while her brain turned over what he'd said.

The next hour went quickly and dissolved into fits of laughter and stories about the town and how it had changed over the years. It was easy for Kayla to forget that Meadow Lake was a living, breathing entity with people coming and going, changed as time and experiences occurred.

Maybe that's why Christoph had been acting kinder toward her. Was it possible that moving back here, taking on the role of mayor had changed him, softened his edges and his cravings for money and prestige? Her heart wanted to believe that was the case, but there was something in her gut that told her not to trust him. Not to trust the man who'd cheated on her without a second thought.

The emotional upheaval of the day and the copious glasses of wine she'd had were finally getting to her. Kayla couldn't hold back a yawn any longer, though she did her best to try to mask it.

Mark sighed and stood up. "Why didn't you say you were getting tired?"

"I'm not." No, she was bordering on exhausted.

Devin shook his head and stood as well. "You're a terrible liar."

The second yawn came hard and fast. "I'm sorry. I'd been stressed about today, and I think I'm crashing."

Mark already had his keys out. "I'll pull the car around to the front."

Carlo nodded toward the array of empty tasting glasses around Mark. "Are you good to drive? I can always get someone to take you guys back to where you're staying."

"I can take us." Devin held his hands out for the keys. "I've only been taking small sips."

Of course, Devin would come to everyone's rescue. Kayla leaned her elbows on the bar and smiled at him. "Do you even know how to drive a limo? You realize you do need a special license."

"I'm just getting us to the B&B, so that should be fine, right? And Mark can sit in the front with me and make sure I don't do anything wrong." The look of glee on Devin's face was enough for Kayla to know that there was no way she'd be able to talk him out of this now.

"Well, if you get pulled over and get a ticket, don't expect me to pay for it."

Devin clapped his hands together. "I'm going to drive a limo."

Kayla rolled her eyes. "Carlo, I'd love to order a few cases of wine to be shipped to my home in Toronto."

Carlo straightened. "Of course. Which wines did you like? I'll make sure we get them to you ASAP."

One of the advantages of being filthy rich was not having to decide between different things that you liked. "Send me three cases of all of them. No rush." She tossed her platinum card down and shooed Mark and Devin away as Carlo rang up her order. "Go get my ride, boys."

"Come on, son. I'll give you the rundown on what you'll need to know. Though the road's pretty straight between here and there, so it won't be a problem."

She watched as they left, chatting excitedly as they went. She couldn't remember Christoph ever talking to Mark unless it was to criticize him for a bumpy ride, or having taken a route that took too long. She loved her driver, and it was wonderful to see someone else appreciate him the way she did.

"Everything went through just fine." Carlo returned her credit card. "Thank you so much for your order. It will be an amazing boost for us."

"I have lots of friends who are big wine drinkers. I'd love nothing more than to be able to share some home-grown products with them."

Carlo looked at where the guys had just disappeared. "Your boyfriend seems like a good sort. Carmine, my wife, she's not a big fan of your ex. They dated in high school for a bit, and he didn't exactly treat her right. She was happy to hear that you were okay after things ended. Though when he came back here and ran for mayor, she was pissed. I told her she needs to run against him next time."

Kayla laced her hands together on the bar and took a steadying breath. "I take it Christoph hasn't changed then?"

Carlo shrugged. "As I said, I'm not from around here, so I don't know what he was like before. He's an okay mayor, I guess. A few spending decisions that I don't exactly agree with but can understand where he's coming from. I don't know."

"Thanks." She was no closer to knowing if Christoph had changed or not. "I better go see if they've crashed the car yet."

"Safe drive back to Toronto."

By the time she worked her way through the building, Devin and Mark had pulled the limo in front of the main winery entrance. Devin rolled the window down and stuck his head out. "Wanna ride, pretty lady?"

"'Cause that's not creepy at all." She bent down and looked inside the cab. "Where's Mark?"

"In the back. I'm not going to have any problems getting us back, and I thought he might enjoy seeing how the other half drives." He picked Mark's hat up from the seat and put it on. "You can join him in the back if you'd like, or you can come sit up here with me. Could be fun."

His teasing tone was enough to pull a grin from her. "Don't kill us."

"Wouldn't dream of it." He reached across the car and opened the passenger door. "She's riding shotgun, Mark."

The privacy divider was down, so she was able to look back and see Mark sitting in the middle of the backseat looking uncomfortable. "If you do anything to hurt my car—"

"I've never been in an accident in my life. I've never even got a speeding ticket." Devin waited until she'd clicked her seatbelt into place, before putting the car into drive. "Here we go."

The ride was utterly uneventful, if not amusing. Devin continued to tease Mark the entire short drive back to the B&B, but his eyes never once wavered from the road. It had taken Kayla several minutes to get comfortable sitting in the front of a vehicle; something she hadn't done since she was in her early twenties. Either she had Mark drive her where she needed to go, or she'd take the occasional Uber.

Glancing over at the console, she narrowed her gaze at the lights and indicators. "I should get my license someday."

"Waaaa?" Devin put the blinker on before turning into the parking lot of the lodge. "How can you be in your thirties and not have a license?"

"I didn't have the money for driving lessons when I was a teen, and then I got rich. I haven't needed to know." But his surprise served to reinforce that this was a life skill that she should probably work on. "Maybe when I have some free time I'll go for my beginner's permit."

In truth, she'd thought about doing this once before. Christoph had discouraged her, going on about *how would it look for a millionaire CEO to be driving herself all around—horrible!* She'd backed down and hadn't given it much thought until now.

Devin put the limo into park and turned the engine off. "Not a scratch."

"Thank God." She heard Mark sigh from the back. "You know, you did pretty well. You could always go for your limo license and start driving. Good money in it."

Devin's smile faltered. "I'll take that under advisement." He slipped the hat from his head and looked down at it. "Maybe I'll be your driving instructor instead."

"I'd like that." She put her hand on his thigh, enjoying the warmth of his body. "Though I can't claim that I'd be a very good student, I do not doubt that you'd be an excellent teacher."

"Why do you say that?" There was no anger or snark in his tone, only genuine curiosity. "So many people have told me that they think I'd been good teaching others. But no one has seen me in the classroom. Even as a teaching assistant at the university, the most I did with the few students who'd show up was some one-on-one stuff. That's not the same as working with kids day in and day out. In knowing how to explain algebra or quadratic equations to high school students. So, what is it that people see that I don't?"

Kayla hadn't been expecting the depth of the question, but it was clear to see how important this was to him. "Can I ask you something?"

"Sure."

"Do you *want* to be a teacher? Not do you think you'll be good at it, or should do it, but do you *want* to? Because it seems like you do. It seems like this is a thing that you're fighting against for some reason, that it's your secret desire, but you're not able to reach for it. And I know we haven't known each other very long, but clearly this is important to you. Depending on if you're honest with yourself, then you'll have the answer."

She then leaned in and kissed his cheek before getting out of the limo. She'd been in a situation like that before and knew the best thing was to be given time.

Mark was standing outside the car and frowned at her when Devin didn't get out immediately. "He okay?"

She nodded. "Nothing some thinking and a few games of crib can't fix." Her earlier exhaustion came roaring back. "I'm going to nap. I'll see you later."

Some time alone for herself might be a good thing too. Because right now, her heart didn't know which direction to go in either.

Christoph—a past mistake that might have self-corrected, or Devin—an unexpected and uncertain future. There was always the third option, the one that had served her well in the years since her divorce.

Being alone.

That was safe, easy to manage and familiar. One more day to get through and then things could get back to normal.

Normal and alone.

Chapter 17

Devin balanced the tray of food carefully as he slid the key into the room lock. Kayla had disappeared hours earlier, and he didn't want to risk waking her. But when Mrs. Babineau brought him a large meat and cheese board to nibble on, he knew it was probably time for him to check on her.

Especially since she'd done her best to try to help him.

The room was dim, so it took his eyes a moment to adjust to the low light coming from the side lamp. Kayla was curled up on her side, the blanket from the bottom of the bed pulled over her body. She looked so helpless there, so small, yet peaceful as she slept. He hated to wake her but knew she might like to have some food too.

After setting the tray on the small table in the room, he dropped to his knees beside the bed. The position put his face close to hers, and he took a moment to memorize as much of her sleeping expressions as he could. Reaching out, he tucked a strand of her black hair that was stuck across her cheek, behind her ear.

The contact was all it took to stir her, and with a sleepy blink, she opened her eyes. "Hey."

"I'm sorry. Mrs. Babineau sent me with some food. Want me to let you go back to sleep?"

"No, I'm good." She pushed herself up and stretched. Her shirt tugged tightly across her breasts, and Devin had to force himself to look away. Because as much as he wanted to see Kayla completely naked, he knew this wasn't exactly the right time.

He retrieved the meat and cheese board from the table, and set it up on the bed, taking a seat opposite her. "Okay, so Mrs. Babineau was very excited about this assortment of cheese. I'm more of a cheddar and Ritz cracker kind of guy, but she assured me that this was a far better quality than anything I've probably tried. I think she's convinced I live off of Kraft Dinner and canned beans."

Kayla cocked an eyebrow. "Do you?"

"Only sometimes. I do alright considering. My mom makes sure that I'm invited home for supper at least three times a month. She'd like me to come more, but I'm a bit old to be eating her out of house and home." His mom would probably kill him if she had even an inkling that he was struggling financially and hadn't told her. "If things ever got too bad, I'd grab some food at the soup kitchen where I volunteer."

Kayla had popped a piece of cheese into her mouth and spoke around it. "You volunteer at a soup kitchen?"

"Yeah, why not? I try to help out when I can. Which isn't as often as I'd like."

Kayla stared at him, shaking her head after several long moments. "Has anyone told you that you're a bit too good for this world?"

"What's that supposed to mean? I'm not doing anything that hundreds of others do on a regular basis."

Kayla cut off some cheese and put it on a thin cracker that looked as though it would crumble under the slightest of touches. Then, she reached out and offered it to him. "Most people I know don't volunteer. Not even a bit."

"I'm sure they do other things. Like, don't rich people host fundraising auctions? Big parties where you schmooze them and then some person will throw out a twenty thousand dollar bid on a hand-drawn picture from a poor child?"

"That hasn't exactly been my experience. Though I've made more than a few donations to good causes over the years." Her face grew pink, and he could only assume she was thinking about the dedication ceremony today.

"Well, there you go. We both like to help out. We just do it in different ways. The only ones that are available to us." He then picked up a slice of meat, rolled it up and held it out for her to eat. "It's hard to believe the dance is tomorrow. Our little fairytale adventure is coming to an end."

"I know." She reached up and touched the side of her neck. "I thought this week was going to be horrible, but it's turned out to be good. Things have changed here. I guess, I've also changed, which has let me see Meadow Lake with different eyes."

"And that's a good thing?"

"It is." She looked at him, and there was a sparkle in her eyes. "Thank you."

"For what?"

"I wouldn't have come here on my own. Thank you for agreeing to come and be my pretend boyfriend for the week."

God, how he would love if he could become her real boyfriend. To be able to wake up to her face day after day. To hold her when her world got to be too much for her. "I'm happy to have obliged."

He didn't know when it happened, but suddenly something in the air changed between them. He became painfully aware of every inch of her body, her scent, the deepening flush on her skin. It had been too long to blame this on the effects of the wine, or the emotions of the ceremony that morning. No, this was something primal, an attraction that he'd been fighting—poorly—since they'd first climbed into the limo.

Reaching out, he cupped her cheek, enjoying the feel of her soft skin against his calluses. "I'm going to miss this. Being with you."

"I…" But her words died.

Fine, she wasn't obligated to say anything. It was probably better for them both if she didn't. It would make things easier when they parted ways. Still…

He moved the meat tray to the floor, shifting closer to her now. "I promised you I wouldn't break your rules. But I'm finding it hard not to kiss you right now."

Her breath caught, and for a moment, he hopefully thought she might relent. "I'm sure you'll survive."

"Yeah. I will." He slid his hand down the side of her neck to her shoulder. The skin there was just as soft as her face. "Is it still okay if I kiss you other places?" He kept his voice low, loving how she shivered as he spoke.

Kayla swallowed, nodding once quickly. "Yes."

Knowing that they only had tomorrow, and then the fantasy would be over, Devin wanted to be sure to take his time. To draw this out, to enjoy every second of being with her until their time was up.

"The last two times I didn't get the chance to see you completely naked. Can I do that now? Can I strip you slowly and kiss every single inch of skin I see?"

"Not my lips."

"Never your lips." Kissing her mouth would be a fantasy that would haunt his nights for years to come. "I promise."

Using both his hands, he carefully undid each button of her shirt, slowly exposing her pale skin beneath. The fabric was delicate, and he felt little more than a clumsy oaf as he worked carefully, pushing the buttons free. He made sure not to touch her skin, wanting to draw the tease out as long as he could—for both their sakes. Only once the tails of her shirt opened wide did he lean forward and push the airy fabric down her arms, exposing her lace-clad breasts to his eyes.

"You're perfect." God, he wanted to cup and squeeze her, to pinch her nipples until he heard her gasp of pleasure.

Not yet.

Slowly. Purposely. That's how he wanted to do this. If it took him all night to seduce her, then that's what he'd do.

After dropping her shirt to the floor, he paused long enough to pull his own off. There was no sense in her being naked if he wasn't as well. Kayla's gaze shifted to his chest, and he took a moment to flex his muscles. She giggled as she reached out and threaded her fingers through his chest hair.

"Not everyone likes the body hair thing. But that's who I am."

"I don't mind it." She gave a gentle tug, before resuming her caress. "It's soft, and I like that."

Shit, he was going to come in his pants, and she hadn't even touched his cock yet. "Pants. I need to take your pants off."

He stood too quickly, and nearly put his foot in the middle of the meat tray on the floor. Kayla laughed, as she stretched out on the bed. "Here. I'll help." She lifted her hips and gave him a wink.

"Thank you." It was far easier freeing her of her pants, and he even paused long enough to trail kisses across her belly.

Kayla moaned as she squirmed beneath his touch. God, he loved how sensual she was. How she responded to him was so unlike any other woman, Devin didn't know how he was going to ever move beyond her.

Enough of that.

She reached down to pull at the front of his pants. "Take these off. And get a condom."

"Yeah. Right, I need a condom." Shit, he hadn't brought that many, and he was trying to remember how many he'd had with him. "One minute. Don't move."

Once again, he found himself scrounging around his shaving kit in search of the one thing he needed to ensure they were both going to have a good time. His heart danced with joy when he found one single condom left in the bottom of the bag.

Kayla hadn't moved an inch from when he'd left her, which was perfect. Taking a moment to relocate the now abused meat and cheese tray from the floor to the table, Devin took his pants off and held up the condom for her to see.

"This is all we have to work with." He grinned and held it out for her to take. "We'll have to make this count. Unless you want me to leave and ask Mark to take me to the pharmacy?"

"Get over here."

He stopped himself from climbing on top of her immediately, not wanting to rush things. Instead, he crawled beside her and shifted so he could help her sit up. "Let's get that bra off first."

"Demands, demands." But she reached behind her back and quickly dealt with the clasp. When the straps loosened, she reached around and held the cups in place, continuing to deny him of the sight he so wanted to see. "But it will cost you."

"You're such a wonderful tease." He sighed, reached out and ran a finger down her cleavage, teasing the skin with his fingernail. "I love that."

Her expression changed, softened as she leaned closer to him. "You love that I'm a bit of a tease?"

"I love that you're playful." He moved his hand to the side of her head and carded his fingers through her long hair. "I love that you're all serious toward others, but when it's just you and me you relax. It's like I see a part of you that you normally hide away from the rest of the world. It makes me feel special."

Devin opened his legs and shifted, so she was now bracketed between them. He leaned in and kissed her bare shoulder. He rained kisses across her skin until he hit the edge of her bra strap, then he kissed down alongside it. He let his fingers brush back and forth across the top of her thigh, simply touching, caressing.

Kayla sighed and let her hands fall away. The weight of the cups had her bra slip down her arms, finally exposing her breasts to him. They seemed to turn toward one another at the same time, as Devin pulled the bra free and tossed it to join the rest of their clothing on the floor.

It took everything in him not to immediately suckle her. But he managed to show some restraint, and instead caressed the side of her breast with the back of his hand. Her nipple tightened as her skin flushed as she shuddered.

"You're going to kill me with all of these light touches." Her chuckle was throaty and went straight to his cock. "I've never been with a man who likes to take his time the way you do."

"I can't speak for them, but I want to be sure that I remember every single moment, every single thing about you." *Because I don't think I'll ever see you again.*

Kayla's gaze snapped to his, and he couldn't look away from her. *I should be kissing her. I should be showing her how good we can be.* But he didn't. Instead, he leaned back on the mattress and stretched out. "Want to do a little exploring of your own?"

There was her smile! "That sounds like a good idea."

He loved being at her mercy, but it was harder than he'd anticipated to hold himself back from doing what he wanted. Thankfully, Kayla was as good at teasing him as she was at just about everything else in her life.

She ran her hands over his chest and down to his stomach. He tried not to squirm when she leaned down and kissed his bellybutton, her fingers shifting to his sides where he was more than a little ticklish. She didn't stay there long, moving her attention to his briefs and his hard cock that pressed obviously against it.

"You're making the fabric damp." She pressed her thumb to the spot, before sliding it down his shaft. "We should get these off you."

"Fuck. Yes, please."

He laughed when she sent his briefs flying across the room. "Don't need those." She then straddled his thighs, placed her hands on either side of his hips and leaned down to lick his cockhead.

He had to grab hold of the duvet and close his eyes to try and hold himself back. Thankfully, Kayla continued licking his shaft; up and down, she teased him with her tongue, until his whole body was a shaking mess. "Too good at that."

"Ummm." She then sucked one of his balls into her mouth.

It took effort not to come there and then. He had to think of every horrible thing he could to try to hold back. Then he moved over to multiplication tables. When he couldn't remember what five times five was, he pulled at her to come up. "Stop. God, please stop."

The smug look on her face was more than a little unnerving. "Too much for you?"

"You still have panties on. I was hoping we'd both get naked."

"How about I put the condom on you first, then I'll take these off?"

"Yes. That's a thing you need to do now. Please now."

The condom wrapper was torn, and the condom slid into place by the count of five. Kayla then stood up and slid her panties down her legs, all the while maintaining eye contact with him. His cock pulsed at the sight of her finally naked body, standing before him in all her glory.

All for him.

Just for tonight.

"So?" She cocked her eyebrow and put her hands on her hips. "Now what are we going to do?"

A flurry of thoughts and positions flew through his mind, but there was only one that he wanted to experience. One that he knew he'd never forget. "Ride me?"

"Oh, I like that." She climbed back on the bed and straddled him with ease.

But she didn't put him inside her. Instead, she rubbed her pussy against his cock, siding his shaft against her clit. Her eyes fluttered shut as she repeated the motion. Her heat penetrated the condom, another tease of what was to come.

Finally, she lifted her hips up high enough to position him at her opening, and she slowly slid herself down his shaft until they were completely joined. Their eyes met, and neither of them moved for a moment. Devin's body was a live wire waiting to spark, and from the look on her face, he knew Kayla was nearly as far gone as he was.

Without lifting herself off him, Kayla swiveled her hips as she clenched her inner muscles around his cock. The dual action sucked the breath from him, and he wanted nothing more than to pound up into her.

Hold back. Calm. You can do it.

It didn't take long for Kayla to set a steady rhythm, riding his body purposefully. With effort, he forced his eyes to stay open, so he could watch her face, the sway of her breasts, the contraction of her stomach and thigh muscles as she moved. The look of ecstasy on her face and the sounds of pleasure coming from her imprinted on his heart and soul.

"Come closer," he managed to mutter. "Kayla, please."

She fell forward, her hands landing hard on the bed on either side of his head. There she was, so close, her mouth a temptation he needed to resist. He shifted his focus to her breasts, capturing one with his hand so he could lift it to his mouth. The moment he sucked her nipple, her pussy tightened around him. Yeah, there she was, close to orgasm, her body primed and ready to be pushed over the edge. With his free hand, he pushed against her clit, adding a bit of pressure for her to move against.

Kayla groaned and pressed the side of her face to him. "Yeah, yeah. Harder."

He felt her pussy clamp down on his cock before a cry of pleasure erupted from her. All semblance of restraint dissipated as she continued to come on him. He couldn't wait, couldn't hold back any longer. He picked her up and flipped her over, so he could pound into her hard and fast.

Logic, emotions, his fantasies and desires mixed as his pleasure rammed through his body. A cry so primal that he didn't recognize it as his voice ripped from him as his cock pulsed and twitched in her body, filling the condom. His body shaking long after the pleasure had passed, Devin knew he was about to pass out. He was able to pull out and slide to the mattress beside her before blissful sleep washed over him.

His last thought before darkness claimed him was that he wished he had another condom.

Chapter 18

The feeling of Devin snoring against her lulled Kayla into a light sleep as well. She didn't know how long they'd lain that way, but she woke to the feeling of wetness against her leg. She looked down to see the condom they'd forgotten to dispose of stuck to the side of her thigh.

Her first thought—*disgusting.*

Her second thought—*holy shit I passed out.*

Her final thought—*I need to get cleaned up.*

Devin was still snoring, and apparently a deep sleeper because she was able to slip out from under his arm and go to the bathroom without him moving an inch. She turned the bedside lamp off, letting the soft gray light from behind the curtains bleed into the room. It gave the place a serene look, as a strip of brightness splashed across the carnations on the table, highlighting their color as she passed them.

After a quick pee and heating up a facecloth, Kayla cleaned herself up. Her neck sported the faint brush of razor burn from Devin's stubble. She touched it, but there was no discomfort, which meant the marks would be gone before anyone noticed.

A quick glance at the clock told her that it was at least an hour before anyone else would be awake. But soon, the Babineaus would be up and make breakfast for them and their other guests. Then Kayla would have to find something to do until it was time for them to get ready for the dance tonight.

And tomorrow morning, they'd head back to Toronto, and this fantasy would officially be over.

The sudden wave of depression hit her hard, even as she reheated the facecloth. Devin would also be a mess, and it was only fair to help clean him up. Even if all she wanted to do was to stay in bed with him all day, make love and drink wine. Which they couldn't do.

She stopped to stare at him when she came back into the main room. He'd rolled onto his side, his arm thrown across the spot where she'd been sleeping moments earlier. The air in the room had cooled, and she had no doubt that he was chilled as much as she was. So, she leaned down and pressed a kiss to his bare shoulder, to check.

That was the only reason she kissed him. Honest.

When he didn't stir, she gave him a soft shake, until he rolled onto his back and blinked sleepily up at her. "Hey."

"Hey. We fell asleep." Holding out the facecloth for him, she nodded toward his groin. "You'll want to clean up."

"Oh shit." Devin sat bolt up, taking the cloth from her. "Wait, where's the—"

"I got rid of it." She wasn't about to tell him where she'd found it. Knowing him, he'd be embarrassed that he hadn't disposed of it before passing out. "It's nearly time to get up."

"Wow, really?" He got up and dropped the facecloth in the laundry bin. "I don't normally fall asleep like that after sex."

"Neither do I." Normally after sex with Christoph, he'd get out of bed to go on his computer or turn over to sleep. Kayla would often lie there alone, thinking about how things had gone wrong between them. Or work.

Both were depressing topics after sex.

Another thing to chalk up as being wonderfully different with Devin— she held on to her afterglow far longer.

They moved around one another, smiling and sneaking glances as Kayla pulled back the blankets of her bed. Climbing in, she tugged down the duvet on the opposite side and patted the mattress. "If you want to get warm, it would be faster if we're in the same bed."

He started to climb in but stopped. "Are you sure?"

"Stop being noble and get in the damn bed." Once they were both snuggled in, she rolled on her side and slid her hand under her cheek to help better look at him. His brown eyes were more than a little sleepy, making him look far cuter than she'd ever seen before. "What do you want to do today?"

"After I have another nap?" She nodded. "Honestly, I'd love to stay in bed all day."

Mentally, she started as she heard him vocalize her earlier thoughts. "That would be lovely."

Too bad they didn't have any more condoms.

Devin looked at the wall, over the covers. "The television works, and I have my tablet with me. If you want, I can cast some movies, and we can just stay here. I'm sure if we asked, Mrs. Babineau would bring our breakfast up for us."

"I know she would. They tend to treat their guests as extended family members."

"God, it's going to suck going home. There's no way in hell I'd be able to convince Ray to bring me a coffee, let alone breakfast in bed."

"Ray's your roommate, right?"

"The one and only. You're lucky you didn't pick his profile when you were on the site looking. He's not half as fun as I am. He doesn't even know how to drive a limo." He winked at her.

"Poor maligned Ray."

"Well, poor Ray. But that has more to do with his mom developing breast cancer again." Devin rolled onto his back and looked at the ceiling. "I promised to help him and his dad when I got back. If it's anything like last time, the treatments take a toll on the whole family."

"You do that a lot."

"What?"

"Help others."

His head rolled to look at her. "Of course. If there's something I can do to assist others, why wouldn't I?"

"Hey, it wasn't a complaint. But you seem to spend all this time putting others before yourself, don't you ever feel like you're getting left behind?"

Devin's brow furrowed, and he looked back up. "I don't think so. Maybe it's a selfish part of me, but I do get something out of helping others. It's a bit of a rush, I guess. I feel good, so do they. It works out in the end."

Kayla often wondered what others got out of their philanthropic works. Hearing Devin's obvious pleasure in his actions was beautiful. "I like knowing that the kids I'm helping are being put on even playing field with the other more financially secure kids. I hated feeling jealous of what the other kids had in school. The family vacations and designer clothing. That was one of the reasons I started making my dresses. I wanted something unique but couldn't afford to pay for the brands I liked."

"Did you make your own knock-offs?" When she grinned, he chuckled. "That's awesome."

"Well, now that I'm the designer whose designs are the ones getting knocked-off, I have a slightly different perspective on things."

"You can't tell me that if one of your big wig executive dudes came to you and said that they learned of a teen who was making your clothing and selling it to his or her friends, that there wouldn't be a part of you happy about that?"

"I'd probably offer them a job."

"There you go. See, we're not that different, you and I." Devin's stomach let out a horrendously loud grumble. "I wonder when I can beg Mrs. Babineau to come up with some food."

"Let me check."

With a single call, Mrs. Babineau, who'd been up for an hour already, promised them a full breakfast and coffee as quickly as she could manage. Far faster than Kayla would have managed at home, their room was filled with the scent of fresh baked goods, fruit, bacon and coffee.

As Kayla walked Mrs. Babineau to the door, the older woman gave her a sideways glance. "Is there anything else you two need?"

"I think we're okay."

"Well, if you need anything. Or need me to get any supplies for you, just call. I can always run out to the store, if you know what I mean." There was no mistaking her intent, especially followed by the not-so-subtle look back at Devin. "It's been many years since I've seen a man that fit."

Oh dear God, Kayla was going to die. "Umm, thanks. I think we're planning on staying in today and watching television."

"Right. My granddaughter calls that Netflix and chill."

Kill me. Kill me right now okay thanks. "You have Netflix?"

Mrs. Babineau grinned. "I'm old, not dead. Have a great day. Call down when you're ready for your lunch."

Kayla had never been so happy to shut a door in her life. Devin was scrolling through something on his tablet, stretched out on the bed, but had slipped on a pair of sleep pants. She'd hadn't seen him in those, though she wasn't surprised that he had something. Running her hands through her hair, she tightened her bathrobe before joining Devin. "I'm never going to be able to look at the Babineaus the same again."

"I heard. Netflix and chill. Good for them." He grabbed a mug and filled it with coffee from the pot. "Series or movie."

It was wonderfully normal, sitting in bed with a handsome man, enjoying breakfast after a night of great sex. It was also something that Kayla hadn't engaged in for many years. There might have been once or twice over the course of her marriage, and those times had been when both she and Christoph had gotten sick.

Devin looked up at her when she hadn't answered immediately. She gave her head a shake. "Sorry. Ah, movie. Unless there's a series with a short season that we can get through."

"Lots of British shows that are only a few episodes. Oh, we could do *Black Mirror*. Twisted technology and crazy people. It's an anthology show, so we can stop whenever we want."

She hardly ever watched television. The time commitment to see a story all the way through to the end wasn't something she could typically afford. "Sure."

"We'll skip the first episode though." He scrolled through the list looking at the descriptions.

"Why?"

The normally easygoing Devin suddenly looked a bit nauseous. "It involves a pig and sex acts. I just…I can't watch that one again. Ever."

"Ah, okay. I'm really fine to skip that one."

"Oh, this one looks good."

Kayla managed to get through a few stories before they switched over to a standup comedian. It felt good to laugh, to hear Devin laugh as they cuddled on the bed, drinking coffee and eating fruit and pastries. They didn't bother to get dressed when it was time for lunch, though Kayla did throw on one of Devin's sweatshirts and hid in the bathroom when she realized it was Mr. Babineau there with his wife.

When she emerged after they'd gone, Devin stood at the new tray of food on the table. "Everything okay?"

He looked up, and for the first time since she'd met him, she was surprised to see him blushing. "Yup."

"What's going on?"

"Oh. I guess they wanted to make sure that we had everything we needed for our day in." He picked up a condom box tucked between the two plates of food. "They even got my preferred brand." He opened his mouth, closed it and frowned. "How did they know?"

"If I had to guess, I'd say they saw the wrapper in the garbage can when they emptied it." At least, she hoped the explanation was that simple. "That was nice of them. Right?"

If he was still embarrassed about the unexpected gift, then he didn't show it. Instead, Devin cracked open the box and pulled out a strip of condoms. "I'd hate for their investment to go to waste."

A shiver of anticipation raced through her. Kayla took a step closer, ignoring the television laughter from the crowd. "It would be a shame. I did tell Mrs. Babineau that we are watching Netflix *and* chilling. I wouldn't want to be accused of being a liar."

Devin picked up the television remote and pressed mute, cutting the comedian off mid-joke. "Never a liar. You might hide the truth, but that's because you never seem to want to take credit for your accomplishments."

Kayla pulled the sweatshirt off, dropping it at her feet. "I'm here this weekend. Letting everyone know how awesome I am."

He snorted. "Please. You're still hiding from everyone." He came closer, his erection visible through his pajama pants. "But I'm getting closer to seeing the real you."

Close enough to touch her, he ran the back of his hand gently across her cheek, down her throat to the top of her breasts. God, she couldn't believe how quickly he could make her come undone. How within a matter of a heartbeat she went from laughing and having fun, to her pussy throbbing and wanting to feel him inside her. She'd never been with a man who could do this to her. Not with this sudden intensity, this primal need to press against him and feel every inch of his body on hers.

She didn't want to let this go but knew she had no choice. Reaching out, she put her hands on his hips just above his waistband. "You better get one of those condoms ready."

"Yes."

"I want to suck you first." She dropped to her knees, taking his pants with her.

"Kayla." His hands went to her head, his fingers into her hair. He seemed to love playing with her hair when they had sex.

"Bunch up my hair. Hold it out of my face for me."

He did as she asked, making her feel more exposed than she had with her legs spread wide before him. She looked up at him as she ran her tongue up the length of his cock. His eyes went wide, but he didn't look away as she continued. She had power and riches, but there was something incredible about being able to reduce a man to a quivering pile with her mouth.

Devin squeezed her hair in his hand, a gentle counter-tug as she sucked on his cock. Her body hummed, her legs spread wide for fear that she'd get too aroused and come without even touching herself. It wasn't long before he pulled away, sending her chasing after him, wanting more.

"I'm too close for that." She barely moved, and he was lifting her up on the bed. "Want to try something."

"Yes." Anything, she'd do anything with him.

"Get on your hands and knees."

She hadn't done doggy style in a long time. Getting into position, she was ready to feel his hands on her hips as he slid inside her. Instead, she was surprised when he got onto his back, his head now between her legs.

His hands found their way to her hips alright, but from an entirely different angle than she was expecting. It was easy for her to look down and see his face as he sucked on her clit.

The different position opened up her body, and she responded immediately. Her breasts hung heavy as sweat broke out across her skin. Devin moaned as he licked and sucked; he added a finger into her body, working her into a sexual frenzy that threatened to throw her completely. It was too much everything; pleasure, intimacy, desire, her wants and needs for more of this man.

Her body shook, and Devin must have sensed how close to her orgasm she was. Instantly, he increased the suction on her clit and added a second finger. Kayla sucked in a breath, tried to hold back the oncoming storm, but knew failure was at hand. She cried out, her body curling in on itself as her orgasm ripped her apart.

He finally slowed down and released her as his upper body fell back against the mattress. "Fuck."

A bubble of laughter popped from her. "Yeah. Fuck."

"I need to—"

He slid out from beneath her, grabbing the condom. She listened as he opened the condom and rolled it on. She didn't move, wanting to feel him pound into her body from behind. When she felt him hesitate, she opened her legs a bit wider and wiggled her ass. "I'm waiting."

"You're..." He did as she asked and pressed into her pussy with a single thrust.

They stayed that way for a moment, and Kayla was thankful. Her body still hummed from her orgasm, her pussy primed to come again, something that rarely happened. So when Devin set a slow, but steady pace, she reached between her legs and circled her clit with her fingers.

"Are you...are you playing with yourself?"

She closed her eyes. "Yeah."

"Think you can come again?"

"Not sure. Maybe."

Devin groaned. "I'll try to hold back. Let me know if you're close."

Her brain shouted at her that Christoph had never done something like that for her, would have waited for her to come, or tried to push her over that beautiful precipice more than once during sex. But when Devin increased the pressure of his thrusts, the remaining of her logical brain shut down. All she was aware of were his fingers squeezing into the flesh of her hips, the sweat of their bodies mingling wherever they touched, his gasps and moans as he made love to her.

The weight of her head grew to be too much, and she let it fall forward as she increased the pressure once again on her clit. She was so close to coming again, so closing to feeling that heaven she chased it with renewed purpose. Thankfully, Devin didn't change a single thing, making it easier.

"You're close. I can feel your pussy clamping down on my dick. That's it, pretty lady. Come on my cock. Come hard for me."

She gasped, her body shuddering at his words.

"You like me talking dirty." He picked up the pace. "I love your ass. Touching it." He dipped his finger into the top of her ass cheeks. "I could fuck you here if you wanted. I could make you feel so good, make you come. Or I could come on your breasts. Rub it across your skin as I pinched your nipples. You like that too."

Hearing the litany of filth coming from Devin—kind, generous, sweet Devin—did things to her brain that she didn't want to examine. On his next thrust, her world came apart a second time. She cried out, pressed hard on her clit as pleasure tore through her body.

Devin's thrust grew erratic, and he cried out as well. His fingers bit into her hips, no doubt leaving a mark in the wake. He unexpectedly leaned his body against her back, and they fell forward in a heap of arms, legs and sweat. His cock slipped from her as he rolled off her. "I'm sorry."

"It's okay." She laughed into the mattress. "God, you've got a dirty mouth."

"I have no idea where that came from." He threw his arm across his eyes. "Seriously, I never do that."

"I guess I bring your inner bad boy out."

"Apparently." He got up and went to the bathroom, coming back moments later with the condom gone and a warm face cloth in his hand. "Lay on your back. Let me clean you up."

That was the biggest turn on of them all. The way Devin wanted to make sure that everything was fine, that she was looked after and cared for. It made her feel unique in a way that she'd never felt before. There wasn't an award or illustrious recognition in the world that could compete with the feeling of Devin looking after her.

And it would all be over tomorrow.

They lay on the bed together, and Kayla couldn't help but lace her fingers with his, wanting to extend the intimacy as long as she could. They must have dozed off because she jumped at the sound of the room phone ringing. Devin got up and answered it. "Hello?"

His eyes widened, and he looked down at the clock. "Yeah, thank you. Can you tell Mark that we'll be down in a half hour?"

Shit, the alumni dance! "An hour. I need to shower and get dressed."

"Make that an hour. Thanks so much. Ah, yes. We did get your present. Yup. Yeah. Again, really appreciate that. Thanks." Devin hung up and looked frantically around. "I didn't realize the time."

Kayla had more than enough experience at getting ready quickly. "I'll shower first. Then I'll get dressed while you shower."

"I can skip it." He took a sniff of his armpit. "Or not. I'm quick though."

"Let's do this."

She'd have to worry about what would happen between them later. Right now, she had a dance to get ready for.

Chapter 19

The gym had been transformed from the impromptu breakfast hall, to look as though a glitter bomb had exploded across every surface. Devin had purposely avoided any and all of his school reunions, mostly because he'd still been in school and didn't see the point in celebrating something he was still actively engaged in.

Based on what he saw here, he would do his best to avoid all potential reunions going forward.

Kayla's hand was firmly in the crook of his arm, her fingers digging into the fabric of his dress coat, a reminder of why he was here at all. The registration line was moving nicely, as a group of women took names and smiling handed out name tags to the attendees.

"I thought you guys had a pretty small graduating class? Why the name tags?"

She let out a breath, but her gaze didn't move from the point she was staring at on the wall ahead of them. "It's not just one graduating class. It's easy to forget the names of the people who weren't in your grade."

"Right." Maybe he was more nervous about coming here tonight than he realized. "Do you know many people?"

"A few." She nodded at someone off to the side when they called out her name. "But they all know me."

He hadn't seen many issues with her and her former classmates up to this point, but then again, they hadn't been in many social situations that allowed for one-on-one conversations. When they made it to the table, Devin turned on the charm, hoping to deflect some of the attention from her.

"Well, hello there." He winked at the women behind the table. "I hope you two lovely ladies won't be stuck here all night. Bon Jovi won't dance to himself. Well, maybe he will." He shrugged and grinned. "Devin Ford and Kayla Arnold."

The blonde smiled at him, leaning forward just enough to give him a glimpse of her cleavage. "You're not from around here."

"Nope. City boy here. Though I'm going to have to convince Kayla to bring me back soon. It's been an awesome week."

Despite having said her name twice, neither woman acknowledged her standing there. *Nope, that's not going to happen.* He reached around Kayla's waist, pulled her in and kissed her cheek. "You like to dance to Bon Jovi, right?"

That got him the eye roll he'd been hoping for. "Whoa, whoa, living on a prayer." She said it so deadpan he couldn't help but laugh at her.

The blonde behind the table sat up straight and finally looked at Kayla. "It's wonderful to have you back. Here are your name tags and drink tickets. It's a cash bar, and the proceeds will go to help send the boys hockey team to camp this summer. I'm sure you can afford to buy a drink or two. Or ten."

Devin's mouth fell open. Dear God, didn't she do enough for these people? No wonder she didn't want people to know about her contributions.

Before he could say anything, Kayla tugged him away. "Thanks. I'll be sure to do that."

He looked over his shoulder at them even as Kayla pulled him farther away. "Did she say that? What the actual fuck is wrong with some people?"

"Not everyone likes it when a local girl makes good." She turned him around and pinned his name tag to his lapel. "And even if they do, only so far as for what that person can do for them. Not everyone is like you." She patted the name tag. "There you go."

"Do you want me to put yours on?"

She shook her head. "Everyone here knows me. I don't need to announce it."

A quick look around and he noticed that all of the women had pinned corsages along with their names. Kayla's didn't have one attached. An oversight—either intentional or not—that he needed to correct. "Don't move."

He had to wait for the couple currently being registered to move before he slid in front of the registration ladies. "Hello again."

"Hello, handsome." This time the brunette smiled at him. "What can I do to help?"

"Well, it seems Kayla's name tag is missing her corsage. I was hoping it had fallen off here so I could give it to her."

The blonde turned her attention to the next couple in line, which the brunette faced him. "That's too bad. We don't have any extras, so she'll have to go without." There was no sympathy in her voice.

Devin mentally reset himself to try again. "I'm sure there's someone who won't be showing up tonight. People always last-minute cancel their tickets for these things." He upside-down scanned the list in front of her until he saw a name he recognized. "There. Carlo and his wife I know aren't coming. I talked to him about it the other day. We can snag hers."

"I'm sorry, I can't do that."

"Can't or won't?"

The brunette's smile didn't waver. "I'm sure our millionaire can survive without a three-dollar flower. Now, if you'll excuse me."

She turned away from him, leaving Devin shocked.

How could anyone treat Kayla like that after everything she'd done for this town? He looked over to see her standing there watching him. She must have anticipated the outcome and gave him a sad smile.

No, there was no way he was going to let them do this to her. Fuck that.

He turned around and grabbed an elastic band that was sitting on the registration table, ignoring the brunette's protests as he walked away. There were some tables lining the edges of the gym where people could sit, relax and chat if they were so inclined. Most people were still arriving or were already at the bar or on the dance floor, which meant no one would notice him.

Walking past each one, he didn't stop until he saw the perfect flower. There! A pink carnation bud that was opening up. He pulled it from the flower vase and broke the bud off the stem. He marched back to Kayla, ignoring the strange looks people were giving him.

When he looked back at her, he saw that a man was engaging in conversation with her. Based on her body language, she didn't want to be talking to him. Shit, he was supposed to be acting as a buffer for her and here he was off on a foolish side quest.

Eye on the prize. Protect the princess.

He had to dodge some dancers as he crossed the floor and made it back to her side just in time to hear the end of what must have been a business pitch.

"...so then all the profits would come from outsourcing the labor to third world manufacturers. Right? That's the best way to do it these days."

"Hey, sorry about that." He stuck his hand out to the man. "Devin Ford, Kayla's boyfriend."

The man looked at his hand, then at Kayla before shaking it. "Tim."

"Sorry to interrupt, Tim. But they lost Kayla's corsage, and I was on a mission to fix that." He then turned, so his back was mostly to Tim and smiled at Kayla. "Could I have your name tag, pretty lady?"

"Everyone knows who she is." Tim then tapped his shoulder. "I haven't finished my pitch."

Devin wasn't known for his temper, but the people here tonight were undoubtedly putting that to the test. "What's your widget?"

"My what?"

"What are you selling? The actual item?"

"A new flashlight. One that would work on Mars." Tim grinned, his chest puffing up. "It will change the world."

"That's great. You know she sells ladies' clothing, right?"

"I'm looking for investors to get in on the ground floor." Tim then pushed Devin to the side. "You'll make your money back in six months. Eight tops. All I need is a million dollars to get the manufacturing—"

"Are you insane?" Everyone looked around at Devin, but he didn't care how loud he was. "She's here for a dance. She's not going to give you a million dollars."

"Devin, it's okay." Kayla grabbed his hand and tried to pull him away. "Tim, why don't you send my office a proposal and I'll look at it when I get back home."

"Yeah sure." Tim glared at Devin. "Don't let your asshole boyfriend ruin your chance to get rich." He turned and stomped away.

"She's already rich!"

"Devin, please. It's okay." She squeezed his hand, before turning him around. "I'm used to it."

How could anyone get used to always being the object of everyone's wants? "That's something that you shouldn't have to get used to."

She lifted his hand. "So that's my corsage?"

Right! "Let me see your name tag."

Without question, she pulled it out from the tiny purse she'd insisted on bringing. He took it and pulled the pin from the plastic. "After everything you've done for them, they couldn't even give you a three-dollar flower."

It took a bit of fumbling, but he attached the carnation to the pin using the elastic band. Holding it up to inspect his work, he was happy when she chuckled. "What? It's pretty good considering what I had to work with."

"It is." Her shoulders relaxed, and her expression softened. "Thank you."

Careful not to stick her with the pin, he pierced the fabric of her dress and fastened it in place. "There. Now, you're ready for your reunion."

She blinked rapidly, before looking away. "Thank you. I guess the next thing we need to do is get a few drinks."

There wasn't anyone waiting at the small bar set up in the back corner. "A beer would be a great idea." Thankfully, he had a few drink tickets because he had a feeling that more than one beverage might be required to get through tonight.

The distance between where they stood and the bar wasn't much, but it took them a solid fifteen minutes to make it. If felt as though with each step they took, someone else got in their way to talk to Kayla. Some were friends wanting to reconnect, people who genuinely seemed to like her. Others thanked her for her donations to the school, the scholarships. Devin was shocked at how many of those people were looking for money to help their children.

"I know you've already setup a fund, and my son has applied, but it would be great if we could get a bit extra. I'd love for him to be able to go to Toronto."

Kayla's smile never wavered. "I don't select the students who win the scholarships. Ms. Simon normally does that. I'm sorry I can't help more."

"Of course. Thanks." The woman didn't bother to hide her annoyance before she left.

Devin pulled Kayla to the bar and slapped down two drink tickets. "Whiskey. What do you want, hon?"

"The same."

He pulled her into a hug, waiting for her to relax into his touch before finally letting her go. "I'm sorry."

"For what?"

"I didn't understand what it would be like here for you. Nothing like this happened all week. What makes people think they can demand things from you? Money and time, God, you give them so much already."

She shrugged as she took the drink from the bartender, sliding a fifty to her before walking away. Devin followed her to one of the tables and waited for her to speak. "I think it has to do with the dark. People seem to do and say things they normally wouldn't when they don't think others will notice. Honestly, they're just trying to make a better life for themselves. I don't blame them."

"And you think I'm the nice one." He shook his head before draining his glass. "Let's dance."

"Nope." She placed both her hands flat on the table. "Remember the rules?"

"Remember the sidewalk?" He put his glass down and unbuttoned his jacket. "Maybe people would treat you differently if they saw you as a person rather than whatever preconceived notion of you they've created. Let's show them how amazing you are."

The muscles in her jaw jumped as she leveled him with a glare that could strip paint. "I'm not dancing."

"Okay then. But I'm going to." He backed away from her grinning, hoping his plan would work.

He wasn't precisely into music from the two-thousands, well, at least not the pop stuff. Thankfully so far, the DJ had a solid mix of older and modern music, which meant the night wouldn't be too painful. Besides, if he had to dance to Brittany Spears in a gym to try to win Kayla over, then by God that's what he'd do.

Devin was many things, but a smooth dancer wasn't at the top of that list. He wasn't exactly horrible, but he wouldn't be winning any awards either. Instead of worrying too much about what other people thought, he kept his gaze on Kayla and gave the song all of his best—and very limited—moves.

Kayla was watching, even though she kept turning her head to look away. It was funny watching her emotions, clear even from this distance, shift from embarrassment to amusement. He risked looking away from her, turned his back and gave his ass a shake. If that didn't give her something to laugh at, then nothing would.

A few people around him clapped and cheered, while others gave him a thumbs-up. Well, if nothing else, he'd leave an impression on the locals. When he turned around to see what Kayla thought, he was shocked to see that she wasn't at the table anymore.

"What the?" He stopped and moved to the edge of the crowd to look for her. Had someone tried to corner her again? Shit, he shouldn't have left her alone. Not after everything else they'd gone through since they'd gotten here.

Shit, he was such a fucking idiot.

A light tap on his shoulder had him turning back to the dance floor, and face-to-face with Kayla. She smiled at him, the tendrils she'd pulled down from her hairdo, bouncing as she swayed to the music. "I'm ready to show the world how I dance."

Explosions of warmth and joy ricocheted in his chest. He took her by the hand and moved them farther into the now large dance crowd. Her moves were jerky, nearly robotic as she tried to step in time with the beat. It was hilarious and some of the best fun Devin had in a while. When the music changed to a slow song, Kayla started to move away. He captured her by the hand and spun her around until they were swaying together.

Kayla cringed. "I'm going to step on your toes." Then she proceeded to do precisely that.

"Thankfully, I have dress shoes on, and you can't hurt me." Not his toes at any rate.

He tugged her closer until she relented and pressed her cheek to his. "I rarely got to dance like this in school."

"That sucks. Everyone should get to waltz at a dance."

"I wasn't exactly everyone."

"Thank God for that."

She pulled back to look at him, but all he was aware of was how close her mouth was to his. The bright red lipstick she'd put on was a beacon to him as the disco ball above them cast streaks of light across her skin.

"Devin?" Her tongue darted across her bottom lip, leaving it moist.

He forced his gaze up to hers. "I want to kiss you."

Her lips parted, but she didn't say anything.

"I know it goes against your rules. I know I promised you that I wouldn't. I won't. But I want to more than anything."

"Devin." Unshed tears filled her eyes, making them glisten. "I—"

"Mind if I cut in?"

Kayla stepped away from him as Devin's gaze snapped over to where Christoph stood, decked out in a suit that looked as though it could have come from one of Kayla's collections. Hell, maybe it did.

"I'm going to steal her away from you for a moment." Christoph stepped between them, took Kayla in his arms and moved them fully into the crowd.

The entire thing happened so quickly, Devin didn't even have the chance to move. What the hell had just happened? Scanning the people, he found them dancing in the middle of the floor. Several other couples were looking at them, smiling and nodding as though the two of them together was the most natural thing in the world. Maybe it was? Kayla certainly didn't owe Devin anything beyond their agreed upon money for his time.

Despite her comments to the contrary, maybe she did miss her ex-husband. He could have changed since their divorce and was looking for the chance to get back into her life. She had a history with Christoph. She'd only known Devin for a few weeks.

He should cut back in. Worst case she'd give him hell for butting in. But best case she'd thank him for helping her out of a bind. All he managed was a single step forward when Christoph stopped moving, took Kayla's face in his hands, leaned in and kissed her.

Not a little light peck on the lips. Nope, this was a full-on passionate smooch, long enough that more than a few people stopped dancing and looked at them and to where Devin stood.

Shit.

Operation: Seduce a Millionaire was officially over.

A woman and her friend stood next to Devin. "They make such a cute couple. I hope they get back together."

"Right? The mayor and the millionaire. I bet they could get their own reality show."

"I know I'd watch it."

Devin turned his back and stepped off the dance floor. He started toward the bar, but stopped, turning sharply to head for the door instead. He found Mark reading a book in the limo, parked at the far end of the lot.

He tapped on the window. "Hey."

Mark got out with a grin. "She's done already? You managed to keep her here an hour. I'm impressed."

"She's still in there dancing."

Mark's eyebrows shot up beneath his hat. "Dancing? Kayla?"

"With Christoph."

"The hell you say." He pulled his hat off and gave Devin a hard look. "So why are you out here?"

"I didn't want to get in her way." Not to mention he was more than a little terrified that he'd fire off and hit Christoph for absolutely no reason. Kayla hadn't objected to that kiss, which explained why she'd been so against Devin doing that to her. She was probably still in love with Christoph. "I should head out."

Mark looked back at the school, before nodding to the car. "I can drive you back to the B&B."

"Thanks." He'd get his things and be ready to head back to Toronto first thing in the morning. It was time to get back to reality and his life.

Time to put his feelings for Kayla in a small box and tuck it away, never to be opened again. "Let's go."

Chapter 20

The air vacated Kayla's lungs as she stepped away from Christoph, even as the crowd around them burst into applause. She lifted her hand to her mouth, staring at him. "Why did you do that?"

Christoph took her by the hand and pulled her to the side of the gym. Not that they were out of sight of curious eyes. No, if anything their illusion of privacy seemed to act like a spotlight on them. She tried not to look at the groups of people looking their way, which only left her with Christoph.

When he tried to take her by the hand, she pulled back. "I asked you a question."

"I kissed you because you're my wife and I missed you."

"I'm *not* your wife. I'm your ex-wife because you couldn't keep it in your pants. I'm on my own now, because your love of my money was far greater than your love for me. So no, you don't get to kiss me. You don't even have the right to *talk* to me."

It had been a long time since she'd felt this sort of anger. It had taken her a long time to deal with her rage and embarrassment after she'd left him. Simone had always accused her of still harboring resentment and based on how desperately Kayla wanted to knee Christoph in the balls, she might be right.

But of course, Christoph didn't see her side of things. That had been a critical issue with their marriage from day one. Even now, she could tell from his annoyed look that he thought she was overreacting to the situation.

"Baby, you're overreacting."

Asshole.

He tried to retake her hand, and she batted it away. Christoph frowned. "Look, you're right. You have every reason to be angry with me. I'd screwed up with you, with our marriage. I was angry at you for leaving me, which is why I moved back home. It took me a long time to realize that I'd been the one who'd made the mistakes, not you. I'm sorry for that."

Oh. In all the years they'd been together, she'd never once heard him apologize to her, or accept blame for one of their fights. Maybe he had changed over the years. "Thank you for that. But it doesn't change the fact that you'd cheated on me. That you were more interested in what my money could get you than having an actual relationship with me."

"I didn't know what I had until you were gone." He let out a huff, and his gaze dropped to the floor. "But seeing you this week with that man, it hurt."

Devin. Shit.

She looked around, but there was no way she could pick him out in the crowd. There was no doubt in her mind that he would have seen the kiss. And while she didn't owe him anything—well, except for ten grand—he'd been too kind to her, too caring for her to hurt him that way. She needed to get away from Christoph and find him, to apologize for what happened.

Christoph took advantage of her temporary distraction, stepped in and wrapped his arm around her waist. She tried to pull away, but he held her tight. "Let me go."

He leaned in, his gaze locked to hers. "You're the most beautiful woman in the world. I'd made a horrible mistake when I'd cheated on you. It took me a long time to realize that. Moving back home, becoming mayor, it all served to make me realize how much I'd screwed up with you. I'm sorry, and I hope that someday you'll be able to forgive me."

And then he kissed her again.

It was a masterful one as well. Christoph cupped her cheek even as he held her tight against him. It used to make her feel as though she were the most important person in the world. But God, not anymore. Knowing people were watching, knowing that *Devin* was watching, turned her stomach and cranked up her embarrassment to levels she hadn't felt since she'd been in high school.

This time she let her baser instincts rule and brought her knee up sharply. "I said let me go."

Christoph gasped and stumbled back, finally releasing her.

There were a few gasps from the people who'd long given up the pretense of not watching their unfolding drama. Kayla no longer gave a shit. Christoph had his hands on his knees, bent over as he tried to catch his breath. She should feel some remorse for having hurt him. Then again, no meant no.

"I'm leaving. Don't follow me."

Ignoring the shocked looks of the people she passed, Kayla searched the crowd for Devin. He wasn't near the bar or in the crowd dancing, which meant he'd witnessed everything that had happened and had left.

Shit.

The registration desk still had the women sitting there, so Kayla made a beeline for them. "Excuse me, did you see Devin leave?"

The women exchanged looks before the blonde smiled far too sweetly for Kayla's liking. "You mean Mr. Let-me-make-her-a-corsage? Yes, he marched out of here about ten minutes ago. He didn't look pleased, did he, Sue?"

The brunette smiled as well. "No, no he didn't. Looked a bit angry and maybe even hurt. I wonder why he was angry and hurt, May?"

"Can't imagine. Unless it was because his date was kissing the mayor. Maybe that was it?"

Kayla turned her back and walked out of the gym, ignoring Sue's parting comment. "Bitch."

The night air was fresh after the stuffiness of the gym. The music was a steady beat behind her, bleeding through the walls and down the hall as she stood in the foyer of the school. She pulled her phone from her purse and texted Mark.

Did Devin come to the limo?

When he didn't respond immediately, she knew he was probably driving. Which, if she had to guess, meant that he was taking Devin back to the B&B. Shit, she needed to get over there and apologize to him before things got bad. He hadn't deserved to witness what had happened, not after everything that they'd done and shared this week.

She fired off another quick text to Mark.

I'm taking a cab. Wait at the lodge.

Her phone immediately dinged a reply.

Heading back now. Stay there, and I'll be back in fifteen minutes.

God, she didn't want to wait to talk to Devin. She wanted to get back to him, to explain that none of this was her fault, that she hadn't wanted Christoph's kiss. She hadn't wanted a relationship at all before this whole sugar daddy site thing had begun. But now that she'd had a glimpse of what things could be like with someone who wasn't preoccupied with her wealth, with someone who saw her as a person and not merely a means to an end, she knew she wanted more. That she could have more. And if that made her selfish, then fuck it, she'd happily be selfish.

"Kayla!"

She turned as Christoph marched toward her down the hall. No, this wasn't something that needed to happen. "Stay the hell away from me."

"I'm sorry." He held up his hands and kept his distance, but it was clear from the look on his face that he wasn't going to leave her alone. "We need to talk."

"No, I don't think we do."

"I'm sorry. Again." He grimaced as he took another step closer. "It's been so long since I've been with you, I couldn't help myself. You're still one of the most beautiful women I've ever met. I needed to feel your kiss again."

"It's always about what you want, isn't it?" She looked down at her phone. Ten minutes, that was all she'd need to wait for Mark's rescue. "It was never about me or my needs. You wanted to kiss me. Just like you wanted me to take time off so you could go on vacation or a cruise. You wanted me to buy you things. You wanted to do things in the bedroom. It was never about what I wanted or needed."

"I'm selfish. You're right." He sighed and let his hands finally fall to his sides. "Being mayor here has shown me that I've spent too much of my life putting myself ahead of others. I don't have that luxury now. I spend most of my days helping the community, running meetings and committees, going to events to help celebrate accomplishments. It's opened my eyes."

"So, what was that in there?" She pointed toward the school, her rage rearing up again. "Those kisses weren't about me."

"I don't know." And for the first time, she believed him. "It's like I see you and I slip back into old habits."

Another look at her phone. Five minutes. "Then I think it's probably best for you to stay away from me. If you've changed for the better, who am I to show up and let you self-destruct."

Silence fell between them as Christoph stared at her long and hard. "I hurt you, didn't I?"

"I caught you in bed with another woman. Of course you hurt me." The fact that he was only coming to that realization now sickened her.

Thankfully, she looked over as the limo pulled into the school driveway and made its way to her. "I'm leaving."

"Can I call you? I'd like to try to work things out."

"No."

"Kayla—"

"No, Christoph. We're done. Live your life here. Help the town and the people. Find someone else who you can love. But leave me alone." She didn't wait for Mark to get out of the car, instead yanking the door open and climbing into the car.

Mark started driving away without her saying anything, and even though the privacy screen was down, she let out a sob. God, who the hell did Christoph think he was, trying to worm his way back into her life? He didn't deserve her tears, but she was so freaking angry, she couldn't stop them.

"Are you okay, sweetheart?" Mark said once they stopped at a red light. "I saw Christoph there. Did he do anything to hurt you?"

"I'm fine. Just pissed off." She angrily wiped away her tears. "Is Devin okay?"

"He seemed hurt, but he didn't tell me what happened. I assume it had something to do with the asshole?"

She let out a surprised laugh. "Yes. The asshole kissed me."

"I hope you kneed him in the nuts."

"I did."

Mark spun around. "Wait, seriously?"

"Yup."

He grinned. "Good for you. It's about time he got what was coming to him."

"He did." She took a breath and finally felt herself start to relax. "Now all I have to do is make it up to Devin."

"You will."

The rest of the drive passed quickly, but the second Mark pulled the limo up in front of the lodge, Kayla didn't know what to do. Even when Mark got out and opened her door, she didn't move. Looking up at Mark, she clasped her hands together and squeezed them. "I don't know why I'm nervous."

Mark dropped to a squat beside her. "Because for the first time in a long time, you've found someone who means something to you."

"But I just met him. We've only known each other for a few weeks. You can't fall in love with someone that quickly."

"I did." He smiled as his gaze flicked to the side. "When I saw Alex for the first time at a party, I fell in love. Didn't even know if he was gay, but my heart didn't seem to care. It was like I recognized a missing piece of myself from across the room."

"Did he love you back?"

"Alex? My practical, by the book husband? Hell no. He was polite and talked with me, but it took me a long time to convince him that we were meant to be together."

"But you did." Mark and Alex were her gold standard for relationships.

"I did. And based on how that boy looks at you, I don't think you'll have to try as hard as I did to win him over."

She reached out and hugged him, placing a kiss on his cheek. "Thank you."

"You're welcome. Now, I suggest you head in there and go talk to him."

He helped her out of the limo and Kayla took a moment to take a deep breath before heading inside. There was no one at the front desk, so she headed right up the stairs, her nerves driving her on.

But when she unlocked the door, she was surprised to see that the room was empty. "Devin?"

The bathroom had been cleaned out on his side, but more importantly, his suitcase was gone. She sat hard on the edge of his bed, pulled out her phone and sent him a text.

Where are you?

She waited, staring at the screen for a hint that he was okay. It took nearly ten minutes before a response came back.

I didn't want to get in the way of your reunion.
I had Mr. Babineau drive me to the bus station.
Heading home tonight.

No. The pit of her stomach soured, and for a moment, Kayla didn't know what to think. Devin had left her. He hadn't waited for an explanation or to hear her side of the story. He'd made an assumption, placed his blame and left her on her own.

Maybe everything she'd felt this week had been nothing more than an illusion. A vacation romance that was paper thin and meaningless. It had been a long time since she'd been the center of someone's world the way she'd been with Devin this week. But it wasn't real.

She held up her phone, not sure what to say. Finally, she typed the truth.

I didn't want him to kiss me. I'm sorry you got
hurt.

Devin's reply was again slow coming.

It's okay. None of this was real.

Seeing her thoughts written on the screen cemented everything. Their time together had been little more than a fantasy, one that had run its course.

> *I'll setup the e-transfer for the money I owe you.*
> *Thank you for everything. I'm sorry it ended this*
> *way.*

She didn't wait, and quickly sent the first installment of money to his account. She received the notification that the transfer had gone through, and that was that.

Thank you, Kayla. Be well.

Tossing her phone on the bed, she lay down, pulling her body into the fetal position. The week was now over, and she was free to return to her normal routine, her normal life. Tears slipped from her eyes to soak into the duvet cover.

Yup, everything back to how it was. Her life under her control.

Exactly how she liked it.

Chapter 21

Two weeks later

Kayla sat at her office desk, staring at her computer screen, barely aware of the words. It was past suppertime, and her stomach had been protesting for the past half hour. Sooner or later she was going to have to get up and get something to eat, even if that meant she'd have to continue reading this report at home.

But the last thing she wanted to do was go back to her empty home, to sit in her empty kitchen drinking wine and reading a report that she couldn't focus on.

The sun was still shining bright even at seven o'clock, the longer days making it easier for her to stay at work. Any other summer, she'd be out with Simone or some of her other friends. They'd go to events around the city, and she'd had a good time. But since she'd come back from Meadow Lake, the last thing she wanted to do was be social.

There was a knock on her office door that pulled her out of her thoughts and back to reality. Rhianna had left hours ago, so Kayla wasn't sure who it would be. "Come in."

Simone poked her head through the door. "Ah ha! I knew I was right. You're still here."

"Yes, I am." Kayla relaxed back against her seat. Well, at least she now had an excuse for not getting any more work done. "Is that food I smell? Tell me you brought food."

Simone pushed the door all the way open, stepped inside and held up a bag of take-out and a bottle of wine. "Dude, did I bring food."

"You know you're my best friend and I love you, right? Because you are and I do."

Simone giggled as she closed the office door with her foot. "I've barely seen you since you got back from the reunion thing. And you've been avoiding me—"

"No, I haven't."

"—but I wanted to see you. So I texted Mark, and he told me that you were still working, so I got you supper, and here I am."

Simone set the bag and the bottle down on Kayla's desk. The smell of hamburgers hit her hard, and her stomach growled its appreciation. "God, are these Works burgers?"

"With extra fries. And the wine has a screw top, so we don't have to find an opener, though I totally know a trick for getting those out without one." Simone fell into the guest chair, pulling it up close as she pulled out the food for them both. "So, whatcha been doin'? How did the week back home go? Did you have any fun with a hot guy who you've now fell head-over-heels in love with?"

For half a second, Kayla forgot that she hadn't told Simone about Devin. She'd kept her contact a secret because the last thing she'd needed in her life was Simone going ape-shit over a mental pairing that wouldn't have her desired result—seeing Kayla fall in love. But now that the week was over, that her little fling with Devin was over, there wasn't any point in keeping things from her friend. If anything, maybe it would help to talk them out.

God, who had she become over the past month?

Simone poured wine into two plastic take-out cups and put one down in front of Kayla. "You're taking way too long to answer that question. That leads me to believe that something amazing happened." She put her elbows on the desk, bridged her fingers together, and rested her chin on them. "Spill."

Right. Okay. Kayla took a deep breath and slowly let it out. "Do you remember Devin?"

Simone frowned. "Devin? Is he one of your old boyfriends or *oh my God* he's the guy from the dating site!" Simone stood up, her eyes bugged out. "You did the sugar daddy site! Oh, my God, that's awesome!"

"Will you sit down and hush. Or else I won't tell you what happened."

Simone sat back down hard, swallowed down all the wine in her cup and refilled it. "Talk. Now."

Kayla drank down her wine, waited for a refill and then let the floodgates open. She told Simone pretty much every single detail, from the CN Tower to the Babineaus leaving them a box of condoms, to Christoph and his ill-timed kiss. By the time she got to their final few texts, Kayla was ready to go home, crawl into bed and stay there for the rest of her life.

In a completely out of character kind of way, Simone said nothing throughout her entire story. It wasn't until Kayla finished that she leaned back in her seat and stared at her oddly. "And that's it?"

"What do you mean, *that's it*? That's a whole pile of shit that I've had to deal with. Oh, and I didn't tell you the best part."

"What?"

"Christoph has been emailing me almost daily since I've gotten back. He wants another shot at our relationship. Says that I should consider stepping back from the company and moving back to Meadow Lake to stay with him. Can you imagine?" She'd been furious when she'd received the first email from him, but after the fifth, the tenth, it had merely grown sad.

"You're not going to do that right?" Simone shoved a huge fry into her mouth. "Because I'll have to kick your ass if you do."

"Hell no. Christoph can screw himself, or anyone else for that matter. Going home and seeing him again only reinforced that he and I aren't suited for one another."

"Excellent!" Simone grinned before devouring the rest of her burger. "Next question. How are we going to win back Devin?"

"*We* are not going to do anything at all." No, she did not need Simone getting involved in her love life at all.

"Okay fine. What are *you* going to do? Because that boy was clearly in love with you and I'll never forgive you if you don't find a way to win him back."

"He wasn't...I mean, I don't think he was in love with me. He liked me, certainly. I liked him as well. It was us against the world while we were away. But that doesn't mean we had a chance at a real relationship."

"Tell that to Marissa and Vince. I heard he made this gigantic public proposal to her, and there were balloons and—"

"I'm not Vince Taylor." Kayla was on her feet before she knew what she was doing. "I'm not going to take out an ad in the paper or make some huge YouTube video begging Devin to forgive me for something that wasn't my fault in the first place. We had an arrangement that he fulfilled. I paid him for his time, and now he's gone back to his life."

She hoped that he'd soon figure out what he wanted to do with his life, or at the very least, permitted himself to be a teacher and put the specter of his father's career behind him. Devin was a good man who deserved to have a good and happy life. But he didn't need her to do any of that.

Even if she wanted to have a place with him.

"Can you sit down? You had your scary Kayla face on, and now you look sad, and that's very confusing to me."

Kayla sat and downed her wine. "This is good."

"I got it at Metro for like ten bucks."

Kayla refilled her glass. "It's good."

"And you're changing the subject." Simone shook her head. "Why won't you let yourself be happy? You're an amazing human being who does so much for others, but you never want to do something for yourself."

"Fashion Finds was my something. It's my special thing in my life."

"That doesn't mean that you're not allowed also to have a good relationship. To have a family if that's what you want. Just because your business took off, that doesn't mean that's all life is allowed to give you."

"Maybe."

"Not maybe," Simone growled, got up and started pacing. "Seriously, you're maddening. I mean you donate money and time and things. You're like the best friend I could have ever asked for, and you're an awesome boss, and you're always so sad all the time. That's not right, and it needs to change."

"Hon, it's not going to work between us."

"Why not? You like him, and it sounded like he liked you. Why won't you even give him a chance?" Simone finally came to a stop beside her, crossed her arms and glared down at her. "Text him."

"What? No."

"You don't know what he's thinking or feeling because you haven't spoken to him. So, text him. You'll know where you stand depending on his response."

This was a horrible idea. But based on Simone's expression, it was either send Devin a text or be subjected to another tirade. She pulled her cell from her desk drawer, held it up for Simone to see, then pulled up Devin's number. She'd nearly deleted it from her contacts a few times now, but something had always held her back. A refusal to let the one good thing that had happened to her in a while go, or pure stubbornness, she wasn't sure.

"Text him." Simone crossed her arms and waited.

"Fine. But if this backfires, you owe me."

"It won't."

Kayla pulled up his number and opened SMS app. She typed quickly, not wanting to overthink about what she was saying for fear of not getting anything out at all. *Hi. I know things didn't end the best for us. I wanted to check in and make sure you were okay. Hope all is well.*

She tossed her phone on the desk. "There. I texted him. But I'm not expecting a response."

They both jumped when her phone buzzed. Kayla's heart pounded so loud and hard in her chest that she was sure Simone could hear her. With a shaking hand, she reached up and retrieved her phone, only for her stomach to sink. "Not him. Just Mom letting me know she and Dad have arrived back home safe and sound."

Simone looked nearly as disappointed as she felt. "He'll text you. I know he will."

They spent the next half hour making small talk while they finished off their food and wine. Every time her phone would beep, they'd both look, only to be disappointed when it wasn't Devin. Maybe he'd been the one to block her, or thought she was sad for reaching out to him, much the same way she felt about Christoph.

She hoped not.

By the time they cleaned up, and Simone was getting ready to leave, Kayla had given up hope that he'd reach out to her at all. Simone pulled her in for a hug. "Don't give up yet."

"It's okay. He's moving on with his life. I don't blame him either. It was a clear-cut arrangement. He lived up to his side of the bargain, and that was it. He doesn't owe me a thing."

Simone had a look on her face that told Kayla that she didn't believe her. "I'll talk to you later, okay?"

"Yup."

Alone once again, Kayla sat back down in front of her computer. She lasted another five minutes before calling Mark. "I'm ready to leave."

* * * *

Devin was exhausted. He'd spent the better part of yesterday with Ray at the hospital, only to crawl into bed that night and find himself unable to sleep. Since he'd gotten back from Meadow Lake, he'd thrown himself into the task of helping his friend and his family deal with his mom's cancer. They'd had a scare that had Devin driving Ray to the emergency room and staying to make sure they didn't need anything else.

He'd made sure to call his mom this morning. He couldn't imagine anything happening to her, not after having lost his dad. But life was rarely fair, and he wanted to tell her that he loved her as much as possible. But it was now Saturday, and he had nothing to do.

Ray was staying at home with his parents to help out, which meant Devin was alone in a far too quiet apartment. He'd lasted an hour fumbling around the place before he got dressed and caught a bus down to the soup kitchen.

Angela greeted him with a giant hug. "It's not your Saturday to volunteer."

"I know, but I found myself with a bit too much free time on my hands. Thought I'd make myself useful. If you need me."

"I always need you, my beautiful boy. We're cooking chicken for supper tonight. Why don't you help with the trays?"

"Thanks."

The tension eased from him as he fell into the familiar routine of working. Once he'd completed the food prep, he helped hand out food to their guests. Devin didn't do this aspect of the job very often, but he enjoyed meeting the people, making them smile and maybe even laugh a bit when serving them. It wasn't the rush time yet, but they never turned anyone away, not when they needed it.

He was surprised when an attractive blond woman with black framed glasses bounced into the soup kitchen, smiling as she walked. She paused long enough to look around at everyone until her gaze landed on him. There was no mistaking her excitement as she came up and stuck out her hand.

"Hi. I'm Simone, and you're the man I'm looking for."

He gave her hand a shake, even as something in the back of his mind told him that this was not going to be an encounter that he was going to like. "Hi, Simone. You don't look like one of our regular customers. Is there something I can help you with?"

"You're Devin, right? Devin Ford?"

There was something in the way she said his name that set alarm bells off in his brain. "Yes. Why?"

"Can we go somewhere to talk? I won't take too much of your time. Promise."

"We have a lounge outside." He nodded toward the back door, and she followed him. "What's this about?"

Simone crossed her arms and kicked her hip out to the side. "I was curious why you broke my best friend's heart?"

Chapter 22

All the pieces slotted together, as Devin remembered why her name sounded so familiar. "You're Kayla's best friend."

"I am." She pushed her glasses up the bridge of her nose and nodded. Her blond hair bounced around her shoulders as if it were alive. "And I wanted to know why you didn't respond to her text?"

In the two weeks since he'd left Kayla in Meadow Lake, Devin had worked very hard to push every fleeting thought he had of her out of his mind. Sometimes he'd think he'd see her in a crowd on the street, or sitting in the back of a car, but every time he did a double-take, it wasn't her. To distract himself, he'd thrown all of his attention into helping Ray and his family. The reception in the hospital was horrible, and it had killed his battery.

"I haven't seen a text from her. When did she send it?"

"Yesterday." Simone crept closer to him when he pulled his phone out from his pocket. "It didn't ding? Mine always makes the little ding sound."

"It didn't ding. But I was at the hospital yesterday, and then my phone died. I haven't looked at it much today." He quickly scrolled through the messages from Ray, his mom and a few of his friends.

There it was. Sitting toward the bottom was a phone number without a contact name—Kayla's number. He'd never entered her full information into his phone, scared that by having it there would be too much of a temptation to get in touch with her. Or worse, it would curse their entire relationship.

Which seemed to have happened regardless.

"Why were you at the hospital?" Simone reached up and pressed the back of her hand to his cheek. "Are you sick? Do you need anything?

Because if you're sick and you need something, I know Kayla would be more than happy to help you."

"I'm fine. I was there helping out a friend."

"Aww. That's sweet of you." Simone's goofy grin set him instantly at ease. This wasn't going to be a crazy confrontation like he'd initially feared. She sat down on the chair and looked up at him. "I'm a reporter, so I tend to need to find out what's happened when things don't go the way I expect."

"And you expected me to text her back?" Devin leaned against the wall, crossed his arms and looked down at Simone. "I'm not sure why you'd think that."

"Well, because she told me what happened, and I could tell that you totally had feelings for her, and so when she texted you, I'd kind of hoped that you would have reached out to her right away. I think she did too."

Devin ignored the way his heart pounded and the unexpected flutter of excitement that flooded through him. Wanting something, and that something working out for him were two entirely different things. He might have thought that he and Kayla had a chance at being a couple, but the night of the dance only proved that they were in two very different places in their lives.

He sighed, looking back toward the soup kitchen. "Look, thank you for coming. I know you think that this relationship with Kayla was something that might work out, but you weren't there. You didn't see her and Christoph together. The way they kissed—" He closed his eyes for a moment, before steadying himself. "That wasn't a kiss of regret. The look on her face said it was something else."

"She doesn't love him."

He wanted nothing more than to believe her, but deep down, he knew there was more to what Kayla felt than what her friend thought. "You didn't see her." He ran his hand down his face, trying his best to squash his frustration. "She was clear from day one about what our week would entail. This was a fake relationship, nothing more. If she wants to start something back up with her ex, then that's completely her business."

Simone stood, getting right into his personal space. "She didn't want Christoph to do what he did. He hurt her bad back when they were married. I didn't know him, I met her afterward. I saw the damage and tried to help her pick up the pieces."

"If I've learned anything about Kayla over the past few weeks, it's that she's more than capable of looking after herself."

"You leaving the way you did hurt her as much as Christoph kissing her did." Simone huffed, hugging herself. "Look, I didn't know anything about you until yesterday, so you'll have to forgive me if I'm more interested in protecting my friend than hurting your feelings. But you owe her a conversation. If, after that, you don't want to talk to her again, fine. But you walked out on her without giving her a chance to explain her side of the story. That's not cool."

Simone then headed for the door, but paused for a moment. "And by the way, she kneed Christoph in the balls for that kiss, before coming after you. So you might want to think on that."

Devin's stomach flipped as he watched Simone leave.

That revelation was more than a little unexpected. He should have known that Kayla hadn't asked for Christoph's attention, but knowing and coming face-to-face with them kissing were two entirely different things. He pulled out his phone once more and looked down at Kayla's message.

He should contact her. Simone was right that he owed her the opportunity to at least defend herself. But beyond that, the chances of them developing any lasting relationship was unlikely. She was rich, and he was a PhD graduate with mountains of debt.

Well, a bit less debt as soon as he took the money she'd paid him and put it toward paying off his loans.

Noises from the kitchen reached him, and Devin knew that he needed to get back in there to help. It would be getting close to rush hour soon, and they'd need all hands on deck. He took a step before stopping. No, he needed to deal with this Kayla situation first. He opened up the text, took a breath and typed out a response.

There. The ball was now back in her court.

* * * *

Kayla was running full tilt on the treadmill in her home gym when she heard her phone buzz. The temptation to stop running and check to see who'd emailed her was huge, but she'd promised herself that she'd spend at least an hour on herself, and not let work interfere.

If her time in Meadow Lake had proved nothing else, it was that it had been far too long since she'd put herself first. Meetings for work, charitable acts, even dinners with Simone and her other friends, everything was about other people. Devin had been right that she needed to take more time for herself, for her own needs every now and again.

By the time she hit the ten-kilometer mark, her legs were protesting loudly, as were the soles of her feet. She hit the cool down button and took a moment to swallow down as much water as she could manage without spilling it everywhere. It had been a long time since she'd run that far, and it felt good to stretch her muscles. Still, the moment she stepped off the treadmill, her body was immensely thankful.

Yeah, she'd likely pay for this in the morning.

She wiped down, grabbing her phone as she did her towel so that she could take a quick look at the emails. There were several from her VP of production, commenting on her thoughts regarding what she'd seen at the German plant a few weeks earlier. Rhianna had sent her a joke—a not so subtle hint that she thought Kayla needed to relax. And some update reports that sooner or later, she'd have to go through.

There was another indicator on her phone that caught her attention; she'd also received a text message. Her heart was already pounding and her hands shaking from the rush she'd gotten from her run, so when she saw that the text was from Devin, all she could do was stare at it. He'd finally gotten back to her, and only a day later than she'd hoped for. Still, she didn't know if his reaction to her out-of-the-blue communication would be positive or not.

Well, this was Devin she was talking about; while he might not want to talk to her, he was far too kind to be rude. At least, she assumed he was.

She took a breath to steady herself before she opened his message. It was simple and direct, a bit more pointed than she'd expected.

> *Hey. Your friend Simone tracked me down to*
> *let me know that you'd texted me. I was at the*
> *hospital with Ray yesterday and missed it. It*
> *wasn't an intentional snub.*

And that was it. No *hi, how are you doing* or *hey, I've missed you and want to get back together.* A simple statement about what had happened so she wouldn't be upset with him. Not to mention he'd told her about Simone—which was another problem for another day. So, now it was up to her to respond to him, to find out where they stood, if anywhere.

Right. Okay. She could do that.

Typing a message, she quickly deleted it and started over. Then again. And a third time. Finally, she tossed her phone on the chair and went to have a shower. What the hell was she going to say to him about what had happened? They'd been living in fantasy land for a week, nothing more. He had his life to live, his friends to help. She had a business to run. While Devin was the farthest thing away from Christoph, she still couldn't guarantee that he wouldn't grow to resent her the way Christoph had.

She couldn't guarantee that she wouldn't end up alone once again.

As she got dried off and dressed, her brain kept turning over what to do about Devin. Could she take the chance and see where this relationship went? Or did she say screw it and reach out to another guy on the sugar daddy site? That was always an option, a chance to have some companionship for a while and when things got too complicated, she could just walk away. No doubt, that's what a number of the men on the site did, so why should she be any different?

Because she was, and that was all there was to it.

At the very least, it would be nice to see Devin one last time, to talk to him and say how sorry she was in person. Right? That was the grown-up thing to do, and despite everything that had happened, they were both adults who deserved respect.

It took her another minute to collect her thoughts and type out what she wanted to say.

> *Sorry about Simone. She is a tad overprotective of me. I hope Ray's mom is doing okay. If there is anything I can do to help, please let me know. I was hoping to take you to supper as an apology for how things ended at the reunion. No other obligations. I feel I owe you that at the very least. Let me know if you'd like to go. If not, no worries.*

She closed her eyes as she pressed send. There, that was that. And if he didn't get back to her, well, she'd at the very least attempted—

Her phone buzzed in her hand.

> *Supper would be nice. I didn't like how I left, the unresolved things. It's a date.*

A date. He said yes!

Kayla's grin was so wide her cheeks hurt.

Well, this was going to be something. Maybe things would work out after all. Maybe if she were very lucky, she wouldn't be alone any longer.

Chapter 23

Devin had tried to pick the restaurant this time, doing his best to convince her that the burgers at the Pear Tree were really great. While having her rent out an entire banquet room at the top of the CN Tower had been cool, he wanted to make sure they were on slightly more even footing this time around. Not to mention, Kayla had been terrified of the elevator ride up, even if she hadn't said anything directly.

That hadn't worked out the way he'd hoped—mostly because Kayla had insisted on taking him to a better spot than his typical local pub.

"You have to let me make this up to you somehow," she'd said on the phone last night. "There's a place that's come highly recommended by a friend. I haven't eaten there, but he swears it's good."

That's how Devin found himself standing in front of a restaurant called the Catch, waiting for Kayla's limo to arrive.

That had been something else he'd insisted on—no car rides. While he'd enjoyed sitting in the back of the limo eating Twizzlers, he didn't want that luxury to influence his view of Kayla. Didn't want to be subjected to Mark's disapproving looks. He'd take his Uber to the restaurant, and that would be that, thank you very much.

The summer heat had kicked up to full blast, making his decision to wear a dress shirt and tie more than a little shortsighted. There was no sense in not looking good, even if he suspected nothing would come from their dinner.

Even if maybe there was a small part of him that wanted *something* to happen.

Devin was about to text Kayla to see where she was when the limo turned onto the street. Even as his tension faded, his nerves kicked into high gear, making his chest feel tight, and his palms sweat. There was no reason for him to be nervous, this was still Kayla. Still the same woman he'd made love to and laughed with. Who he'd danced with on the sidewalk and teased regarding her inability to play mini golf.

Still, the same woman who didn't look to be over the man who'd broken her heart.

The limo came to a stop in front of the restaurant, and Mark immediately got out. He found Devin and smiled at him. "Good to see you again."

"Thanks." Devin did his best to not stare at the tinted back window. "I'm honestly a bit surprised."

Mark came around to the back-passenger door closest to the sidewalk, put his hand on the handle, and turned to face Devin. "I'm not." He then gave him a wink before opening the door.

Devin held his breath as Kayla took Mark's hand and got out of the limo. She was wearing another one of those light, flowy dresses that hugged her body as it swirled around her legs. The light green print was a stunning contrast to her black hair and made her eyes stand out even more.

"Wow." He couldn't stop himself from coming closer, reaching out and taking her hand from Mark. "You look amazing."

She blushed, the color adding to her beauty. "Thank you."

Right, he needed to keep himself focused. This was an apology dinner, not another chance to engage in Operation: Woo a Millionaire. Because nothing good would come of that.

Nope, not a damn thing.

"Ah," he turned around as Kayla shifted her grip to his arm. "I assume the reservation is in your name?"

"It is. They had a private room, but someone already booked it. I'm afraid we'll have to eat in the main restaurant."

"That's fine." Probably for the best. He didn't think he could handle being in a room alone with her looking the way she did. He'd do nothing but drool and make a fool of himself. "We'd better head in."

The Catch was apparently one of *the* places to eat in Toronto, according to all three of the restaurant blogs he'd looked up online. Devin was determined to enjoy himself because based on the prices he saw on their website, this would be his first and last visit. The central area was full, but despite that, there was enough room between the tables to ensure they'd have relative privacy. He wouldn't have to worry about people overhearing their conversation.

Bonus.

The waiter led them to their table and quickly took their drink orders. Devin hadn't planned to have anything, but Kayla ordered a bottle of wine, the same one from the winery they'd toured. Even though the trip ended on a sour note, not everything about the week had been horrible. "I had no idea they even carried that wine here."

Kayla smiled. "They didn't. But I put in a request for a few bottles to be made available and the restaurant was very accommodating. Apparently, they're going to add it to their wine list."

"Carlo will be thrilled." Once again, Kayla working behind the scenes helping people when they don't expect it. He sat back in his chair to look hard at the woman sitting across from him. It was strange seeing her appear nearly as nervous as he felt. "How have you been?"

"Good." She ran her fingers along the edge of her napkin, still sitting beside her. "I had a lot on my plate when I got back from Meadow Lake. Production meetings and conversations with the design team on the winter lineup."

Devin took a large sip of the wine, thankful for the alcohol to help steady him. Because this was crazy and nerve-racking for really no reason. "It must be weird thinking about winter when summer is just getting underway."

"Technically, I'm already focused on spring, but yes. It can be disconcerting always living your life in the future."

"I bet it makes it difficult to focus on the here and now."

She picked up her wineglass, and lifted it to her mouth, but didn't take a drink. Instead, she tilted her head slightly and narrowed her gaze. "Sounds like you're speaking from experience."

"What's that mean? I'm not living in the future."

"No, but you do live most of your life in the past."

He wanted to respond, but that was the moment when their waiter came back to take their orders. What the hell did she mean that he lived in the past? He was always focused on the future, on the here and now. That was why he was in his current predicament of not knowing what the hell to do with his life.

"And you, sir?"

Devin blinked up at the young woman who was waiting expectedly for his order. "Ah, sorry. I'll have the steak. Medium-rare."

"Wonderful. I'll be back with your appetizers shortly."

Frowning, he looked back at Kayla. "You ordered appetizers?"

"You were a million miles away."

"I was." Sitting straighter, he braced his palms to his thighs. "I don't live in the past."

"Yes, you do. Everything in your life seems to revolve around your relationship to your father. Look, this is just my observations here, but I get the impression that you're trying to live up to this unrealistic expectation of what you think your father would want for your life. It's hard to move forward when you're always looking behind you."

"I don't—"

"How many people have told you that you'd be an awesome teacher? How many professors, friends, family members?"

Devin's mom had talked to him about doing his education degree after he'd finished his masters. She'd told him that his father would have loved for him to follow in his footsteps. Devin had considered it, even went so far as to put in his application for the program. But when the time came actually to do it, he'd chosen to do his PhD instead. He'd never questioned why he'd done that, telling anyone who asked that he'd wanted the challenge of the doctorate program.

Had he been lying to himself all this time?

Kayla slid her hand across the table, her fingers brushing his. "I know I have no business telling you what to do with your life. Regardless of what happened between the two of us while we were away, I think you need to permit yourself to do what you want. Because if you keep looking for answers in every place except the one spot you know is the right one, then you'll never be satisfied. You'll never be happy." She squeezed his hand. "Believe me when I say, of all the men I've known, you are one who truly deserves to be happy."

Devin's stomach flipped as though he'd just completed a loop on a rollercoaster. It wasn't that simple. Was it? Sure, he knew in his heart he'd never be half the teacher that his father had been, but he didn't have a burning desire to follow in his footsteps anyway.

Did he?

Kayla didn't say anything else for several long minutes, which was good because Devin wasn't confident he could vocalize a coherent thought then. The silence stretched on until Kayla's phone beeped. She picked it up, looked at the message, frowned and shoved it into her purse.

"That didn't look good. Work bugging you?" *Yes, let's change the subject to something that won't feel like my heart is getting ripped out.*

Kayla's face paled. "It was Christoph."

Or not. Let's pull that heart out and stomp all over it, shall we?

And yet, there wasn't any trace of joy in her expression, even as she couldn't meet his gaze. Apparently, they were going to deal with all of the shit tonight. "You don't want to talk to him? Or bad timing because you're with me."

She shook her head, as her eyes grew wide. "I didn't want anything to do with him at all. Not back at Meadow Lake, and certainly not now. He hasn't changed. He kissed me, pulled me to the side to talk to me, all because that was what he wanted. He wanted to try to convince me to come back to Meadow Lake, back to him. He never once cared about what I wanted. He never bothered to ask."

Deep in his heart, Devin knew that was true. She'd never once indicated that she'd wanted to get back together with her ex or had any intention of moving back to her hometown. He'd been the one to have overreacted to what he'd seen that night, even if he hadn't wanted to admit it.

Shit, he'd been a complete asshole.

Getting up, he moved his chair, so he now sat at the spot beside her rather than across the table. He took her hand in his, holding it in his lap. "I'm sorry."

"For what?"

"For having overreacted to Christoph. When I saw him kiss you—" Anger caused his throat to tighten for a moment. He had to take a breath and force himself to relax. "It doesn't matter what I thought. You didn't owe me anything. We weren't a couple."

"But we were." Her voice was so soft that he wasn't sure he'd heard her. "We were a couple. Or at least we'd been acting like one. We'd just spent the entire day alone together in bed. You'd made me a beautiful corsage when mine wasn't there. And I repaid your kindness by not putting a stop to Christoph's behavior sooner than I did."

"You're not responsible for his actions. Just like you're not responsible for mine." He lifted her hand to his mouth and kissed the back of it. "I'm sorry."

She smiled, her eyes glistening with unshed tears. "Me too."

Their supper arrived shortly after that, making the rest of their confessional awkward. "I better move back to my place. There won't be enough room for you to eat."

"You're so good that way," she said as soon as he moved his chair back. "Looking out for other people."

"So are you."

"No, I'm good at throwing money at things when I see there's a problem. You instinctively seem to know when something needs fixing, and then you do it."

"I guess that's the advantage of not wanting to examine your issues. You tend to focus on everyone else instead."

They both seemed to relax after that, and Devin finally felt as though they were slipping back into the natural back and forth they'd had before the alumni dance. The more they talked, the more animated Kayla got. The more animated she got, the more Devin wanted to reach out and touch her. The more he wanted to touch her, the higher the chances that he would fall irrevocably in love with her.

Was that a good thing? He didn't have a fucking clue.

But more than ever, he wanted to see where things might go.

By the time dessert came, Devin had formulated in his mind a new Operation: Woo a Millionaire. Pretty much it was the same as his last plan, except he wouldn't let kisses from ex-husbands throw him off track. He watched as she took a bite of a chocolate concoction that probably had enough sugar in it to kill a large mammal.

Kayla's eyes rolled before she closed them and moaned. "Dear God, that's amazing."

"You're going to be hyper later." He took a bite of his dessert, a creme brulee that had him moaning as well. "I'm never getting to sleep tonight."

Kayla chuckled, low and deep, a sound that shot straight through him. "If we're both going to be high on sugar, maybe we should find something to do together. Seeing as we're not going to be sleeping anytime soon."

Was that a proposition? Devin's now hard cock was reasonably sure that it was, but the rest of his brain wasn't entirely certain. "Ah, yeah."

"Unless you don't want to." Her eyes were wide and far too innocent looking for him to believe she wasn't teasing him. "Given how things ended between us a few weeks ago, I wouldn't want you to feel obligated."

Ha ha, that's funny. "You already paid me, remember? I'm here tonight because you invited me, and I wanted to be here. Not because I felt any obligation. Not because I think I can get something else from you. I came because, despite my insecurities, I enjoyed our time together. I enjoyed being with you." He let his gaze travel and stopped on her exposed cleavage. "And if I only get one more chance to be with you, then I wanted to make sure that I took it. Because despite everything that happened, how this whole thing between us started, I can't get you out of my mind. I think that maybe, I might be developing feelings for you."

Kayla's mouth snapped shut. She looked around until she found their waitress. "Check please."

Chapter 24

Kayla managed to hold herself in check until they fell into the back of the limo. The second Devin shut the door—because neither of them had waited for Mark to get out and open it for them—she pulled him close and kissed him hard.

At first, he didn't respond, staying unmoving beneath her. It threw her off so much that she pulled back. "What's wrong?"

"You're kissing me." The wonder in his voice was plain as day. "Kissing *me*."

His statement didn't make sense to her at first, but then she remembered her stupid rules. "I had been trying to make sure that there was a buffer between us. That I wouldn't let myself fall into the trap of thinking that I might have feelings for you if I didn't let you kiss me." She'd been an idiot if she'd thought there was any way she'd have prevented herself from falling for him.

Devin took her by the face gently, leaned in and kissed her softly. Their previous encounters had been passionate, but his gentle press of lips on hers, the exploring swipe of his tongue darting effortlessly along her teeth, across her tongue, had her body ready to explode.

The car jerked as Mark pulled into traffic, but Kayla hardly noticed. She didn't bother with seatbelts, not wanting to let go of Devin for even a moment. "More," she whispered against his mouth. "More."

Devin growled, his arms coming entirely around her to pull her onto his lap. He didn't stop exploring her mouth with his, even as he ran his hands along her arms and across her thighs. He didn't touch her in the sensitive places she wanted him to—her breasts, between her legs—but came close enough that the tease easily got her aroused.

"Where...is...Mark taking...us?" He kissed his way down her throat until he came back and kissed her mouth again.

"My home. He's smart like that."

"Thank God." He pulled back and swallowed hard. "Condoms? I didn't bring anything because I didn't think we were even doing...God, I want to get you into bed."

She laughed a full body chuckle that was two-parts therapeutic and one-part release. "Yes, I do have condoms."

"Good. That's so so good."

The look on his face was more than a little painful, not surprising given the massive erection she could feel through his pants. As carefully as she could, Kayla reached between them and pressed down hard on his cock. Devin sucked in a breath, his eyes squeezing shut. "Killing me."

"As long as you don't come too quickly." She leaned in and sucked his earlobe into her mouth. "I want to drag this out as much as we can."

"I'll come fast. Then the second time I'll come slow. And in between, I'll make it so you come a whole bunch of times. Fair?"

"More than."

They made out like teenagers for the entirety of their drive back to her place. She'd been so distracted by Devin's mouth that she hadn't realized the limo had stopped until she heard Mark knock on the door's window. They both let out a yelp, scrambling to get untangled from one another before Kayla finally reached for the door and opened it.

Mark stood there, smiling down at them. "Hello there. We've arrived. I assumed you wanted to come home. Unless you'd like me to take Mr. Ford here somewhere else—"

"Nope, we're good." Devin gave Kayla a little shove to get her moving. "Her place is perfect."

When they were both standing on solid ground, Devin slipped his arm around her waist, and Kayla's whole body relaxed. She did her best to ignore Mark's knowing smirk. "Thank you, Mark."

"Will you need me again tonight?"

"No. No, I think it will be fine for you to head home." God, she wanted to giggle. Kayla never giggled. Well, not when she wasn't around Devin. "Say hi to Alex for me."

"I will. Have a good evening you two."

Kayla barely remembered fumbling with her keys to shove it into her lock. She had a vague recollection of dropping her purse and kicking off her shoes as Devin spun her around and kissed her again. It was long, hard and did things to her body that she'd never experienced before in her life.

It was awesome.

"Where's your bedroom?" He toed off his shoes, maintaining contact with her the whole time.

"This way." Taking him by the hand, Kayla marched him up the stairs to her room.

Her house, while far too big for one person, wasn't so large that she felt out of place in it. When she and Christoph had lived here, she'd often been thankful for the added space, the room to hide when she'd wanted. But right now, she wished that her house was a single story.

The master bedroom was huge, one of the features that she loved the most about it. There was nothing better than having a fireplace in front of a king-sized bed. Knowing that there was a giant soaker tub in the en suite, for those moments when she wanted to stretch out and relax.

Maybe, if she played her cards right, Devin would want to share a soak with her after they had sex. Because that was a dream of hers, one that she had yet to fulfill.

Devin whistled the moment they walked into her bedroom, stopping long enough to look around and take in all the details. "This is amazing."

"I'm glad you like it."

"Shit, it's nearly as big as my entire apartment." He ducked into the bathroom briefly, whistling again. "I keep forgetting how rich you are."

"That's one of the things that I love about you."

She stopped short as Devin spun around to stare at her. "What did you say?"

Nope, that was so not the right thing to have said. "I meant, it's one of the things that I like about you. You genuinely don't seem to care at all about my money."

Devin's smile made his eyes sparkle. "I don't care about your money. I mean, it's pretty awesome to get to ride around in a limo, but that's not the be all and end all." He began to unbutton his shirt as he moved closer. "But can we back up a bit to that *love* part."

She rolled her eyes, knowing he wouldn't let that go. "It was a slip of the tongue."

"Was it now? So, you meant it, but didn't mean to say it?"

"Don't get cocky." The second he was within reach, she ran her hands along his bare chest. The hairs covering him caught on her fingers, and she tugged at them just the way she knew he liked it. "I'd hate to have to take you down a peg or two."

"We wouldn't want that, would we?" He yanked his shirt off, leaving him dressed in just his pants. Without a word, he picked her up and carried her over to the bed, before unceremoniously dropping her in the middle of the mattress.

Kayla laughed, for once knowing she didn't have to keep her guard up. With Devin, she could finally be herself—Kayla from Meadow Lake. Her dress flared around her legs, riding higher than was proper.

She stretched out, thrusting her breasts high. "So."

"So?" He yanked off his socks and made fast work of his pants, pushing them to the floor. "Where did you say those condoms were?"

"Nightstand drawer. A whole box of them." Though, now that she thought about it, she didn't know how long they'd been there. "Might want to check the expiry date on those before you use them."

"Yeah, I don't know about you, but I'm not ready for any little Devins to be running around quite yet. No offense."

"None taken."

It only took a moment for him to find the box, check the date and pull a strip of condoms out. He grinned as he waved them around. "We're ready to go."

"Excellent." She spread her legs.

Devin's gaze snapped to her thighs, but instead of moving to take her, he instead shook his head. "Not yet. I didn't think I would ever be here with you again. I want to make sure we take our time and do this right." He climbed onto the bed beside her, his erection poking out against his briefs. "I want to kiss every inch of your body the way I wanted to back at the lodge. I want you to know that I'm maybe more than a little in love with you as well."

Kayla didn't know where the sudden rush of tears had come from, nor could she stop them from spilling down her face. "Really?"

"Of course." He brushed them away with his thumb, kissing her face where it had been wet moments earlier. "How could I not love someone like you? You're kind and generous. You care about other people, even when you don't have to. You're beautiful and amazing."

She reached up and kissed him hard. There was no way she could let him continue, could hear any more of his kind words without her heart exploding. He might have wanted to take things slow, but there was no way she'd be able to do that. Sitting up, she rolled him over, so she was now on top, continuing to kiss him until her head swam from lack of oxygen.

Devin groaned, his hands running up and down her back, before he unzipped her dress and helped her slide it free of her arms, and up over her head. Her bra only lasted a minute longer than her dress, before it too went flying across the room.

Now free, her breasts swung low, and her nipples brushed against his chest hair. The light contact sent shivers through her and made her nipples hard and her pussy wet. Even still, she ignored it in favor of letting Devin kiss her anywhere and everywhere he wanted. It was liberating and arousing.

It made her happy.

And that was the best thing, the most important thing since she'd reached out to him on the sugar daddy site—Kayla was finally, unequivocally happy. With a sigh, she pressed her mouth to the side of his throat. "Make love to me. Please."

She felt him reach for the condom wrapper, which meant she was going to have to move or else they weren't going to be able to do much of anything. She slid to the side and watched as Devin made short work of putting the condom on. It was too much of a temptation to resist, so she grabbed his cock and squeezed it.

"Now what do you want to do?"

Devin rolled her onto her back and with a single thrust moved inside her. He laughed at her shock, which had her laughing as well. "How's that?"

"Good. That's good." She clenched her pussy on his shaft and grinned again at the blissed-out look on his face. "That's better."

"Please, can we do this again?" He thrust into her at a steady pace. "And again some more? Because I'm getting hooked on you and I don't think there's a support group for broken hearts."

"Yes." She didn't want to let him go, didn't want to be alone anymore. "As long as you want."

"I…" His words died, and he lowered his mouth to hers, kissing her once again.

Every place their bodies touched felt electric and Kayla wasn't sure if she would ever get tired of feeling him against her. Of knowing that there was someone else out there who loved her for her, who was just as taken with her as she was with him.

It was a new experience.

Devin's thrusts grew stronger, the contact with her clit pushing her arousal up with every brush of skin on skin. He slid his hand up to cup her breast, to tease the nipple even as he deepened their kiss. Her head was spinning as pleasure throbbed through her. She wanted to come, wanted to scream her release out for the world to hear, but she also wanted to drag things out as long as possible. She never wanted this moment to end.

Devin apparently had other thoughts.

He shifted his hand from her breast down between them. Breaking their kiss, he pulled back enough to make room for his fingers to press against her clit as he rolled his hips. The dual pressure was enough to do her in. Kayla tried to fight her orgasm, not wanting everything to be over, but she couldn't. A cry escaped her as her eyes squeezed shut and her body shuddered beneath Devin.

"Yes, shit you're so perfect." He pulled his hand out and braced himself on either side of her body, pounding into her as hard as he could.

Moments later, he roared as his orgasm hit him. Kayla was too wiped out to do anything but let him thrust into her. When he finally stopped and fell forward on top of her, she wrapped her arms around him. She could feel the pounding of his heart against her body and closed her eyes to enjoy the sound of it.

This, this was what she'd always longed for. Who knew that she'd find it with a man who under normal circumstances, they would never have been able to meet. Simone and her suggestion to sign up for the sugar daddy site didn't seem quite so stupid now.

She couldn't stop a chuckle from popping from her. Devin slid to the side and looked at her questioningly. "You okay?"

"I just realized that I'm going to have to buy Simone a thank you gift."

"Dare I ask why?"

"It was because of her that I signed up for the sugar daddy site. I thought it was stupid, that people only used it for sex and that you wouldn't find someone to have a relationship with." She leaned over and kissed him. "I was wrong."

Devin's eyes sparkled, even as he tried to maintain a serious look. "Well, we'll have to show her our appreciation. Maybe we should sign her up, and she can meet a sugar daddy of her own?"

God, Kayla could only imagine how that would go. "I'm not sure she'd be the right person for that. Knowing her, she'd end up researching the hell out of the man she picked and would do her best to find them someone else to fall in love with. She's a bit of an aggressive romantic that way."

"Well, I hope she finds her happy ending as well." Devin rolled onto his back as he grabbed the condom. "I know I have." The dopy-sex look was a good one on him.

Kayla's body was still tingling, and she knew that their night was just getting started. "Why don't you go get rid of that and then come back here for a cuddle. Also, make sure that the rest of the condoms are good to go."

"Oh?" His eyebrows shot up high, and for a moment he looked as though he was going to go for a sprint. "Ah, yes. Right. Give me a minute, and then we can do another quality control test of those condoms."

"For science." She made sure to nod with the greatest sincerity. "Better hurry."

As Devin dashed for the bathroom, Kayla stretched out, letting his lingering warmth soak into her skin. This was what she'd always wanted, had always dreamed of having with another person. And finally, the last piece she'd been missing from her life slotted into place.

She was finally happy.

Chapter 25

Had it only been a few days since Devin had finally gotten his wish and found himself back with Kayla? Two days of laughter and sex and cuddling while watching television, followed by more sex. He nearly cried when she told him that she had to go into the office because she was a responsible adult who had a job and people who relied on her. Not that he didn't want her to do what she was undoubtedly amazing at, but because he was apparently selfish and wanted more of her than he could reasonably have.

He did get to watch her get dressed though, and that was nearly as arousing as watching her get undressed. He had no idea how intimate it was to watch a woman pick out her clothing, to put on make-up, how she'd smile in the mirror to see what overall impression she was giving the world. It was a look at her personality, who she was at her core in a far different way than he'd ever considered possible. Another thing he'd learned about women from her, something that would stick with him forever.

When she'd finished, she turned and held out her arms. "Well?"

"Perfection." He looked at the pile of his clothes that they'd moved to the chair in her room. "I need to get dressed so I can go home and change."

"I can have Mark drop you off." She nodded toward the door. "I'll go put the coffee on. Meet you in the kitchen?"

"Yeah."

Unlike the care that he'd just witnessed, it only took him a minute to slip on his several-day's-old clothing. He needed a shower and a shave, but other than that, he wasn't horrid.

Yeah, no, he looked awful.

The smell of coffee hit him before he made it all the way to the kitchen. Unlike the old drip coffeemaker he and Ray had bought at a yard sale last year, Kayla had a significant industrial looking thing that seemed to do everything with the press of a button. She was already sipping what looked to be a latte, as he came in.

"That's…wow, you made that fast."

She shrugged. "One of the first things I bought when I realized I had more money than I knew how to spend was this super amazing thing. What do you want? It can make anything."

"Ah, an Americano?"

She grinned, slipped a mug under the spout and pressed a button.

Moments later, Devin was sucking back the best Americano he'd ever had. "I'm now ruined for life."

"You're welcome." Kayla's phone buzzed, and she looked at it as if on reflex. Whatever the message was, she must not have liked it, because she was frowning deeply.

"What's wrong?"

"Nothing." She set the phone face down on the counter.

Lord, she was a terrible liar. "I won't pry because it's none of my business, but it didn't look like nothing. If you need to talk, I'm here for you—"

"It was Christoph." Her mouth snapped shut, as though being forced to say his name left a bad taste in her mouth.

He took a breath and did his best to keep his frustration at bay regarding the ex that never seemed to want to go away. "What did he want?"

"Nothing."

"Well, if you need me to—"

"He wants to come talk to me." She threw up her hands and started to pace. "God, I'd pretty much put him out of my mind for years and now because of that stupid kiss at the dance he's under the impression that he somehow has a chance to get back together with me. I mean, he cheated on me and tried to take all my money for himself. Why the hell would I want to get back together with someone like that?"

Devin's mind was screaming *danger, danger Will Robinson* even as his mouth opened. "I'm sorry he's bothering you."

The buzz of joy that they'd both seemed to be riding on for the past few days petered out as Kayla snatched her phone. "It doesn't matter. Mark is here with the car. We better go."

But it did matter, and he was more than a little tired of Christoph ruining Kayla's life.

When they walked outside, Mark was standing by the back door smiling. "Good morning, you two. Nice to see that you're wearing the same clothing, Devin. Rumpled is a good look on you."

Kayla didn't say anything and climbed into the limo. Mark looked at him frowning, and Devin could only mouth *Christoph* before getting in the back with her. Another look at her frustrated face, and he knew there was no way he could let this go. "Mark should drop you off first. Traffic near my place is pretty horrible this time of day. You'll be late if you take me there first."

"Are you sure?" She looked down at her phone. "I do have a meeting in an hour."

"Seriously, it's good. Not like I have anywhere I need to be today." And that was an entirely different issue for him to deal with on another day. "We better get you to that meeting, pronto."

Mark had the privacy screen down and gave them a thumbs-up. "To the office."

Devin's mind didn't shut down the entire time they weaved their way through Toronto traffic. Kayla was also quiet, but he was excited when a few minutes into the drive she took his hand in hers and squeezed it. The tension he'd been holding in his body eased, as he looked over at her and smiled.

Everything was going to be okay because he was with her now. Not that she needed someone to save her from her ex, but he still wanted to help. His gaze shifted to Mark, and at that moment, Devin knew what to do. When they pulled up in front of Kayla's office, he made sure to give her a long, slow kiss, just for good measure. "I'll call you later?"

Her smile made his heart skip a beat. "Sounds good. Say hi to Ray for me."

"Will do." Though if all went according to his plan, it wouldn't be Ray that he was planning on meeting.

He waited until Kayla shut the door and Mark got back behind the wheel before he moved to the seat closest to the privacy screen window. "So, I have a question for you."

Mark turned around to look at him fully. "I know we haven't known each other long, but that's a tone of mischief if I've ever heard one."

"Kayla keeps getting texts from Christoph. Apparently, he won't leave her alone and seems to think that they have a shot at getting back together."

"That's the most ridiculous thing I've ever heard." Mark frowned. "After how he treated her, she'd never get back together with him. Ever."

"That's…good. I don't feel like I have any right to get involved, but I want to try to help her. If I could talk to—"

"That's a terrible idea." Mark sighed, and Devin knew he wasn't going to like what was coming. "I'm sure you could talk to Christoph, and you might even have a chance to make him see reason. But the man I knew was an arrogant asshole who was only interested in what he could get for himself. Anything you do, he'll find a way to turn it around to benefit himself."

"Right. I get that." The little bit of interaction they'd had back at Meadow Lake had made it clear to Devin that Christoph was only out for himself. "I'll just do nothing. I guess."

"Smart man." Mark put the blinker on and pulled into traffic. "Let's get you home."

Devin hated not being able to help Kayla. Despite this not being any of his business, there was still a part of him that wanted to make everything better for her. But if he did that, in a way he'd be no better than Christoph.

Traffic was heavy, and they ended up sitting in line waiting for cars to creep through the intersection. To try to distract himself, he pulled out his phone and logged in to one of his neglected mobile games. He was about to blast through another space mission when a text message popped up on his phone from a number he didn't recognize.

He flipped over to the text, reading it twice to make sure what he was seeing was correct.

Is this Devin, Kayla's arm candy?

Someone thought he was arm candy? That's so not how he'd ever expected to be described by anyone ever. Smiling, he typed out a quick reply.

The one and only. Who's this?

A friend of Kayla's. I'm in Toronto and was hoping to talk to you. I'm concerned for her.

Alarm bells started screaming in his head that this was a huge mistake.

Which friend? How did you get my number?

Another pause while the response was typed out, taking far too long for Devin's liking.

I got it from Ms. Simon. I'm in Toronto today.
Can we meet?

Not unless you tell me who you are?

The next pause was even longer than the previous ones. Finally, he got an answer.

Sue from the dance. Please?

Devin didn't have a clue why that woman would want to meet up with him. From what he'd been able to tell, Sue didn't care for Kayla even a little bit. Then again, maybe something had happened after they'd left that involved Christoph and Kayla. It wouldn't hurt to hear her out.

Where do you want to meet?

The Fairmont. In the bar. Say at noon?

A quick look at his clock told him that there was no point in heading home if he was going to do this.

I'll see you there.

"Ah, Mark?"
"Yup."
"Slight change in plans. Can you take me to the Fairmont?"
Mark frowned at him in the rearview mirror. "Seriously? Why?"
"Looks like I'm meeting a friend."
At least, he hoped this would be a friendly meeting. Because the potential for something to go wrong was far too high for his liking.

* * * *

Despite having been born and raised in Toronto, Devin had never once set foot in the Fairmont Royal York hotel. It was classy and for people who had a bit extra money to spend than what he had in his pocket. Even the bar was a bit outside of his price range. Thankfully, they had beer, and even he could drop a few bucks on that. So, there he sat at a table facing the door waiting for Sue to arrive.

The longer he sat the more he started to doubt the wisdom of agreeing to meet this woman. Because really, who the hell was he to get involved with Kayla's personal life?

A boyfriend? Did a week of playacting followed by a weekend of sex on repeat qualify him as a boyfriend now? They hadn't exactly come to that agreement at any point in their togetherness, which now that he thought about it, probably meant that he really shouldn't be meeting Sue and risk upsetting Kayla.

Shit.

He should go.

Devin swallowed down the rest of his beer and stood to leave when Christoph walked in. His stomach bottomed out as a swell of anger rose inside him. "What the actual fuck."

The bar wasn't busy this time of day, which meant it took Christoph all of three seconds to see Devin. The grin on his face sent alarm bells off in Devin's head.

"What are you doing here?" Devin's voice was loud enough to draw looks from the bartender and the few other patrons present. "That was you and not Sue?"

Ah, that made a whole lot more sense. Christoph knew Devin wouldn't show up if he thought it was him, so he'd pretended to be Sue. Shit, Devin should have known there was no way in hell Sue would have driven all the way to Toronto to talk to him about Kayla. *Idiot.*

Christoph pointed to Devin's chair as he took the one opposite him. "Have a seat and let's talk."

"I don't give a fuck about you or what you want to say. I'm leaving."

Christoph leaned back and laced his hands on the table. "You're not wondering why I came all the way here? Don't you want to know why I've reached out to you?"

"Not really." Though he was more than a little curious.

"You're a grad student, right? Let me get you a drink. What do you want? Beer?"

"It's barely noon."

"Clearly, you've already had one." Christoph shrugged. "Let me get you another."

"Yeah, fine." He jerked the chair out and sat down as Christoph motioned the bartender for two beers. "You have until the bottle is gone. And then so am I."

"I don't think I'll need that much time." Christoph waited until the bartender dropped the bottles off.

The bartender gave Devin a concerned look before turning around and leaving. "I think the bartender is worried that we're going to get into a fight."

"I wouldn't lower myself." Christoph gave him a good onceover, and Devin could tell that he was being found lacking. "What the hell does she see in you?"

"Lots of things. I make her laugh, I don't care about how much money she has, and I'm hella good in bed." He couldn't help but smirk as Christoph frowned. "But none of that is your business. You need to back off and leave her alone. She moved on from you a long time ago."

If Christoph was upset or thrown off by Devin's dig, he didn't show it. "How did you meet? Because there's no way you run in the same social circles."

"Why would you say that?"

"Look at you. You don't have any real money of your own. I don't care what you say, someone who doesn't have money is always interested in dating someone rich. So you can stop with that bullshit right now."

"I don't. I really don't." But Devin also knew there was no way he could prove that to anyone. Well, not easily. "Again, that doesn't matter. It's between Kayla and me."

"It does matter because I don't trust you."

"You don't need to trust me, because we're not dating." Devin took a long pull of his beer, downing a third of the bottle. "And you're running out of time."

Christoph cocked his head to the side and narrowed his gaze. "How did you meet?"

"Why the hell is that important? We met, we're a couple. I came with her to the reunion. It's not like she'd bring a total stranger to an event like that." *You're a lying liar who lies.*

"I've known her for a long time, and yes, she absolutely would bring a stranger to an event like that if she thought it would save her some headaches." Christoph took a sip of his beer. "I'm not going to stop. I'll keep texting her, talking to her. I want to be back in her life and if I have to get rid of you in order to do that, then I will."

"You lost that chance when you fucked around on her."

"I fucked around on her because she'd frozen me out. Our marriage had been having problems long before I fucked around. She'll do the same with you. Everything will be going along well and then next thing you know she's spending all her time at the office and you haven't seen her in a week. The weeks get lonely."

Devin didn't know much about marriages, but in his limited experience, it took two people to make one successful. And the ones that fell apart usually had more problems than both sides were willing to admit. "That was your relationship. Not ours."

"So why won't you tell me how you met? Kayla and I have common ground, and we're both from the same place, know the same people. You're an outsider who didn't know her background at Meadow Lake. Every time I saw you, you were looking surprised. Learning some new revelation about her every five minutes. Me knowing her for years, makes us far more compatible than you having met her as, what? A blind date? Was it fucking Simone who set you up? That sounds exactly the thing that meddling little…person would do."

"We met online. Simone had nothing to do with it." The second the words left Devin's mouth he knew it was a colossal mistake. The look of devilish glee on Christoph's face only confirmed it.

"Online? Really? I can't imagine Kayla having signed up for an online dating app."

"I think she said Simone encouraged her." Shit, this was not going well. "And what the hell does that matter? Lots of people meet online. There are like a thousand apps out there."

"Because I know she hadn't been dating for years." He picked up his beer and held it high. "What, do you think I haven't been keeping tabs on her? She's my ex, but I wasn't happy with how things ended between us. I want to make sure that if someone else tries to take my place that they're not going to screw things up."

What, what? "Screw things up how?"

"We had a prenup, one that didn't entitle me to a fucking penny." He shifted the bottle to his chin, holding it there. "But kind, sweet woman that Kayla is, she agreed to give me a monthly stipend. And I plan on keeping it coming."

Devin's mind tried to work through the implications of what Christoph was getting at. "I don't care what she agreed to do for you. It's none of my business. But you harassing her is. Leave her alone."

"Right." Christoph finished his beer and got to his feet. "You don't even know what you're getting into. I suggest you take your shit and run because I'm coming for you now, asshole." With another glare, Christoph turned and marched out of the bar, leaving Devin sitting there more confused than when he'd arrived.

Devin had the sneaking suspicion that he'd somehow made things worse for her. Shit, he'd never intended to do anything that would have hurt Kayla, let alone throw blood in the water to drive Christoph wild.

Devin groaned and put his head down on the table. *What the hell have I done?*

Chapter 26

Kayla had spent most of the day moving from meeting to meeting. They'd finalized the spring lineup, which took a lot of the pressure off. The next thing she needed to make sure was done was the exploration of the new manufacturing plant. If things went the way she'd wanted, this was going to be her way of releasing her specialty designs and it not impacting the broader line production.

She was so close to getting back to her roots with the company that she could practically taste it.

She hadn't felt this good at work in a long time. Not only were things finally starting to go her way with the VPs she spoke to, her body still held a pleasant ache from her weekend activities with Devin.

Oh, Devin.

She couldn't hold back her smile, even as she continued to speak on the phone. "That's fantastic news, Ronald. If you could get us a timeline and some financial figures along with expansion projections by the end of the month, that would be great. I'd like to start moving forward on this as soon as we get board approval."

"No problem, Ms. Arnold." Kayla hung up the speakerphone and turned to Alicia, her VP of production. "What do you think?"

Alicia flipped her notebook closed and smiled. "If the German facility is as good as you say, then the costs to get our plant up and running should easily offset the smaller production runs. It might run close to the line for the first few cycles, but a personal high-end brand should be financially viable. Well, as long as the numbers you showed me are correct."

"They are. And if the line fails, we can shift the plant over to expand regular production. It's a win-win."

Alicia smiled. "It sounds as close to it as I'm willing to concede. Nothing is a sure thing in business."

"I know." They both stood, and Kayla followed Alicia out to the main office. She'd spent too much time today sitting and talking. She needed to get up and stretch her legs. She was shocked to see that Rhianna had already left for the day and that most of the office was empty. "Wow, I had no idea it was this late."

"You've been going full speed ahead since you got in today. Time to call it a day."

The elevator door dinged, and Kayla looked up to see Devin walk out. The tension and exhaustion she'd felt only moments before were suddenly gone. Alicia also saw him and made a soft humming noise. "Stranger on the floor."

"That's Devin." Kayla's face heated even as she forced her expression back into her normal detached mask. "He's a friend of mine."

Alicia gave her a side glance before looking back at Devin. "A friend, eh? I hope he's more than that, for your sake."

Great, I'm blushing more. "Ah, well, he's a good friend."

"I bet."

Devin saw them and gave her a smile and a small wave. He didn't come any closer though, and she could only imagine it was because he didn't want to interrupt them. Kayla turned to her VP and held out her hand. "Thanks again. I'll touch base with you a bit later in the week."

Alicia squeezed her hand and winked. "Have a good night with your *friend.*"

Devin smiled and said hi to Alicia as she walked past him to her office, only coming over to Kayla once she was entirely alone. "Sorry about that. I didn't want to get in the way of your meeting."

Another difference between Devin and Christoph. Her ex would have barged in and made it so uncomfortable for everyone involved, Alicia would have walked away far sooner. "It's fine. We were all done and just chatting. Though I'm surprised to see you here. I was going to text you and see if you wanted to get together tomorrow for dinner or something. Thought it might be too late for you tonight."

Devin's smile faltered a second before he reached up and pinched the bridge of his nose. "Dinner would be great, but we should probably talk first."

Her good mood began to fizzle around the edges. No, she didn't want something bad to happen now, not when everything had been going so well.

"Why don't I get my things from my office, and we can go somewhere to talk."

"Sure." He didn't follow her in, didn't make any moves to indicate that he wanted to renew their previous closeness.

Shit.

Kayla collected her things, continuously looking out her office door to see that yes, Devin was in fact still standing there. Why she got the feeling he was about to bolt on her she didn't know, but if something was wrong, she wanted to deal with it now rather than have things fall apart in a public place.

"Devin?"

He poked his head into her office. "Yup?"

"Maybe we should talk here." She set her jacket and purse down on her desk and sat in her chair. "It's more private, and I get the feeling we might need that."

"Yeah." He sighed, but came in, shutting the door behind him. "I screwed up."

There were many ways that he could have screwed up and every single scenario she could think of raced through her mind in a microsecond. Still, this was Devin, and his idea of screwing up was no doubt having been rude to someone, or not giving a hundred and ten percent when helping out a friend. "What did you do that makes you think that?"

He didn't sit but moved to her guest chair and leaned both hands on the back of it. He didn't look her in the eyes, which was a very un-Devin-like thing for him to do. "I met with Christoph."

She gave her head a sharp shake. "You did *what*?"

"I didn't intend to meet him. He'd gotten my number from Ms. Simon and told me it was Sue, the woman from the registration desk at the dance—"

"I know who Sue is."

"Yeah. Well, I thought it was her, but it turned out to be Christoph. I should have left the minute I saw him, but I didn't. Though now I wish I had."

Anger she hadn't expected, welled up inside her. "What did you do?"

"I tried to tell him to back off." He stood up straight and held both his hands up. "He was being an asshole and doing his best to piss me off. I know you don't need anyone to come and try to rescue you. But he'd been bugging you all weekend, and I didn't mean to say anything, but having him there in front of me all I wanted to do was make him back off and leave you alone."

Ten, nine, eight... She forced her hands to relax, flattening them out on her desk. "I take it that didn't go the way you'd anticipated."

"No." Dropping his chin to his chest, Devin sighed. "I don't know how, but I let it slip that we met online through a dating app. I didn't say what the app was, or anything about our initial arrangement—"

Kayla stood so quickly her chair fell over. "You told him *what*?" She was shouting, and she didn't even care. God the last thing she needed was Christoph having ammunition to use in the rumor mill back home.

"I screwed up. I'm sorry."

"I can't believe you did that." Kayla struggled to calm down. There was no way Devin could have known about her arrangement with Christoph. While she'd had him sign a prenup and didn't owe him anything, she'd been giving him a stipend over the years. The money kept Christoph far away from her, so she could get on with her life.

But now he had a thread of information, he'd try to make her miserable, because that was exactly the sort of thing Christoph would do. He'd always hated that she'd left him, that he'd been cut-off from her deep pockets, even with the money she'd been giving him. God, this was going to suck.

Devin ran his hand along the back of his neck. "Look, I'm sure this won't be bad. I mean, he's not going to know what site we met on. I'm sure everything will be fine."

If the board found out that she'd been active on a sugar daddy site, if that got out to the public, it could ruin her reputation. Christoph was just bitter enough to threaten to expose her if he learned the truth, which would cause chaos at Fashion Finds.

While Devin meant well, he was yet another person who thought they knew better than she did about what to do with her life. Christoph, Simone, Devin, hell, even her parents to a certain extent, always seemed to think that they knew best. If she'd just stuck to her guns and ignored Simone and her *I know you'll be so happy with this sugar daddy site* routine, then she wouldn't be in this mess.

She looked up to see Devin standing there, looking confused and sorry. Without intending to, he'd proved to her that she was far better off being on her own than having to worry about trusting that another person wouldn't screw her over—intended or otherwise. She'd handle Christoph, get him out of her life once and for all, then go back to her normal controlled life.

"Thank you for letting me know." She turned and picked her chair up off the floor. "I'm going to ask that you stay out of this. I'll deal with Christoph."

"If there's anything I can do to help—"

"You know what you can do? Stop trying to fix everyone else's life and straighten out your own." She barely recognized the venomous voice as her own.

Devin took a step backward. "What?"

Kayla took a breath, but it did nothing to calm her. "You're so busy trying to help others, the soup kitchen and Ray's family and Christoph. But you're not doing that to be magnanimous. You're afraid. You don't want to look at your issues. You refuse to move forward in your life because you're too scared of being compared to a man who's been dead for years. So maybe, you should fix your shit before you meddle in someone else's."

Kayla's labored breathing was making her head spin. It didn't help that she was suddenly crying either. But if Devin noticed her distress, he didn't say a word. Instead, he nodded and took another step backward. "Wow. Right. My mistake."

The look of pain on his face broke her heart. "Devin I'm—"

"No, you're right. I'm…far from perfect. I've let the memory of my dad overshadow my life. I thought that maybe despite our differences that there was a chance we could make things work. I was wrong." He took another step backward. "But you need to start letting people into your life, or you'll continue to be miserable."

"I have people in my life."

"Mark doesn't count."

"Yes, he does. And I have Simone and my parents." Sadly, that was probably it.

"Your parents? You didn't even invite them to your award ceremony. I can't imagine how hurt they'll be when they find out."

"They'll be fine." Her stomach was churning to the point where Kayla thought she might be sick.

"I should leave."

"For the best." *No, it's not!*

The muscles in his jaw jumped. "I'm sorry if I've caused you problems with your ex-husband. But I'm done with this. It wasn't something that was ever going to last, I mean not with how we met. This was never supposed to be about anything other than a week away. That was it."

"You're right." A giant sob stuck in the back of her throat, but she somehow managed to swallow it down. "This was never about being a couple."

"No." Devin wiped at his cheek so hard and fast that she almost didn't see the tears. "I wish you well in your life. Please never contact me again."

And then he was gone.

Kayla continued to stand long after she heard the elevator doors slide open and then closed. Devin had left, and she was still here, still standing.

Still alone.

The anger that had been holding her upright finally faded, and she picked her chair up off the floor and gently sat down on the edge of it. Her throat ached, squeezed by emotions she didn't want to acknowledge.

He'd been right that she'd always had a wall up between her and the world. Her parents had tried to talk to her about that once, years ago. They'd claimed that she'd grown distant, that she'd kept things from them. She'd thought she'd been looking after them, giving them a life that they'd always wanted and could have never afforded before.

So why hadn't she invited them to the dedication?

For the first time in a long while, Kayla didn't have an answer. Hell, she hadn't even spoken to them since they'd gotten back from their cruise. What kind of daughter did that make her? They'd been nothing but kind and supportive of her and her career, never asking her for anything other than a bit of her time. And recently, that had been the one thing she'd been unwilling to give.

Picking up her cell phone, Kayla turned it over in her hand until she pulled up her contacts and looked at the one that said *Mom and Dad*. It still took far longer than it should for her to press that button and wait for the ringing to begin.

"Hello?" It was her mom, sounding the same as she always did.

"Hi." Kayla sucked in a breath.

"Kayla, hon, is that you?"

"Yeah."

"What's wrong, baby?"

"I...I don't know."

"Where are you?"

"At work. I'm so sorry."

"For what, sweetheart? You didn't do anything."

"I did. I..." How the hell did she tell her parents that she'd pushed them aside for no damn good reason? That she'd denied them the chance to see her recognized? That she was miserable and lonely and needed someone to love her just for herself.

Someone like her parents.

Someone like Devin.

The sob that had stubbornly refused to leave her finally escaped. "Can I come over?"

"Yes, of course. I was baking some banana bread. It will be ready by the time you get here."

"It's not too late?"

"Never for you. You're my little girl, and I'm here for you no matter the time of day."

"Okay. I'll be there soon." She hung up and let the wave of emotions wash over her.

Devin was right; she'd been selfish. But it wasn't too late to make things right, starting with her parents. She'd then deal with Christoph and his inevitable demands. Maybe Devin's mistake would help push her on the path to making things right.

Maybe she'd be able to step out from behind that wall and see what she was missing.

Chapter 27

Devin sat at the kitchen table staring at his empty coffee mug, but not really seeing it. His mind continued to play his fight with Kayla on a loop, even though it had been nearly a week since he'd last seen her. They'd both said some things that had hurt, but that wasn't why he couldn't get her words out of his head.

Mostly, it was because she'd been right.

Ray came out of the bathroom and made a beeline for the fridge. "Dude, did you eat the leftover pizza? I'm starving, and I can't cook when I'm hungry."

"That makes absolutely no sense." Then again, this was Ray talking. "And no. It's there."

"Awesome." He pulled the box out and shoved most of a piece into his mouth as he walked over to the table. "Mom said thanks for the books. She hadn't read most of those, so it should keep her busy during her chemo."

"No problem." It had been so easy to fall into the pattern of helping Ray and his family, just as it had been easy for him to volunteer at the soup kitchen.

If he was busy, he didn't have to think about his future.

"Man, are you okay?" Ray flicked the pizza box open and rescued another slice. "You've been off for days now."

Devin knew he wasn't exactly a guy to hide his emotions, but he must be way off for Ray to have noticed. "Do you think I'm letting the memory of my dad impact my life?"

Ray swallowed down the bit he'd been chewing, looked at him for a moment before folding the piece in two and lifted it to his mouth. "Yes." He shoved the whole thing in and grinned.

"Wait, really?"

"Yes." He held up his hand and swallowed, coughing as something got stuck. "Dude, you have a PhD in math, not because you're brilliant—which you are—but because you wouldn't do your education degree. You wanted to, but you won't because your dad was awesome years ago."

Shit, as much as it had hurt to hear, Kayla had been right. "Why didn't you say anything?"

"Wasn't my place. Besides, I figure you'd clue in sooner or later. As I said, you're a smart guy." Ray pointed at the last piece of pizza, but Devin shook his head. "Awesome."

If he was so freaking smart, he should have figured this shit out a long time ago. "I fucked things up with Kayla."

"The rich girl?"

"Yes, but don't call her that."

"Sorry. What'd you do?"

It took a surprisingly short period to fill Ray in on everything he'd done, ending in their shouting match at her office. "I have no idea if her ex ended up causing her problems or not. I mean, she can handle herself, but depending on what he does, it might screw her up at work."

"Wow." Ray had stopped eating his last piece of pizza. "I take back what I said; you're a stupid idiot."

"Thanks, dude."

"Seriously, you met with her ex? What the hell did you think would happen?"

"I don't know? I didn't plan it, but when he was there taunting me, I just couldn't shut up. But she was right. I have my own issues to deal with and should have stayed the hell out of hers."

"You're a great guy, Dev. I mean, you've helped my family out, and we'll never be able to repay you. Not really. But you need to start putting yourself first. And that can't happen until you let go of this crazy idealized memory of your dad. I'm sure he was great, but I'm sure he was a jerk too. And funny but maybe told off-color jokes when he shouldn't have. He was just a guy, the same as you."

Devin nodded. It wasn't going to be easy, but Ray was right. "Mom always said that I should be a teacher. Apparently, when I was little, I would play teacher all the time. Dad would come home from school and be my student for a while before supper. Then I'd pretend to grade papers the same as him." His mom always got teary-eyed when she told him that. "Maybe it's time I do something about making that dream real."

"Well, you'll be one hell of a math teacher. I would have loved to have had you in school. God, Ms. Easterbrook was my advanced math teacher. She was a great person but tended to teach lessons incorrectly. After she'd assigned homework. It was hell."

Devin couldn't help but laugh at the pained look on Ray's face. "I can imagine."

"You know it's not too late to see about getting into a program for the fall. You might have to sit on a waitlist for a bit, but people tend to drop out. I bet you could find something."

"Maybe." But for the first time since he'd started down this path, he knew this was finally the right direction. "I'll do some poking around today."

He should also give his mom a call. She'd want to know that he'd finally started to figure things out.

"Good for you." Ray stood up as he clapped Devin on the shoulder. "Now all you have to do is make up with your hot rich girl, and your life will officially be a thousand times better than mine."

Shit. "I'm sorry. But your mom is going to be okay." Keeping some perspective on these things was important. Going for his education degree might be a big step for him, but in the grand scale of life issues, it was minor.

Ray shrugged. "I know. We got some good news from the doctors yesterday. It looks like they caught it early this time and that the cancer is pretty localized. They hope that the one round of chemo will be all she needs. They'll get it all, and she'll be back on the mend again. I have faith."

"Good for you."

"Speaking of which, I better get over to the house. Dad was threatening to cook, which will drive Mom up the wall. I was going to get some takeout and bring it over."

"I'll see you later then."

Devin didn't wait for Ray to leave before he opened his laptop and pulled up York University's online education program page. He lost himself reading up on the course descriptions, his mind already picturing him walking into a classroom for the first time. He might never live up to the mental image he'd created of his father, but that didn't mean that he couldn't aspire to that ideal. He owed it to himself to at least try. And if he failed, well, then he would know that he gave it his best effort.

Regardless of how he did, both of his parents would be proud of him and what he'd accomplished in his life.

More importantly, he'd be proud of himself.

He was on the phone with the registrar's office when his phone made a strange noise. Ignoring it, he was thrilled to learn that it wasn't too late to apply for the fall term.

"We can't guarantee that you'll get in where you're late applying, but the numbers happen to be in your favor. You're lucky."

Maybe his dad was still looking out for him. "That's fantastic."

"You'll need to get your application into me today though, along with your deposit."

"I'll do it right now. Thank you so much."

The next hour was lost to completing forms and figuring out where to get a background check, and when the next first aid course was going to be offered. By the time he finished the online application through the portal, Devin had forgotten entirely about his phone and the strange sound.

His back ached as he straightened from the awkward angle he'd been sitting at. When there was a knock at his door, he was thankful for the chance to stand and stretch his legs. "Just a minute." Hopefully, it wasn't a cable company coming to try to sell him a package. They didn't have any money for that shit. "Yes?"

But instead of a salesperson, instead, Mark was standing there dressed in his full formal attire. "Hello, sir." Mark tipped his hat.

"What are you doing here?" While a part of him was thrilled that Kayla was reaching out to him, another part was wary of letting her back in.

Neither of them would be ready to get back together after what had been said.

"Well, I'm either here to pick you up and take you to a location, or I'm just exploring a building that I'm not familiar with and thought I'd randomly knock on this particular door. I'm good with either story."

Devin frowned. "What?"

"I take it you haven't checked your phone." Mark leaned back against the wall opposite the door. "I'll wait here until you do that. Please, don't leave me hanging if you're not coming out. No explanation needed, just *no thanks* will do. Go ahead and shut the door. I won't go anywhere."

Devin continued to frown as he did what Mark said. His cell was on the table, face up and screen on. The moment he picked it up and looked, he saw the message indicator from millionairesugardaddy.com.

"Oh." That had been the sound earlier.

His hands were shaking as he pressed the button and waited for the app to open up and log him in. As he'd anticipated, there was a message from Kayla.

*Hi. I need to start by saying that I'm sorry. I
lashed out at you when you told me that you'd
met with Christoph. Just so you know, he wasn't
able to figure out which dating app we'd met
on—mostly because he wouldn't have considered
me signing up for something like this. As I'd
expected, he wanted more money from me. I
said no. I also said that the payments I had been
making were now done, and that I'd decided to
enforce our prenup.*

He didn't like that too much.

I don't care.

What I do care about is you.

I was wondering if—

Devin's phone shut off. "No!" He raced into the kitchen, scrambling for his charging cable. "Shit, shit, where the fuck is—dammit. Right." Ray had taken the cable the last time they'd gone to the hospital to sit with his mom. He'd forgotten to put it back. With a growl, he banged his phone on the counter, then quickly checked to make sure he hadn't hurt it. He'd need to turn on his laptop to check his messages directly on the site.

Or...

After running to the door, he jerked it open to reveal a slightly startled Mark. "My phone died. What did she say?"

"Don't know the specifics. I was just supposed to come here and see if you'd read the message and if you were going to come."

"Shit. I..." What the hell was he going to do?

Mark smiled. "Son, I don't know what happened between the two of you, but whatever it was she's changed."

"She has?"

"Yup. She's been at her parents' house three times this week. That's three more times than she'd gone in the past six months. She looks—well for the first time in forever she looks happy—calm. That's it; she looks calm. I'm not sure if you're the reason for that, but if you are, I suggest you get your coat and come with me. That is unless you don't want to see her. In which case you can—"

"Let me get my wallet."

"Don't bother. I have a feeling you won't need it."

"My keys at least. Give me five minutes." And he shut the door again.

Devin only needed three to quickly brush his teeth, change his shirt and throw on some deodorant. He didn't know what was going on, but the last thing he wanted was to look like hell if he was going to see Kayla.

He grinned when he stepped out into the hall and locked his apartment door. "All set."

Devin was surprised not to see the limo waiting downstairs, but a Honda Civic. "This is different."

"It's my personal car. Where we're going the limo won't fit."

"Okay." Well, apparently this was going to be an adventure. "I'm in your hands."

It was easy enough to make small talk with Mark, finding out some of the little details of the past week that he'd missed. They'd gotten laughing at something when Devin realized that they were pulling into a neighborhood he wasn't familiar with. "Where are we?"

"Almost there. Just need to take the next right, and it's only three houses up on the left."

The small bungalow wasn't a fancy house similar to Kayla's, but he knew in this market, the price would still be far from what he'd ever be able to afford. He would have asked Mark what next, but Kayla stepped out of the front door, her hands shoved into her back pockets.

For a moment, he forgot how to breathe.

She looked stunning dressed in little more than jeans and a band T-shirt, her hair pulled back into one of her low ponytails. Smiling, she gave him a short wave.

And just like that, Devin was nervous.

"Are you getting out?" Mark unlocked the doors. "There, I'll even make it easy."

Right, there was no point in coming all this way and not getting out of the car. "Okay. Right. Thanks."

"No problem. Good luck."

Mark pulled out of the driveway while Devin slowly made his way up the walkway to the steps. He stopped at the bottom and looked up at Kayla. "Hi."

"Hi." She bit down on her bottom lip. "I'm sorry."

"I am too."

"You were right." They both said in unison, before breaking out into equally big smiles.

He chuckled. "I just signed up for an education degree."

"I've been talking a lot with my parents. I didn't realize I had as much anger in me as I did. None of it directed at them. Mostly myself."

"Sometimes it takes someone from the outside looking in to see the things that we've grown blind to in our lives." Banging dishes in the house behind her drew his attention. "Whose house is this?"

"My parents. Didn't you read the message?"

"My phone died, and Mark didn't tell me." He would have known this was her parents' home. "I think he didn't want to scare me off."

"He's smart but meddlesome." She came down a step. "Did you want to come in? I don't want you to feel pressured if you're not ready for this."

He took a step up. "I think it would be great to get to meet them."

Looking up at her, coming face to face with her perfect face and lush lips, all Devin wanted to do was kiss her. As though she read his mind, she bent down and kissed him softly. "I'd like that. And for the record, they already like you more than they did Christoph."

"Awesome for me." He reached up and took her by the hand. "Do they know how we met?"

"They do."

"And they still like me more?"

"They do. I do too." She waited for him to step up beside her. "I might even love you."

He couldn't contain his grin. "I love you too. I think I loved you from the moment I laid eyes on you. The real you."

"When was that?"

"At the CN Tower, when you were terrified of the elevator."

She laughed, and Devin knew everything was going to be okay. "Fear, nature's love potion."

He was going to say something else when he caught a whiff of something. "Is someone baking cookies?"

"Mom is making sugar cookies. Yes, she loves irony."

"Well, I now love your mom. Those are my favorite."

"Let's go get some." And Kayla led him inside where his world changed entirely for the second time that summer.

Epilogue

"Kayla, do you know where the Dramamine is?"

She'd been sitting out on their private balcony watching Florida disappear as their cruise ship pulled out of port. There was something beautiful seeing the world fall away, knowing that for the next ten days, their world would be one of pampering, food, and fun.

At least hers would be. "Devin, we're not even out of port yet. You shouldn't be seasick. Besides, it's a bit late if you're feeling ill. It takes time to kick in."

"I'm not. It's more preventative." He stepped out to join her, decked out in a T-shirt and board shorts. "I'll get used to this right? Because I don't want to get sick and then ruin the whole trip—"

"Sit down and have a drink." She patted the chair beside her, which he quickly fell into. "Is your mom all set in her room?"

"Are you kidding? She spent all of three seconds in there before finding your parents and going off to explore." He sighed in that big dramatic way that made her smile. "Are you sure bringing them all on this trip for Christmas was a good idea?"

"It is. They'll have fun, and we'll be able to let them know the good news in the best way possible." She'd purposely left off her engagement ring while they'd met up with everyone, but she'd slipped it back on where it belonged the moment they'd stepped into their suite.

"I think Mom suspects."

"You told her, didn't you?"

"No." He rolled his eyes. "I wanted her opinion on how I should do it."

Devin had taken her back to the CN Tower where they'd had dinner that first time, getting down on one knee in the middle of the room despite the fact that the staff had been busy trying to get ready for a function.

"It was sweet." She leaned over and kissed his cheek.

"Well, I couldn't afford to rent the room, but I wanted it to be special. And for the record, Mom hasn't seen the ring."

"That's good." She looked down at the simple stone set in the gold band. It was far simpler than the ring Christoph had given her, and yet, it meant a whole lot more because Devin had saved and paid for it himself. "I love it."

They sat that way for a long time, enjoying the view, the smell of the ocean and one another. This trip might have been about their parents, but Kayla wanted to cement their relationship as well. The past six months had been crazy with her finalizing her new product line of signature clothing and Devin being back in school full-time.

While she wanted to spend every moment she could with him, having the time to follow their passions made their togetherness mean all that much more. She dropped her head to his shoulder. "I love you."

"I love you too."

"We should probably go find the others. Supper will be starting soon."

Devin groaned and put his hand on his stomach. "I'm not sure that I can."

"They have the best desserts on this cruise. All the cakes and pastries you could ever imagine."

The prospect of sugar was more than enough to perk him up. "Oh, that sounds great. Though I doubt they'll be anywhere as good as your mom's cookies."

"Make sure to tell her that, and you'll be in her good books forever."

"I'll do that then. Because I plan on sticking around for at least forever. I'd hate for her not to like me."

"They both love you. Almost as much as I do." Kayla got to her feet and helped Devin out of his seat. "Let's go, before all the cookies are gone."

"Yes, ma'am." He pulled her in for a kiss, moaning softly when she finally pulled away. "I'm never going to get tired of doing that."

"Me either." She looked at the clock by the bed. "You know, the dining room serves food twenty-four hours a day. We could show up a bit later, and I bet there would still be cookies."

Devin grinned. "It's only fair if we try out the bed, to make sure it meets our high standards." He spun her around and gently pushed her on the bed.

Kayla smiled up at him, and without a doubt knew that from now on, no matter what happened, as long as she had Devin by her side, everything was going to be okay. Letting her legs fall open and her dress ride up, she smiled at him. "All aboard."

She didn't even mind missing dessert.

Connecting with a sugar daddy is reserved for a certain kind of woman.
But some men make you yearn to be that kind of woman…

Marissa Roy never thought she would do it. Until she finds herself overwhelmed by debt, college costs—and a vengeful ex-boyfriend determined to ruin her financially. But once she meets multi-millionaire Vince Taylor, the thought of sleeping with her hot benefactor is a major turn-on. Except Vince has one condition to their dating contract: he wants her by his side, but not in his bed. Finding sex was easy, he said, finding someone he could trust was not. Still, his hungry gaze tells Marissa otherwise…

She's the perfect escort—a natural beauty with the kind of savvy discretion that will keep his personal life out of the tabloids. Only Vince doesn't expect his body to pulse every time Marissa steps into the room, every time she stands close. Too close. He doesn't expect to find himself pulling her into his arms, night after night after night. Suddenly he can't get enough of her intoxicating body. And once he's broken that rule, it's only a matter of time until he violates his vow to never, ever fall in love…

About the Author

A romance novelist and short story writer, **Christine d'Abo** has over forty publications to her name. She loves to exercise and stops writing just long enough to keep her body in motion too. When she's not pretending to be a ninja in her basement, she's most likely spending time with her family and two dogs. Visit her at www.christinedabo.com.

www.ingramcontent.com/pod-product-compliance
Lightning Source LLC
Chambersburg PA
CBHW050530260626
47157CB00004B/1547